The Bestman, the Bride and the Wedding

by Michael L. McCoy

with illustrations by Anisa L. Baucke

Book 1 in

The Chronicles of Peniel

published by

CHJ Publishing
1103 West Main
Middleton, Idaho 83644

Library of Congress Cataloging-in-Publication Data
98-072286

ISBN 0-927022-33-8

Printed in the United States of America.

Acknowledgments

An introvert who writes as a hobby does not naturally seek to have a work published. Manuscripts are usually completed and added to an upper shelf collection. External persuasion to put a work in print is required and comes in two forms. First, the aforementioned author needs to be convinced others will find the book worthwhile. Second, constant encouragement is required, especially when there is the great inclination to return the manuscript to its place on the shelf.

Several people have offered comments and encouragement for which I am grateful. Pastor Tim Pauls read the manuscript and added suggestions based not only upon his academic prowess and literary interests, but also from the perspective of his personal struggles as one of the Lord's undershepherds. Clare D. Walker invested his time for two readings of the manuscript. His cogent remarks and personal interest served as benevolent goads. Clinton H. Jones has offered his time, patience and expertise in the preparation of this book.

My sincere thanks are offered to the Bridegroom for two brides. For years, Judy has eyed the dust collecting on a handful of manuscripts in three-ring binders, urging me to take them down and pursue the possibility of finding a publisher for them. During her repeated readings of this manuscript, she has provided helpful suggestions on wording, flow and structure. I also give thanks to the Lord for Our Redeemer Lutheran Church and the members who, each in his or her own way, have let me know what it means to escort the Bride.

To the Reader and the Hearer

This book is story. Wherever the truth of the Word is proclaimed within its pages, there is recitation of *the Story*. The remaining sections are simply part of a story.

While this book may be read on its own, the inquisitive reader or hearer may find a dictionary and/or a Bible dictionary of value. Questions have arisen concerning the characters, specifically, who they are and what their names mean. Many names and titles have meanings, though some are not to be found in a dictionary. For example, *Headbanger* and *Footstomper* are names derived from Genesis 3:15, the place where our story begins. Other names are transliterations from another language. The four horses and riders are from Revelation 6 (once again, the place where our story begins), and their names are from various Greek words (*logos, polemos, limos, loimos* and *thanatos* mean *word, war, famine, pestilence* and *death* respectively). Several names, like *Sonodad*, must be rent asunder.

The story is intended to be edifying, entertaining and thought-provoking. How well these intentions are met is for you to decide. The book will be troubling to some, foolishness for many, a stumbling-block for a few and comforting to a remnant. Therefore, enjoy; but take care, for Peniel is where we live.

Michael L. McCoy
The Annunciation of Our Lord
25 March Anno Domini 1998

TABLE OF CONTENTS

Illustration - The Way to the Wedding

Illustration - Baptized in the Clouds

Illustration - The Black Net

Illustration - In the Light of the Son

Illustration - The End Time

Illustration - The Way Out

for my mother who begat me,

for my brothers with whom I walk

and for the children

CHAPTER 1

CONFRONTATIONS AND CONSEQUENCES

"Stand there. Do not move," the Voice boomed. "I permit you neither leave, nor escape, nor relief."

Footstomper remained motionless with its limbs hanging to its sides. Such immobility was due to the command of the Voice, not the self-restraint of Footstomper. The ground rumbled whenever the Voice was heard. An accompanying, low frequency quaking, never before experienced in this good place, caused all who heard and felt it to tremble with fear.

The Bridegroom stood directly in front of the Violator. "Footstomper, your limbs embraced my Bride. They are no more." The Bridegroom raised his hands and pushed the Violator's shoulders into its torso. The strong hands slid down Footstomper's arms, continuing past the wrists and the backs of the hands and passing beyond the fingers. The entire limb, on either side, from shoulder to fingertips, melted into Footstomper's body. Each arm was blended and welded into place. The side areas were covered by the scaly skin of the creature.

Footstomper's eyes stared in horror.

"With your legs you led my Bride astray. They are no more." The Bridegroom placed his hands on the hips of Footstomper and pressed inward, moving down the legs, passing through the knees and extending beyond the toes. All visible evidence of legs vanished. There remained only a single mass of scabrous, skin-covered meat that tapered from the hips to a single point where Footstomper's toes once were.

"Wait."

"Silence," the Voice thundered, "your mouth is, now and forever, silent. You spoke evil to my Bride. You will speak to her no more as you once did."

Footstomper loathed a thought to the Bridegroom, *We will speak to her in other ways. You may stop our mouth, but we will speak to her.*

With the other two listening, the Bridegroom answered the Violator's thought out loud, "I know, Footstomper, I know. But you will never forget that I am Headbanger. Every dark recess you inhabit will remind you that I am Headbanger."

The Bridegroom shifted his penetrating eyes to the other two standing nearby. With an extended, accusing index finger, he pointed to the limbless one and said, "Footstomper." Retracting his finger, bending his elbow, making a fist and directing a thumb to himself, he declared emphatically, "I am Headbanger." The sound of the Voice reverberated and, as the echo dampened, he continued his proclamation to them.

"I am Headbanger. You two, do not forget it."

They made no reply.

Slowly the Bridegroom turned his head and directed his potent stare back to the Violator's loathing eyes. Footstomper teetered on the point of flesh which had been feet. The powerful Bridegroom inhaled slowly and deeply. As he exhaled into the face of the Violator, he said a long, "Be goooooonnnnnneee." Footstomper seethed in writhing anger, jerked in lost balance and fell to the ground like lightning.

The Bridegroom spoke once more, "What you are going to do, ... go do it!"

Footstomper crawled, slithered and caterpillared in a contorted attempt to pass through the Portal. The Violator hesitated, turned and communicated a thought, *I will kill you, but first I will make you suffer. You will beg to die, but I will prolong your ever increasing pain.*

The Bridegroom thundered, "No more! Be gone! Go!"

The two watched as the crawling creature wormed through the Portal and into the neutral world on the other side. After a few minutes of frustrated and frantic wriggling, Footstomper sprung into the air and fashioned a parabolic vault twenty feet high. Prior to hitting the ground headfirst, the Violator disappeared. The two could not tell whether he dove into the ground or vanished in midair just above the earth.

"Turn back to me," commanded the rumbling Voice behind them. They shivered as their faces met his. The Bridegroom's eyes penetrated beyond theirs. He saw into their minds and souls and spirits and hearts. They gazed upon him, viewing complete justice and holiness and righteousness and perfection and dread and purity.

"Bride, step forward."

With bluish lips trembling from intense fright and overwhelming shock, she stepped forward slightly. Her eyes, now downcast, viewed his feet. Consuming guilt oozed from every pore and her exposed skin glistened with clammy shame.

"Woman, you could have resisted Footstomper, and you did not. You should have done so, and you did not. With you I am greatly disappointed. Woman, you could have closed your ears to Footstomper's evil words, and you did not. You should have done so, and you did not. With you I am greatly displeased."

She remained silent, fully aware that the Bridegroom no longer addressed her as *Bride*.

"Woman, you must pass through the Portal and leave this good place."

Tears flooded her eyes. Her shoulders shook as she sobbed and slowly pivoted in the direction of the Portal.

"Woman, you do not have my leave. You may not go yet. I am not done with you. Turn back to me."

As she did, he stepped forward and placed a pure white cloak around her. He fastened the cloak in the front and gently lifted her chin with his hand, making her look into his ancient eyes.

He blew his soft, warm breath upon her face and dried her pooled eyes.

With tenderness the Voice was heard once more, "I have required the life of the innocent snow leopard in order to cover you with this white cloak. Do you understand?"

She shook her head in negative reply.

"You no longer need these," he said and dead leaves fell to the ground from under the white cloak. "What you could not do, I have done for you. Weep no more, my Bride."

She thought, *Bride? Am I restored?*

He answered her with his word, "Yes."

The woman's mouth parted slightly and tears of joy mingled with ones of guilt. She spoke softly, "There are no consequences?"

The Bridegroom replied, "My beloved, there are always consequences. Do you not see the carcass of the snow leopard?"

"Yes, I see the snow leopard. He rests. Giving me his coat was difficult for him?"

"The snow leopard does not rest. He is dead."

"What is *dead*?"

"The snow leopard no longer is. He moves no more. He breathes no more. He is not."

"I do not like dead."

"Nor I, but there are consequences." The Bridegroom changed his tone and continued, "You will know more of death; however, that will be later. You are restored to me."

Her nose ran and she sniffed, intermingling spasmodic sobs and grateful sighs. She cupped her small palms and placed his hands in hers.

With heartfelt gratitude for his undeserved love, she whispered, "Thank you. What love you have for me. I love you."

"I know," the Bridegroom replied, "but there are always consequences."

The Bridegroom gazed over her right shoulder to the man standing behind his Bride. The man had closed his eyes and willed

12

that this was not taking place. However, his ears had remained unstopped and he heard all that was said between the Bride and the Bridegroom. A great slavish fear, conceived in his conscience and born of guilt, overflowed.

"Return to me." The Bridegroom spoke with the authority capable of making it happen. "You represent the greater disappointment. With you there is greater displeasure."

The man, unable to resist, was drawn alongside the Bride. His eyes reflected shame causing him to close them as he took a deep breath of the clear air. His rugged chin lifted as his chest filled. The chin did not lower as he emptied his lungs, but remained perched. Silently, upper and lower teeth clamped onto his bottom lip as he thought about what he had done, and especially, what he had not done.

"Open your eyes and look to me. For what is ahead, you must not look to yourself. You will find no hope and no future there. Look to me."

Opening his eyes, the man's heart raced at the sight of the Bridegroom's face. The contrite man replied, "I have failed you."

"True."

"But not you only," the man said, nodding to the woman.

"I entrusted you with my utterances and with my Bride. If you misuse one, you abuse the other. In either case, and in both cases, you failed me."

"I am no longer worthy of your trust," the crushed, somber man confessed.

"True."

"Nor of my duty," the man added, thinking of the woman.

"The task once given to you was not a difficult one. I placed no heavy burden upon you. Not so any more."

Surprised, the man asked, "Do you still have a task for me?"

"Yes."

"You are more gracious than I either expect or deserve."

"True, however my grace is neither prompted by your expectation nor bestowed as your reward."

"Sir, what would you have me do?"

The Bridegroom produced a black robe and put it on the man. The robe extended to the man's ankles. "This is a robe made from the wool of the black sheep." Immediately, brown leaves fell to the ground from under the black robe.

"Is the black sheep also dead?"

"No, the black sheep lives."

"Am I not restored? Does the black robe not cover my guilt and shame?"

"You are restored and covered, but not because you wear the black robe. Remember that. Rather, what I have given to the Bride is also meant for you. The white cloak indicates your restoration too."

The man began to feel a mild itching wherever the black robe touched his skin. He squirmed and asked, "What is this sensation I feel?"

The Bridegroom replied, "The black robe should never be too comfortable on you. I am your hope. When you see the undeserved gift of the snow leopard cloak given to the Bride, think on me. The black robe is a sign of your task and a symbol of your duty."

The Bridegroom brought forth a chain with iron links the size of the man's ear. He placed the middle of the chain over the man's head and on the back of his neck. The ends hung down the front of the man's chest and reached the bottom of the black robe. Attached to the last link at one end of the chain was a metal contraption, dark and ominous in appearance. At the other end, a small, dark brown box with a hinged door was fastened.

A short grunt came from the man as the full weight of the chain and its attachments bore down upon him. He glanced at the burden and raised his head to the Bridegroom in wonder.

"This binds you to your duty. It represents the weight of your task. Yet, it is not merely a symbol or representation. It is

14

quite real. For the work ahead, I have placed it upon your shoulders this day."

"Sir, please tell me, what is my new task?"

"I give you no new task. You are still entrusted with my word and my Bride."

The man pondered his duty, "But that is the same task as before."

"The same and yet different. No longer will it be done on this side of the Portal. Similarly, your duty will no longer be accomplished in a short time. Now, for all three of us, it will be much more difficult."

"Sir, I do not understand."

"What is it that you do not understand? You were the bestman, the one in charge of caring for the Bride and attending to her needs. Though the route and the time have changed, you remain my bestman. Is that so perplexing?"

"Well, yes, it is. And, if you pardon me, sir, you know it too."

"True, but say it aloud. You need to hear it said from your own mouth."

The bestman thought a moment and replied, "You entrusted me with your word and with your Bride in this good place. However, I remained silent when I should have spoken your words and protected your Bride. I permitted her to listen to Footstomper. She was embraced by him and, together, we were led away from you. Is this not true?"

"It is true. Continue."

"What I was then not able to do here in this good place, even for a short time, you are now expecting me to do out there for ... well, for who knows how long?"

The Bridegroom answered the rhetorical question, "I know how long. I also know here and there."

The bestman spoke in resignation followed by frustration, "Yes, you do. But I can not do this thing that you ask. I wasn't able before and I am not able now. You know that, don't you?"

"No."

"Well, if I am not too forward, what is it that you know about this task of mine?"

"It is too forward of you, bestman. However, you will accept this. I do know *how long* and I do know *whether*. That should be enough for you."

The bestman pressed on, "Didn't you know *the how long* and *the whether* the first time, when I failed?"

"Yes."

The bestman thought a moment and replied, "I will try again. When do I begin?"

"I?" replied the Voice.

"We?"

"We.

"When do we begin, sir?"

"Shortly. One must be sent forth first and there are others who must be permitted to go."

CHAPTER 2

PERMITTED ONES AND SENT ONES

With his hand directing them to the side, the Bridegroom spoke to his Bride and bestman, "Stand here and do not block the pathway to the Portal. Behold, the first one I am sending out draws near."

A pounding of the ground was heard and felt. From across that good place, a white stallion galloped, its hooves hammering the green turf. The rider reined the massive beast at the Portal. The magnificent animal stood higher at the saddle than any of the three by the Portal. The stallion snorted fiercely and reared in anticipation of the ride ahead. The Bridegroom did not flinch as the hooves whirled mere inches from his face. Both the Bride and the bestman flinched, raising their arms and backing from the powerful animal.

"Logos! You are sent. Go forth conquering and to conquer," commanded the Bridegroom.

The mighty rider, dressed in a dazzling white robe which flowed in the whirlwind, faced the speaker. His resolute face acknowledged the command and his right arm raised a gleaming weapon, a two-edged sword, in salute. As the front feet of the stallion hit the ground, the rider leaned forward, relaxing the reins. The nostrils of the beast flared and the animal charged through the Portal. A quarter mile on the other side, the stallion stopped and turned. As it reared, the rider raised the sword in a second salute. Lightning flashed from the tip of the weapon to the top of the Portal. The streak of pure light cracked across the gray skies and

17

thunder rocked the deep places of the earth. Seconds later, on a hill far away, the white stallion and its rider, stood waiting.

The Bridegroom turned to the two and said, "Keep your eyes focused on Logos. He is faithful and true. He is the way you must go. Follow him and abide with him. Do you understand me, my Bride?"

"Yes, what you say is what I will do."

"You will lift up your eyes to see this sent one and you will be guided by him, and by him alone. There will be times when he sends his runners to you with my utterances of will and proclamation. Receive the runners who come in my name. Do you understand me, my bestman?"

"Yes, sir, what you say is what we will do. If both stallion and rider remain as clear as they are now, we will have no problem."

"Listen closely, bestman. The stallion and rider will remain as clear, but your eyes will not be as perceptive as they are in this good place. As a result, your task will be neither easy nor trouble-free."

"As you say, sir."

A small, red pony approached the Portal in a gentle walk. The slender rider, clothed in thin scarlet garb, did not take his eyes from the Bridegroom's person. Five feet from the Portal the rider tugged at the reins and the red pony stopped. The red rider, while staring directly at the Bride and the bestman, sent a thought to the Bridegroom, *You have prohibited us from speaking. But by the right of enmity, I am permitted to precede these two.*

The Bridegroom roared aloud, "You have no right save what is granted you! Go through! You are permitted."

The red rider nudged the small pony through the Portal. Immediately the landscape on the other side of the Portal took on a bloody, reddish hue. At a spot twenty feet on the other side, the animal was directed to the side of the pathway. Both beast and rider faced the Portal as if waiting for someone to pass through. Less than thirty feet from the Bride and the bestman, the red pony

18

and rider appeared darker red, though much smaller and weaker than when they were on the good side of the Portal.

The bestman spoke to the Bridegroom, "Why did you send that puny red pair through the Portal?"

The Bridegroom answered, "Bestman, do not be deceived by appearances. They are not weak and I did not send them. The rider is Polemos. I permitted Polemos and the red horse to pass through the Portal to the other side. Their presence in that place is one of the consequences - the consequence of *enmity*. Their doings will be a source of horrific grief for my Bride.

A nervous black gelding trotted its way, often in a sideways gait, to the Portal. The eyes of both beast and rider flashed in obvious discomfort at their surroundings. The rider, dressed in black, avoided eye and thought contact with the Bridegroom. Without stopping, yet slowing down because of uncertainty, the black gelding and rider moved to the Portal.

"You are permitted. Go!"

The land flushed a rust color after they crossed to the other side. The shining appearance of the rider's clothing hazed while the gelding's coat became dull, taking on a drab, sickly appearance. The black gelding was calmed as its rider directed the animal to a position next to the red pony.

"The gelding and its rider are named, Limos and Loimos. They will plague your days and keep you awake at night."

The woman asked the Bridegroom, "Are they also part of the consequences?"

"Yes, the consequence of *endemism*."

From some exposed crease in the good place, a pale horse slowly marched in the direction of the Portal. The animal was strong, giving no sign of fear. A pale rider with albino eyes rode confidently and with an attitude of haughty supremacy. Sharp, pointed teeth glistened as it grinned slyly at the Bride and the bestman. Spittle hung freely from its slobbering mouth. Its colorless eyes focused on them and revealed a lust for them. The pale rider leaned from the side of the saddle in a close inspection of them. The pale horse with anemic eyes was dragging an empty net. The rider extended an ashen arm from its robe and pointed a finger at the two beside the Bridegroom. Slowly its hand arced back and the icy finger gestured to the net, indicating they would be in it. As it rode by the Bridegroom, the pale rider mocked him with wild gestures from its wrinkled, cadaverous, distorted, blanched face.

The pale rider sought no permission to pass through the Portal. On the other side, both horse and rider nearly disappeared from sight. Only by not looking directly at them could they be seen by the Bride and the bestman. The ground turned a dirty, filthy brown as the latest arrival slowly marched past the red pony and the black gelding. The net trailed, etching skid marks in the dust of the earth's surface. The pale rider pointed the ghastly beast in the direction of Logos.

The bestman asked, "Sir, who was that?"

The Bridegroom answered without looking at him, "Not *who*."

The Bride continued, "*What*, then, was that?"

He answered, "Not *was*."

They queried together, "What *is that*?"

"That, bestman, is your second greatest enemy. That is one of your main consequences, bestman - the consequence of *entropy*."

The bestman asked, "Sir, does that have a name?"

"Thanatos."

The Bride asked, "Why does Thanatos drag a net behind?"

"For collecting the dead and taking them along."

She continued, "But Thanatos left the body of the snow leopard."

"Thanatos is not interested in dead snow leopards."

The bestman confessed, "I fear Thanatos."

"My Bride and my bestman, fear no one, no thing and nothing, but me. Thanatos is only able to initiate the first death and cast you into the net, bestman. I alone hold the key to the

20

second death. I alone am able to release you from the net. Bestman, this is one of the utterances you must remember and repeat."

The bestman replied, "At your word, sir. May I ask a question of you?"

"You may."

"You told us that Thanatos is my second greatest enemy. Who is my greatest enemy?"

"Your greatest enemy, bestman, is you."

The bestman asked, "My greatest enemy is me? Is your Bride her greatest enemy?"

"No."

The woman interjected, "Who is my greatest enemy?"

The Bridegroom answered, "Footstomper."

"Why is this so?" asked the bestman.

The Bridegroom explained, "You, bestman, will die the first death. My Bride will not suffer either death. She will never die."

"Then why is Footstomper her greatest enemy?"

"Footstomper seeks to lead her away from me. If it does, many of her children will die the death of the desolate place. Bestman, that is why your work is so important. As you lead my Bride, so will many of her children go. If you speak falsely to her and lead her astray, then many of her children will die the death of the desolate place. They will be lost, but from you will I require an accounting. If you speak the truth to her and lead her in the truth of my utterances, then many of her children will never suffer the second death. Though some will be lost, the fault will not be because you withheld the truth of my word. You do understand the seriousness of your duty?"

"Yes, but it is far beyond me."

"True, however you are not alone. Logos will always be with you. His runners will be sent. Receive them and receive from them."

"And you," asked the Bride, "where will you be as we travel?"

"Logos and I are one."

The bestman continued the questioning, "How will we survive?"

"My Bride, do you feel the pockets inside your white cloak?"

"Yes."

"Reach in the right pocket and take out the small cruse of water." She did and he continued, "This is to be used by the bestman to mark the foreheads of your children, like this." The Bridegroom opened the cruse, applied a drop to his index finger and marked the forehead of the bestman.

"Do you both understand?" They nodded their heads in the affirmative and he continued, "Now bring forth the flask of wine from the left pocket."

As the Bride produced the brown flask from under her cloak, the Bridegroom explained, "This is for a most special use. A blessing is intended. However, abusing it abuses me and results in the opposite of the intended blessing. This special wine heals both body and soul. The bestman is to let you and your children drink of it. Also my Bride, you are to make sure that the bestman drinks a portion for himself."

"Now, dear woman, take the loaf of bread from the large pocket in the center." She did as commanded and he said, "Refresh and sustain yourselves on this bread often. Let the bestman be the steward of this feast as well."

The bestman objected mildly, "Sir, you have given these gifts to your Bride. They belong to her?"

"Yes, these gifts are hers."

The bestman continued, "But I am supposed to administer them. Does she give them to me?"

"No, she entrusts them to you for proper serving. You are my bestman and the steward of these gifts by which the life of my Bride is sustained. In addition to the water, wine and bread, I give her my word. She is to entrust to you the speaking of my word. When her children are gathered about her, you are to speak my utterances to her and to her children. When you are both on the other side of the Portal, she will entrust these gifts to you. Place them within the dark brown box attached to the one end of the chain stole I placed on your shoulders. Use them as needed and as is of benefit to my Bride. Remember that they are intended for you as well."

These words brought another question to mind and the bestman asked, "You said that your Bride will never die, but that I will die. What happens when I die? And who will care for your Bride?"

"You are beginning quite well, my bestman. You are thinking of the welfare of my Bride and what she will need after you have died the first death. This is good and commendable. Bestman, after you die, she will appoint a new bestman. He will continue with your work of serving me by serving her."

The Bridegroom turned to his Bride, enveloped her hands in his and asked tenderly, "Do you understand?"

"I understand the words but not the meaning," she replied.

The Bridegroom spoke as he ushered them to the Portal, "There is a knowing that only comes from experience. You will understand. But lo, the time for you to pass through the Portal and begin the journey has come. You must go for I am now sending you. Bestman, hold fast to the truth that I am Headbanger, that I am always with you and that I am coming. Speak of my presence and my advent to my Bride. Stand firm in the confession of my word. Bride, truly you are my beloved. I anticipate and await the day of the Great Wedding."

The bestman hesitated, "Sir, there is something I do not know; something I need to know. Please tell me, where is the Great Wedding to be celebrated? For certainly, unless I know where it will be, how could I know the way?"

He replied, "Bestman, you are not taking my Bride to a *where*. You are taking her to *the when*."

CHAPTER 3

APPEARANCES AND REALITIES

Two lonely steps after passing through the Portal, an assault was waged against them from the air. Their pristine lungs inhaled a putrid odor, a repugnant stagnation that settled deep into their chests. Uncontrollable fits of coughing erupted in fruitless attempts to rid their lungs of the foul, contaminated atmosphere on this side of the Portal.

"Agh," the Bride hacked and choked, "What is happening to us, bestman?"

He gagged and answered in coughing spasms, "I don't know. I am being invaded and overcome. I can't hold my breath. We have no choice but to breathe this foul air. Perhaps this is one of the consequences."

The Bride noticed he had fallen to his knees and asked, "Are you dying, bestman?"

"I don't know. I have never died before," he replied with fear. "No doubt this is one of the consequences. But, I don't feel like reclining on the ground like the snow leopard. I must not be dying."

"There is no other air for us to breathe here. We must adapt to this contaminated atmosphere we are inhaling," declared the Bride.

Indeed, the Bride and the bestman began controlling their coughing fits. The bestman attempted to stand, but found it difficult to do so. The chain stole was heavier, digging into his neck and pushing his head forward slightly. The black links rattled together and clanked against the dark attachments.

Covering her ears in reaction to the harsh grating, the Bride complained, "Oh, please, stop! That sound hurts my ears."

The bestman ignored her for a moment, stating he could taste the air. Bending over with the veins bulging from his reddened neck, he vomited. Stunned at what he had done, he focused on the fruit of his mighty heave. The Bride's hands covered her mouth in horror. Her eyes widened in shock.

A loud, dry laugh came from their left side and an arid voice was heard, "Taste the bitter gall on the edge of your teeth and welcome to our world, oh you bestman. This is our kingdom. I am going ahead of you to prepare the way for you. You are not the king here. You may be bestman, however you are but dust. So begin scratching out a living, before you die." The wiry, gaunt rider of the calm, black gelding released a guttural laugh and began a slow stride in the direction of the hill far away. As they traveled, the black rider sowed the seeds of thorns and thistles along the way, casting kernels from horizon to horizon.

"Was that Limos or Loimos?" asked the Bride.

"Uh, perhaps both," bestman answered cautiously.

"Ha!" boomed a thundering voice, "He doesn't know the answer. Woman, strike him dead for not being able to give you true and certain counsel. Run him through with a sword. Pike him. Find the jawbone of an ass and crush his skull."

Startled by the voice and trembling at its depth, the bestman and the Bride fearfully turned to see the one who spoke. The rider of the red horse scowled at them with utter disgust. The Bride and the bestman backed away from the red pair before them. Polemos' mount was no longer the little red pony they had seen on the other side of the Portal. The imposing, massive creature stood twice as high as the bestman. Taut muscles bulged against the animal's red hide while flaring nostrils sent forth mighty whirlwinds conjuring dust devils across the land. Polemos, now completely clad in red, heavy metal armor, wielded an imposing spear the size of a beam. The pointed weapon had a curved hook on the end.

The rider commanded, "Too late, woman. Oh man, smite her for being weak and unwilling to kill you. In this world, the rule is the survival of the strongest, the quickest, the fittest and the one who acts. The one who hesitates, dies. It is only fitting. Man, be the warrior!"

A moment of silent waiting passed and the rider boomed again, "Too late, pacifist. Neither of you are ready. So I will act on your behalf. I go to prepare the way for you, and where I go you will be. You will rue this day when neither of you were strong enough to do the deed."

The red horse snorted, reared and charged to the far left horizon. In its wake a cloud of dust billowed around the Bride and the bestman. Once more they coughed. Polemos and the red horse were nearly out of sight when the dust cleared and the couple looked up. The red beast turned and raced across the plain. Polemos hung the spear to the side and dragged the hooked end across the face of the land. The hoe-like spear dug into the ground and a trench formed. The trench lengthened in a snakelike fashion, extending as far as the east is from the west. The red horse turned and made another charge, skewing slightly. Back and forth they traversed the terrain, forming a zigzag of trenches across the land. The hook continued to carve the earth before them as the red pair prepared the way. While they were soon far away, the battlefield of enmity, carved in the weed-infested land of Limos and Loimos, was before the bestman and the Bride.

A voice spoke to them from the side, "I am ready and I will follow you. So, please proceed."

They turned to see the speaker but saw nothing at first. The Bride glanced to the side and in doing so, caught a glimpse of the horse and rider. She looked directly at them and saw nothing again. Moving her eyes away once more, she could see them only in fleeting glances.

"Do not look directly at the voice," she told the bestman and added immediately, "Gaze to the side."

He did and announced, "Yes, there, a glimpse, I see Thanatos and the pale horse."

With seething satisfaction, Thanatos hissed, "Oh, you have seen nothing yet. The time will come, worstman, oh yes, the day will descend upon you, the moment when you will see me face to face. I feed on your terror and feast on your fear. I will slowly, ever so slowly, savoring each moment of terror, swallow you up, savoring the process of your dying and craving the owning of you after you die. My black net drags behind me. It is empty now. Oh, who will be the first to be gathered into it and dragged behind me? Will it be you, Worstman Dirt, or perhaps it will be you, abandoned woman?"

With a false bravado, the bestman countered, "The Bride can not die."

"Who said?" replied Thanatos and continued before the bestman could answer, "No matter. We will see. I am so very patient. My beast and I pursue slowly, but we pursue. I will speak no more to you, but know that we are never far behind you ... waiting and pursuing, always waiting and always pursuing. The pale horse is strong and pulls a heavy load. I am quite patient and will wait to gather you into my net. And though I say no more, I will haunt your darkening nights and make bleak your miserable days. You will run far and fast, but I will catch up to you and put you into my black net. It shall be so. I speak no more. We follow. It is time for you to go. And do not forget, we are never far behind you. Go! Be gooonnnne." It repeated the command several times whispering softer each time, "Go ... go ... go."

Completely terrified, the bestman grasped the Bride's hand with the intention of running back through the Portal. She thought the same and began to move with him. At that instant a streak of lightning flashed from the hill far away to the top of the Portal. The white bolt remained fixed between the two points. The bestman raised his arm, pulling the black wool robe to eye level. The Bride remained still as her eyes spanned the length of the lingering lightning. In seconds, the white flame consumed the Portal. The lightning bolt receded slowly from the place where the Portal had been, withdrawing across the dark sky and back whence it came, to the horse and rider on the hill far away. The Bride focused her attention on Logos, but she trembled and wavered with fear.

The bestman quickly turned his head back and forth from Logos to the place of the Portal. He caught a glimpse and glanced to the side. Thanatos was salivating in anticipation. It raised an arm in the direction of the trenches and sown seeds. Slowly it swung its gaunt arm back to the net. An awful grin remained until Thanatos brought forward the hood of the pale cloak causing its face to be somewhat hidden. It placed a similar hood over the head of the pale horse. Together the ashen pair stood and waited.

The bestman lowered his eyes below the shield of his black robe. He closed his eyes and with trembling lips, willed all this be gone. He whispered, "Please, oh Bridegroom, please, I can not do this thing you ask. Get us out of here. If there is some other way for this to be done, let it be that way."

The Bride spoke, "Bestman, quick, look at Logos and the white horse. What do you notice about them?"

"What?" he asked, his eyes still hidden below his black robe.

"They have changed. Open your eyes and look at them. What do you notice?"

The bestman peered from the black robe. A moment later he spoke, "Yes, they are no longer white. Both are gray. What has happened to them? Have they changed or have we?"

The Bride continued without answering him, "Look closer, bestman, not just at the gray. Do you see what I see?"

"Yes. Oh, how can this be? The rider is a servant wearing gray or even dirty clothing."

She added, "And there is a gray donkey where the white stallion used to be."

"The Bridegroom told us our eyes would not be as perceptive in this land as they were on the other side of the Portal. I believe they are still Logos and the white horse. Our eyes see things in a different way and we should not trust in appearances only. Polemos' horse was a little red pony on the other side. Now the animal is a churlish brute."

"Who is the ruler of this world? Is it Polemos or Limos or Loimos or even Thanatos? Which of these, do you think, is the most powerful?"

The bestman responded with some doubt, "Bride, we do not even know how to define power. The more powerful might not be the strongest physically, or the fastest, or the loudest talker. In the names you listed, where would you put Logos and the white horse? Where would you put the servant and the donkey?"

She replied, "I do not know. On the other side of the Portal, the Bridegroom was the ruling lord and king. But, as we are well aware, this is a much different place. It does not appear that the Bridegroom is the strongest here, if indeed, he is here. Logos and the white horse are not as impressive and majestic in this land. But in saying these things, are we not doubting what the Bridegroom told us?"

"Hmm, yes," bestman answered, "I think you are correct. If Logos is here and that is Logos on the hill far away, then that is where the Bridegroom is. He said that he and Logos were one. We should trust the Bridegroom in spite of what we see and hear, especially in spite of what we feel."

The Bride continued his line of thought and added, "Will you trust him, bestman, in spite of your own death?"

"Yes."

She asked further, "Do you say that because you have no alternative, or because he can be trusted?"

His eyes rose in slight bewilderment, "Are you trying to plant doubt within me, Bride?"

"No, I am only trying to know why you trust my Bridegroom when much of the appearances and evidence here seem to bear witness against such trust."

"To be honest with you, Bride, there are some of both churning within me. There is no alternative, is there? Yet, I also have his past actions which forgave me instead of taking revenge on me. The Bridegroom restored me to my place and sent me forth with you. In addition, and just as important, we have his word."

The Bride glanced in the general direction of the pale horse and saw Thanatos directing them to the open land of trenches and sown seeds. She nodded her head in the direction of Thanatos and asked the bestman, "What do we do now?"

He caught a glimpse of Thanatos' pointing arm and turned hood. "We wait here."

The Bride was surprised and queried, "Why?"

"There are three reasons, Bride. First, I am inclined not to follow the directions of Thanatos. Second, I speak to you of the advent of Headbanger. We are not going to him, he is coming to us. Finally, I am not to escort you to a *where* but to *the when*. This seems an adequate spot to stay until the time of his advent."

The Bride answered as she looked to the hill far away, "Well reasoned, bestman. I think you are right about this. The Bridegroom will be pleased."

At that moment Logos turned and began moving in a direction away from them. Both donkey and servant disappeared behind the hill. The eyes of the bestman and the Bride met in doubt.

He suggested, "Let's wait. He is not too far from us."

"I do not know. Aren't we to follow Logos?"

"Patience."

"As you say," she replied. After further thought, she continued, "Bestman, you said that Logos looked like a servant. How did you know *servant* ?"

He thought a moment and admitted, "I am not able to say. But I do know servant. As you say, Logos does look like a servant. Do you know servant?"

"Yes, but like you, I do not know why."

The gray donkey and the servant appeared on a hill farther away. The two distant ones stopped again. Both were barely visible to the Bride and to the bestman.

The Bride asked, "He does not appear to be coming to us, bestman. What shall we do?"

He glanced at the pointing Thanatos, thought a moment, and said, "I don't know."

CHAPTER 4

THE SERVANT AND THE BURDEN

The bestman and the Bride waited, straining their eyes to keep the donkey and the servant in sight. Minutes passed. A movement was detected on the hill farther away. It vanished for several moments and reappeared at the top of the closer hill. Arms pumped the air and legs churned out long strides as someone in brown raiment dashed in the direction of the bestman and the Bride. The distance runner appeared to be carrying a baton in his right hand. Drawing near, the man leaped the deep trenches without breaking stride. Despite the full sprint over the long distance, the man breathed without exertion. He approached the couple, bowed to the Bride and handed a small, sealed volume to her. With the volume was a card.

> I am Eliathah the Poor,
> a runner from the ancient village of Benedicamus
> at the base of High Mountain.
>
> (Please imprint your right thumb on the other side of this card
> and return it to me. Please keep and read this volume.)

Eliathah the Poor focused his attention on the Bride, conveying the impression that his duty was most important to him. She turned the card over to press her right thumb on it. Words were written on the back side of the card.

She read the words and asked, "Eliathah the Poor, may I let the bestman look at this card?"

He said nothing and made no gestures.

The Bride leaned to the side, enabling and encouraging the bestman to read the card with her.

> The good land is ahead, not behind,
> Tho' the way to you seems not so kind,
>   You've passed through the Portal,
>   To the land of the mortal,
> The servant now seeks and will find.

The Bride pressed her right thumb against it and an imprint appeared. She returned the marked card to Eliathah the Poor and smiled. He examined the thumb print and, being quite satisfied, saluted the Bride and left without speaking.

"Wait," yelled the bestman to the determined runner. But Eliathah the Poor neither hesitated nor made any indication he heard the demand. His lanky legs quickly carried his slender torso away from the couple in the direction of the hill farther away.

The volume was made from an animal hide. A red thread bound the volume. The ends of the red thread were tied. At the point of the knot, a drop of coagulated blood served as the seal. The signet used to seal the letter left a strange marking, a marking similar to the unknown object at the end of the chain. The Bride pulled the red thread, breaking the seal. A rumble of distant thunder was heard and felt.

Carefully the woman unrolled the volume and read it. The bestman watched her face as she did so. Frowns accompanied heavy sighs. Eventually, a pursed smile and glistening eyes replaced all downcast expressions. The Bride closed her eyes and held a deeply inhaled breath. A moment later, with eyes still closed, she said, "Bestman Dusty, please read the contents of this volume."

He asked, "Bestman Dusty?"

"Yes, Bestman Dusty," she said, her eyes now open wider. "It is in the volume."

He received the volume and studied what had been written. When the bestman finished his initial reading, he rolled the volume and attempted to return it to the Bride. She refused it, saying, "No."

With the volume still in his hand and extended to her, he countered, "The volume rightly belongs to you, Bride."

"Yes it does, along with the water, bread and wine. I entrust this volume to you, Bestman Dusty. Please keep this in the polished box at the end of the chain." She reached under her white cloak, brought out the three items and continued, "Also, I entrust you with the marking water, the bread of life and the wine of the feast. You, Bestman Dusty, use them to nourish, nurture and sustain me, my children and yourself. Study the volume and read it to us. Lead us in the service from, the adoration of and the response to the Bridegroom. You are Bestman Dusty, entrusted with my care. You wear the black robe and bear the chain stole."

"All that the Bridegroom has said and what you have entrusted to my care, I will do and keep," replied Bestman Dusty. "Now, Bride, as we heard on the other side of the Portal and is revealed to us in the volume, our hope is in Headbanger. We are to keep our eyes on Logos and follow him. I believe that is what he was attempting to communicate to us when Logos went from the hill far away to the hill farther away. Don't you remember how Logos stopped, turned around and looked at us? We should have gone to them immediately. Instead, we hesitated and a runner was sent."

The Bride asked, "Do you think the Bridegroom was displeased with us for not following?"

"I don't know," Bestman Dusty answered, "but one thing is most certainly true ..."

"... if we do not start following him now, he will not be pleased," interjected the Bride.

Bestman Dusty agreed. Both checked to confirm the presence of Logos. He had not moved. The smooth door to the small, polished box on the end of the chain opened easily. The four items entrusted to Bestman Dusty's stewardship were carefully placed inside the spacious box.

Cautiously, the Bride leaned toward Bestman Dusty and whispered, "Glance at Thanatos."

Bestman Dusty caught a glimpse of Thanatos and the pale horse. The ashen arm still pointed in the direction of Logos. Bestman Dusty spoke to the faceless one, "We are going that direction, but it's not because of your pointing. We go to Logos because we desire to please him and to be with him. Our path has nothing to do with you or your will."

Thanatos lowered its arm and mockingly bowed its head in a slow, deliberate manner. It touched both hands to the chest, assuming a false position of humility. With head still inclined forward, it raised an arm and pointed for them to go.

The Bride tugged lightly at Bestman Dusty's black sleeve. When he turned to her, she nodded in the direction of Logos. He agreed and they commenced the long journey.

Before them stretched a vast expanse - a land whose face had changed even in the short time since the couple entered it. The red pair, by galloping, charging and jumping across the landscape, had caused Polemos' hooked beam to skip across the ground. The resultant trenches scarred the surface in a rhythmic pattern - a design similar to the travelings of a sidewinder across the sandy desert. The blighted seed from Limos and Loimos had germinated and plagued the land. Even now, the winds of this world carried thistle seeds to and fro. These noxious plants could be avoided by the couple but constant attention was needed to do so. The ground groaned under the infestation.

Bestman Dusty and the Bride descended into the first trench and from its bottom Logos was no longer in view. A dreadful, holy fear overshadowed them, their hearts racing in the twinkling of an eye. They scrambled up the far side of the furrow and were relieved to behold Logos in the distance. Gazing back at the trench they beheld the pale beast plodding along in their direction. Thanatos, pointing no more concerning the way, remained motionless in the saddle and under the hood. The empty black net trailed. The pale rider's words, those ones craving the feelings of despair and the fright of death, resounded in Bestman Dusty's heart and mind. He turned, guiding the Bride's elbow in the direction of Logos, though little effort was required.

The Bride, being of like mind and manner, was already pivoting. They ran to the next trench, a distance greater than five hundred strides. After descending to its depths and ascending its farther bank, the couple surveyed the landscape behind them. Thanatos patiently rode the trudging pale horse. The plodding beast arrived at the first trench. Horse and rider were swallowed by the earth as the black net slipped over the edge and disappeared. Moments passed. No movement came from the deep ditch. Hope was conceived within the couple, for they supposed the ashen rider and beast were trench-trapped. Aghast despair aborted their hope when the pale pair arose from the furrow with the nightly net in tow. Thanatos savored the meal, feasting on the wide, emotional swing from joyful hope to anguished woe.

As his heart pounded, Bestman Dusty spoke. "They travel slowly. Let's run."

"Yes, we might lose them if we ran a great distance," the Bride replied.

The couple ran most of the afternoon, resting only briefly after crossing each trench. When the edge of the earth swallowed the sun at the end of the first day in the new land, seventeen trenches had been crossed. The slow traveling net-draggers had appeared as small dots after the sixth trench and had not been seen since the eighth one.

Reaching the top of the hill far away, Bestman Dusty and the Bride peered into their future and saw the donkey and the servant beyond the hill farther away.

"Oh Bride," said Bestman Dusty, "it doesn't appear that the wedding will take place this day. The light is going away and I do not know what it means. We must stop for we cannot see to run anymore. Maybe this darkening is death coming."

"At least Thanatos and the pale horse are not able to see in this darkness either. They must wait where they are," the Bride exhaled confidently. "This place seems safe."

Sitting on a patch of bare ground free from noxious weeds, Bestman Dusty opened the polished box at one end of the chain and removed the volume. As long as the fading light permitted, he read from the volume, occasionally pausing to reflect on a point. Bread and wine were brought out and Bestman Dusty and the Bride were nourished. They ended by closing their eyes to the distractions of the day and speaking to the Bridegroom.

The Bride made her bed near a smooth stone and pulled her arms under her cloak. Bestman Dusty made ready to sleep ten feet away, near the base of a leafy bush. Neither fell asleep quickly.

"Bestman Dusty?"

"Yes."

"What is *pain*?"

"I know of the word, for we have recently read of it in the volume. But knowing the word pain isn't the same as knowing pain.

"What is pain like?"

"I don't know, but I think a part of what we felt on the other side of the Portal, when we knew we had disappointed and disobeyed the Bridegroom, was pain."

"Certainly I was afraid, but also more than afraid. Perhaps that more I also felt was pain."

"Yes," Bestman Dusty continued, "there was a deep hurting inside of me. I wanted the hurting to stop, but wasn't able to stop it. Perhaps that is part of pain; not being able to stop it or make it go away."

"Bestman Dusty?"

"What?"

"I think we have much pain ahead."

"Yes."

There was silence as each reflected on the events of the day.

"Bride?"

"Yes?"

"What are *children*?"

"I know the word, but knowing the word is not the same as understanding the reality of what children are. Again, I believe we will know about children tomorrow."

"True."

CHAPTER 5

HURTS AND PAINS

Sunbeams broke across the face of the Bride before she awoke. Keeping her eyelids shut, she regained the awareness of who and where she was. Single tears seeped through the downhill corners of her closed eyes as she recalled the good place on the other side of the Portal and the consequences of the place where she was.

The Bride had been a woman only a few days now and her milky complexion and smooth skin, despite the introductory exposure to degenerating forces, remained unblemished. The crow's feet, caused by squinting pain and bitter sorrow, were not permanently radiating from the corners of her eyes. Her youthful, womanly form and lovely maiden features, though now subject to decay in a fallen world, did not yet show the sagging effects that gravity would work in due time.

Still, she had feelings never before experienced. Her feet ached, especially the big toe on which a watery lump pooled. Muscles pulled and knotted down the length of her calves. Her shoulders defined *stiffness* and *soreness* for the first time. She rolled to her back and attempted to stretch the soreness from heel and hamstring.

With eyes closed she mumbled, "Bestman Dusty?"

The Bride was startled that her mouth did not work as she willed. She ran her tongue across her teeth and encountered a foul, filmy coating.

"Ugh!" she moaned as the spittle collected in her mouth. Louder she called to her escort, "Bestman Dusty?"

He groaned and rolled to his other side. Having rubbed the sleep from his eyes with the heels of his hands, he parted his reluctant lids to view the second day in this place. The light of a dawning day momentarily hindered him from seeing properly. Slowly he overcame the brilliance and began to focus on what was in front of him. Accosted by the confronting figures before him, Bestman Dusty bellowed a sound that was somewhat shout, but mostly moan. Upright in an instant, he reached for the Bride in an attempt to escape quickly. Her reaction, caused by his scream, made her willing to run by the time he grabbed her arm. When she saw the figure before them, a groan escaped from her.

The shadow of Thanatos and the pale horse, had there been one, would have cast itself over the place where they had slept. Silently horse and rider had journeyed through the night and caught up with the fleeing couple. Sometime during the pre-dawn hours, Thanatos' unrelenting pursuit of the two ended. Posted like a granite sentinel, the ashen pair waited.

The couple ran, fleeing in the direction of the previous day. Hearts pumped in cadence with the cycling of legs in flight. Soon two trenches separated them from the trudging beast. On the edge of the far bank of the second trench, Bestman Dusty and the Bride sat with their legs dangling. Immersed in personal thoughts they ate bread and drank water. Several minutes later they spoke.

"We didn't run far enough yesterday."

"No."

"What should we do?"

"We did not have a full day to run yesterday."

"That's true. Let's continue running."

"As you say."

Two hours later Thanatos was no longer in sight and after three hours they noticed someone running toward them from the direction of Logos. Arriving within the hour, the runner bowed to the Bride and handed a large, sealed scroll to her. The seal was identical in type and marking to the one on the previously received volume. With the scroll was a card.

> I am Elishama the Mourner,
> a runner from the ancient village of Benedicamus
> at the base of High Mountain.
>
> (Please imprint your right thumb on the other side of this card
> and return it to me. Keep this scroll and sing from it.)

Elishama the Mourner rigidly stood at the ready and patiently waited for the Bride to read and imprint the attached card. Fascinated with the presence of the runner, Bestman Dusty spoke to him.

"Are you permitted to speak to us?"

"Sir, yes."

"What is your name?"

He pointed to the card as the Bride answered for him, "Elishama the Mourner, a runner of the Bridegroom."

Bestman Dusty continued, "When will we arrive at the Bridegroom's location?"

"Sir, that is not for me to know, and thus, not for me to say."

Bestman Dusty spoke, "Will this scroll tell us how long it will be?"

"Sir, I do not know, nor is it my place to speculate on such important matters. The card explains what the scroll is."

The Bride looked at the back side of the card and read the words. After a moment of thought, she spoke, "Elishama the Mourner, are you to deliver the scroll only to me?"

"Madam, yes. The scroll belongs only to you."

"May it be given to Bestman Dusty?"

"Madam, yes. However, the scroll belongs only to you."

"Before I imprint this card and return it to you, may I show this side of the card to Bestman Dusty?"

"Madam, yes."

41

O bestman, who stands in my stance,
My beloved must learn the Great Dance,
To accomplish your task,
And to do what I ask,
I give you my psalms and your chants.

Bestman Dusty read the card several times. The seriousness and extent of his work were sobering. The card received the Bride's imprint and the runner received the card. Upon his satisfactory examination of her thumb print, Elishama the Mourner ran in the direction of Logos.

"Bestman Dusty, keep, read, study and tell me, along with all my children, the words in this scroll. And Bestman Dusty, please teach us the Great Dance."

"This I will do," he said, receiving the three foot long scroll and placing it in the small ironwood box at the end of the chain. He peered through the door and wondered at how so much could be placed into it. The highly polished box, measuring no more than six inches in its greatest dimension, was at least four feet deep as he looked inside it.

He continued, "First, I must learn the Great Dance myself."

"Yes," she replied, "you are not to be excluded from receiving the many blessings simply because you are the bestman."

"Thank you," Bestman Dusty responded with warmth. He continued, "But now, Bride, we must put many trenches between us and the stalkers."

The Bride glanced back at the invisible pursuers. She communicated her agreement with a pursing of lips and a determined nodding of the chin. The two ran until the time of highest sun, stopping only long enough for food and water. Trench after trench was traversed through the course of the day.

Between furrows thirty-nine and forty, the Bride cried out and tumbled to the dry, cursed ground. Bestman Dusty was stunned and came quickly to her aid. She grabbed her foot and twisted it to inspect the bottom of her heel. A spiked kernel remained imbedded in her sole. Short shrieks continued to issue forth from her as she clutched her ankle with both hands. Her attendant steadied the wounded foot with one hand and pulled the multi-spiked kernel from her heel with the fingers of the other.

Breathing heavily, she asked, "What was that?"

"It's a small seed with sharp spikes. When you stepped on it, one of the spikes punctured the thick skin of your heel and penetrated to the quick. This seed comes from a new plant, one found only on this side of the Portal. We should call this plant and its seed, *puncture weed.*"

"Fine," the Bride replied in lessening pain and slight anger, "but that's not what I meant. Not what was in my foot, but what was that I experienced?"

"I don't understand. What do you mean?"

"A sharp feeling enveloped me so that there were no other sensations within me. My mind was filled with complete focus on the point in my heel where the puncture weed penetrated. I could not speak words, only cries. For an instant, nothing else existed. Now, however, that intense experience is gone. I feel nothing except a burning sensation in my heel. What has all of this been which I experienced at that instant?"

Bestman Dusty replied, "I believe you have experienced pain."

"But, it was not like the other pain we felt when the Bridegroom sought us in the good place. Can it be there are different kinds of pain?"

Bestman Dusty opened the small door to the polished box and took out the cruse of water and the flask of wine. As he poured water on her foot and washed it, he answered her, "We have only begun our life on this side of the Portal. For us to think we understand all the consequences of living here would be naive.

You are wise to think there are more kinds of pain. No doubt we will experience them."

The Bride thought a moment and declared, "I do not like this pain."

"Nor I," said Bestman Dusty.

With increasing irritation, the Bride asked, "But you did not experience my pain. How is that you say, 'Nor I' ?"

The bestman was startled and reacted sharply, "When you were pained, I hurt too, though not in the same way. There are different pains that both of us have. Last night I thought about dying. I must die and I don't know even know what that means. But it frightens me and makes me hurt inside. That is a pain you will not have."

The Bride's demeanor softened, "Yes, but as you had to watch me while I was in pain a few minutes ago, I must watch you die and even that thought hurts me. I don't know what that means either, but I am certain it will involve pain. What you say about us having our own pains is true."

With her foot washed and rinsed with water, he took wine and poured a little on the wound.

She asked, "Water is for cleansing. Why have you put wine on my foot?"

"This gift from the Bridegroom purifies. Does your foot hurt anymore?"

"No," she replied while thinking, "well, yes, but it is a tiny hurt compared to what it once was. The pain of the foot may go away after awhile, but the hurt remains elsewhere. One pain leaves only to be replaced by another. The hurts from both remain long after the pain is gone and we are physically able to return to what we were doing. So, Bestman Dusty, while we may continue running, we will do so hurting."

The couple crossed fifty-seven trenches before stopping for the night. After the evening meal, the Bride asked Bestman Dusty to take out the scroll and read about the Great Dance. She wanted to learn the Great Dance before her wedding day. The scroll was carefully removed from the polished, ironwood box and placed on the ground before them. He read to her from the scroll and together they learned the setting for the Great Dance.

According to the scroll, the configuration for practicing the Great Dance was specific. The chain stole was removed from the shoulders of the bestman and fashioned into a circle so that the polished box at one end of the chain was near the device on the other end of the chain. The gap between the two items was to be less than three feet. The bestman entered the circle by stepping through the gap. He built a tiny fire in the center of the circle and placed the containers of bread, wine and water near the fire. With all things now ready, he extended his hand outside the circle, at the location of the gap, and received the hand of the Bride. He led her into the circle and began to sing one of the psalms to her. Taking her into his arms, they began dancing with slow turns and pirouettes. As they danced, the bestman softly spoke one of the Bridegroom's psalms to her. Later, a section from the *Volume of Consequences* was read. In response to the giver of the psalm, the Bride raised her voice chanting a thanksgiving directed to the Bridegroom. The dance concluded with the eating of the sanctified bread and wine. Each step and every response concluded with the affirming words, *ah yes*.

Thus, Bestman Dusty led the Bride in the Great Dance. They were stilted in their steps and clumsy in the twirls. The bestman apologized for having to stop and refer to the scroll during his singing of the psalm. The Bride told him not to be sorry for leading her in the way that the Bridegroom desired and not to apologize for being who he was called to be and doing what he was called to do.

With the Great Dance concluded for the day, Bestman Dusty and the Bride found places to sleep until the dawn of another day. The stars and moon shone brightly on the open plain during that still night.

The next morning Thanatos and the pale horse stood waiting as before. Bestman Dusty and the Bride ran once again, all day long. In the evening, the chain was circled, the gap was formed and the bestman led the Bride in the Great Dance.

Thus were their days and nights filled. Months passed and no matter how far they ran, the pale pair stood waiting for them to awaken in the morning. All things continued as they were with two exceptions. First, they were not able to run as far. The thorns and thistles spread across the floor of the land. Feet became sore as the spiked seeds of puncture weed brought them down. Second, they were not filled with terrorizing fear of Thanatos and the pale beast. They came to expect the ashen pair and were even able to ignore them in the light hours of the day.

CHAPTER 6

SORROWS AND HEARTACHES

A day came when the Bride told Bestman Dusty she could not run. Her stomach had been hurting and she wanted to rest. Bestman Dusty surveyed the area where Logos was. Logos and the white horse stood and made no indication of moving. Secure that he would not lose sight of them, he told the Bride they would camp in that place. Thanatos and the pale horse stood at the ready, but made no threatening moves.

Seven days later, the Bride begat twin sons. The older she named Eli and the younger was called Lo-Eli. She marveled at the tiny babies in her care and the infant sounds they made. The Bride held them in her arms and loved them. Their button noses breathed delicately in the Bride's arms. With little fingers curled and snug, their hands formed small, soft fists.

Bestman Dusty wondered at these tiny creatures. Who were these children and what were their needs? What was he to do in caring for them? Perhaps reading what had been given to him would help. Opening the ironwood box, he removed the *Volume of Consequences* and began reading aloud.

Lifting his eyes as he pondered a section, he noticed a runner from the direction of Logos. The Bride had not seen the man coming to them, but looked up when Bestman Dusty alerted her. The strong runner, with immense power and strength, bowed deeply to the Bride. As he did, his muscular hands held forth a tome with a card.

> I am Elimelech the Meek,
> a runner from the ancient village
> of Benedicamus at the base of High Mountain.
>
> (Please imprint your right thumb on the other side
> of this card and return it to me. Please keep and read this tome.)

The runner returned to an upright stance. Though Elimelech the Meek permitted himself to watch Eli and Lo-Eli, his attention was never far from the Bride. After reading the other side, she handed it to Bestman Dusty. He read the card several times.

> As children are raised in the fold,
> There are stories they need to be told,
> That their voices may sing,
> Of their servant and king,
> Here be odes which are sung from of old.

Smiling, he returned the card to the Bride. She pressed her right thumb in the proper place and left the desired imprint. As she gave the card to the runner, she said, "Thank you."

Elimelech the Meek was surprised.

She continued, "Are you permitted to speak to us?"

Not responding verbally to her question, Elimelech the Meek saluted the Bride and ran in the direction of Logos.

The Bride took enough time to read the tome and handed it to Bestman Dusty. He spent several hours reading and rereading its contents.

That evening the chain was circled with the usual gap. The circle expanded. The small fire was started with great care. The other items were taken from the polished box and arranged in their proper places. The cruse of water, however, remained in Bestman Dusty's hand.

At the point of the gap, the Bride stood on the outside of the circle with her two babies. While inside the circled chain, Bestman Dusty placed a drop of water on his right index finger. The Bride handed Eli to the bestman. He touched his finger to the baby's forehead, uttered Eli's name and marked him a member of the Bridegroom's family. Likewise, Lo-Eli heard the word and received the mark of circle membership, joining his mother and brother. Lastly, Bestman Dusty extended his hand to the Bride and led her through the gap and into the circle. Together the four danced the Great Dance as the edge of the earth swallowed the sun. Bestman Dusty whispered the psalm to those whom he led in the Great Dance. He read to them from the volume, led them in the chants and sang the odes from the tome to the Bride's children. At the end of the gathering, an *ah yes* was spoken.

In the decades that followed, the Bride begat many other sons and daughters. Each received the Bridegroom's watermark. The chained circle expanded to accommodate them as they entered one by one. The Bride, always radiant and glowing with youthful beauty, loved all her children.

One day, years later, while the youngest children were playing near the campsite, the two oldest descended into one of the trenches. There Eli rose up to kill his younger brother, Lo-Eli. The others heard the single curdling cry of Lo-Eli and ran to the edge of the trench. There stood Eli, holding the large rock he used to slay his brother. Eli lifted his defiant face and beheld his mother, her mouth agape and her eyes staring in horror.

"Lo-Eli!" she cried out, "Lo-Eli! You have become like the snow leopard." She buried her face in her hands and she wailed, "I see what *dead* is. Behold, my children, dead hurts the most. Where are you, Lo-Eli?"

The cursed, desert ground inhaled the dripping blood of Lo-Eli and a deep tremor shook the entire land. Bestman Dusty did not know what to do or say, either to Eli or the Bride or the rest of her children. He scrambled down to the body of Lo-Eli. Bestman Dusty watched for a minute and Lo-Eli breathed no more. He touched the body and Lo-Eli had no firmness. Adding to his taut state of mind, Bestman Dusty and the others witnessed an alarming scene. The pale horse plodded a slow, death march to the place of the body and stopped. Thanatos enmeshed Lo-Eli's body in the net and waited.

That evening, Bestman Dusty silently prepared the chained circle for the Great Dance. One by one, the younger children entered through the chain's gap. Quietly weeping, the Bride received the hand of the bestman and stepped into the circle. Eli remained outside. Bestman Dusty extended his hand to invite and receive Eli. The oldest son of the Bride drew near and reached out his hand. At the last instant, he slapped the bestman's hand in disgust. Eli turned and ran into the darkness of this world's night. The Bride never saw Eli again.

Bestman Dusty turned to join the others in the Great Dance. While he danced with the Bride, she whispered a word in his ear. Bestman Dusty stopped and said to the children, "The Bride, your mother, has asked me to make an announcement. Her oldest son is no longer to be called *Eli*. His name now is *Lo-Beni*." Several of the older sons and daughters gasped while others wept at the proclamation.

Later that night, after the Bride and Bestman Dusty had found places to sleep, the Bride spoke, "Bestman Dusty?"

"Yes."

"There are two kinds of dead and I never really knew what pain was until this day. One of the twins has died the first death; the other, I think, is dying the second death. And Bestman Dusty, I am hard-pressed to know which hurts me more."

"Bride, you hurt the most for Lo-Beni, for he has excluded himself from you and the Bridegroom. The true life in him has

50

died. That is the greatest tragedy. You also hurt the most and weep for Lo-Eli, but his essence is not in the net. Each hurt is greater than the other, but for different reasons. Weep for both, but do not weep without hope for Lo-Eli. For I tell you, the Bridegroom has his breath."

She interrupted, "How do you know this, Bestman Dusty?"

"I have read of it in both *The Scroll of Psalms and Chants* and *The Volume of Consequences*. Remember when you heard of this during the times when we gathered for the Great Dance?"

"Yes," she replied, "but to know them by reading is different than to have the results living and dying before you. A stick pierced my very being when I saw that wretched Thanatos and its hideous horse snatch my son away."

"True," he said, "but are you not comforted by knowing what will be for the one who dies only the first death?"

"Yes, and yet I must standby and watch each one of them do so, never dying myself. Bestman, I must even watch you die. Each one of the children I beget will die. For those children, like Lo-Beni, who will leave me there will be two deaths for them. Even for those, like Lo-Eli, who die only the first death, I will be there when each one leaves. I will have to go on. There are so many sorrows in this world; so many different pains. I hurt so much right now."

"Bride, join me in whispering to the Bridegroom this night. He is with us and is listening to us. Let him comfort you as you cry out to him."

"Thank you, Bestman Dusty."

The next morning, one of the daughters of the Bride saw a runner coming from the hill farther away. The little girl ran and told her mother. Children of all ages chattered as he approached the camp. He bowed graciously to the Bride and handed his card to her.

> I am Elika the Hungry,
> a runner from the ancient village
> of Benedicamus at the base of High Mountain.
>
> (Please imprint your right thumb on the other side
> of this card and return it to me. Please entrust the quill
> and the ink to the bestman and scribe.)

"Thank you, Elika the Hungry," the Bride said with hesitation, waiting for a reply.

Rather than speaking, the runner bowed his head in acknowledgement. At no time, however, did he take his eyes from the card. In his hands, Elika the Hungry cradled a chalice of red ink. A white quill from the high-soaring eagle rested in the golden chalice. The Bride read the words written on the back side of the card.

> My belov'd, you need a new link,
> Who'll write down just what I think,
> So call from your tribe,
> A bestman and scribe,
> He'll use my blood as the ink.

After pressing her thumb in the corner of the card, a red imprint appeared. Immersed in deep thought, she hesitated before returning the card to Elika the Hungry. He inspected the card and offered the golden chalice to her. She received it in both hands, smiling to the runner who responded with a salute and immediate departure.

Bestman Dusty watched these events and asked, "Bride, why didn't you let me read the card this time?"

She responded with a touching tone, "Dear Bestman Dusty, the card was addressed to me and I have been given some instructions which I am to carry out. In doing so, my heart bears two feelings. Sadness drains me because the card is a reminder that I will not always have you as the bestman. At the same time, joy overflows, for one of my children will be given a special honor."

"Is my death near?"

"I do not know. The card did not indicate the when of your death."

He asked, "Am I still the Bridegroom's bestman?"

The Bride smiled and said, "Oh yes, Bestman Dusty. In fact, sir, I entrust you with the keeping and care of this golden chalice, the white quill and the blood ink."

The bestman received them with care and placed them in the small ironwood box at the end of the chain.

The Bride continued, "We also have an assignment to complete. We must identify one of my children to become a scribe, writing at the direction and under the impulse of Ruach."

"How are we to decide which of your children is to be given this special privilege of serving?"

"Is there anything in the volume, psalms, chants or odes which may help us?"

Bestman Dusty replied, "I think so. I'll need to check."

"Please do so," she said and added, "Oh, and Bestman Dusty, the one chosen to be scribe will also be the next bestman."

Soberly, he nodded his understanding. The answer to the choosing was found in *The Volume of Consequences* and a young man named Comfy was called forth to be the scribe and next bestman. At Ruach's bidding, Comfy wrote the history of events past and future. The white quill dipped often in the blood ink as account after account was recorded for the Bride and her children.

Comfy read the sacred works entrusted to the care of Bestman Dusty and learned the truths they contained.

The chain when placed on the ground and gapped for the evening gathering grew longer as the Bride begat many children. Each, one by one, was marked with the water and brought into the circle. Thus, each one began to learn the Great Dance.

It came to pass one morning the Bride and her children awoke and discovered that Bestman Dusty was sick. He did not arise and ate no food that day. Comfy sat and read to him from *The Scroll of Psalms and Chants*. Later that evening Bestman Dusty called for the Bride and spoke to her in a quiet, strained voice. Somewhere in the distance, out in the surrounding, silent desert, a hound bayed.

During the first morning hour, when a new day was dawning, Bestman Dusty breathed his last in this fallen world. His breath was taken from the cursed land. As Thanatos and the pale horse moved to claim his body, the wool robe made from the black sheep and the chain stole were removed from him. The Bride said in words written in *The Volume of Consequences* and as if speaking to the man, "Thou art but Dusty."

Just before the noon meal, the camp assembled and the Bride made an announcement.

"Comfy, you are now called to be the Bridegroom's bestman. I place upon you the wool robe made from the black sheep and the chain stole with small wooden box at one end and the unknown thing at the other. I entrust you with the contents of the small ironwood box and direct you to nurture and nourish my children and me. Do not neglect to feed yourself as well. All this do you gladly receive and joyfully intend to do?"

"Yes, under the authority of the Bridegroom and by the power of Ruach," he answered.

"My children, you heard the promise of this man called to be the Bridegroom's bestman. You will no longer call him Comfy. He is now Bestman Comfy. You will recognize the authority of his position and honor him accordingly. When he reads to us, we will listen to him. When he feeds us, we will eat. When he leads us in the Great Dance, we will follow. All this will you do?"

With one voice they answered, "Yes, Mother."

That evening, Bestman Comfy removed the chain from his shoulders and formed it into the familiar gapped circle. After carefully putting everything in its place and starting the small fire, he invited each one into the circle, one by one. When all of the children were inside, Bestman Comfy held his hand through the gap and invited the Bride to enter. The readings were quieter that night and the chants were subdued. As the wind blew softly across the face of the land, the psalm was sung in a still, small voice. The feast was eaten with the mingled tears of joy and sorrow. Nevertheless, Bestman Comfy led the Bride in the Great Dance.

The Bride, alone in the private thoughts of her aching heart, wept into the early hours of the next day.

CHAPTER 7

LOSSES AND RETREATS

In the following two centuries, the descendants of Lo-Beni increased throughout the neighboring land, a hostile territory known as *The Land of the Nephil*. The fruitful generations of Lo-Beni encamped in the trenches and waged two, simultaneous campaigns against the Bride and her children.

The physical war involved crude weapons in battle and attacks by barbaric brutes. The children of the Bride defended themselves, sometimes by withdrawing and, at other times, by seizing the initiative and attacking from the flanks. During those years, Thanatos reaped a heavy harvest in the black net. After horrific battles and prolonged warfare, the net was ten feet wide, six feet high and stretched from one trench to the next. The plodding pace of the pale horse never slowed from the heavy load. Though both camps suffered innumerable losses, Thanatos never tired of enmeshing the corpses of the offspring of men and the children of the Bride.

The other campaign waged against the children of the Bride, while more subtle, was more effective. Children of all ages abandoned the Bride and departed to live in *The Land of the Nephil*. They idolized many things of this fallen world, venerating people, animals, plants, seasons and heavenly bodies. While worldly pleasures tempted and seduced numerous children, self-serving and self-exalting regulations, since they were especially attractive, caused many more of the Bride's offspring to succumb to the forces of the fallen ones.

Bestman Comfy taught and warned against the mass rebellion. In most instances, his proclamations were fruitless.

While the Bride pleaded with her children to remain with her, only a faithful few stayed. The diameter of the chained circle had been, at one time, nearly three hundred feet in order to accommodate the children. Defections occurred daily and the sides became unevenly matched. Physically unable to withstand the barrages of their enemies, the faithful children of the Bride fled in the direction of Logos.

The chained circle shrunk as sons and daughters of the Bride were killed, captured or converted. Chased by Nephilim and dogged by Thanatos, the number of the faithful decreased. Bestman Comfy led them through the thorny plains and across thistle-infested trenches. Hope waned as the number of the faithful decreased to eight: the Bride, Bestman Comfy and six of her children.

The Nephilim increased their search and destroy missions.

The eight decided on a focused and intense effort to leave the Nephilim behind and overtake Logos. Escape from the frenzied hands of the enemy and pursuit of Logos began at night. Feet suffered wounds from the spiked seeds of puncture weed as they ran through the darkness. At the dawn of day, the Bride and her small entourage stopped for three hours in a trench. They tended to wounds, rested as was possible, prayed to the Bridegroom and encouraged one another. Doubly motivated by the love ahead and the hatred behind, they ran the rest of the morning and all afternoon. Quietly, and just before dark, Bestman Comfy removed the chain and formed the gapped circle. It easily fit on the floor of the trench. Bestman Comfy took the Bride in his arms and led her in the Great Dance. Fearing exposure, he lit no fire and spoke softly and tenderly to the Bride and her children. Together, they whispered the psalms and chants. Then they gathered their few possessions and continued pursuing Logos and escaping the enemy. They ran so far and long that Logos was only on the hill far away.

That evening, the service of the Great Dance ended, as usual, with body and soul being fed. The last word spoken to them before gathering the chained circle was *The Psalm of Headbanger's Advent.*

A rhythmic, thumping sound came from the desert floor as the gathering chanted the final *ah yes*. Scarcely breathing, they remained still until they were certain it was not imagined. It wasn't. Someone was approaching. The Bride gathered her children against her snow leopard cloak and held them. Her face showed the first signs of age. No longer the fresh maiden she once was, the young woman had circles under her eyes from stress and lack of sleep. The thumping intensified. Someone was drawing near. The private thoughts of each raced through their individual minds and were similar. They thought of the Nephilim. They hoped for the Bridegroom but, desiring to be undetected as the thumping sound ended, the small, encircled throng remained silent.

Someone stood on the ledge of the trench high above them. Whoever was there knew they were down in the valley of the shadowed trench. No voice called to the eight indicating help. Likewise, there was no victorious cry of triumph splitting the still night to indicate a foe with captured prey. Who was standing there, the enemy or the Bridegroom? Which was it to be?

Several small rocks sloughed from the bank as a spartan man descended to those huddled in the darkness. He cradled a petite iron pot of burning embers in the palm of one hand. The fiery coals within emitted a red glow, highlighting the relieved faces within the huddled mass as well as the ruddy face of a runner. He bowed to the Bride and handed his card to her.

I am Elizur the Thirsty,
a runner from the ancient village of Benedicamus
at the base of High Mountain.

(Please imprint your right thumb on the other side of this card and
return it to me. Use the iron pot of red embers within the circle.)

Without reading it, the Bride handed Elizur the Thirsty's card to Bestman Comfy. As the bestman read the front side of the card, the Bride whispered to the runner, "Would you like some water to drink?"

Elizur the Thirsty gave a puzzled look to the Bride and made no indication he wanted water.

Bestman Comfy extended the card to the Bride and said to the runner, "Now I understand part of what is written in *The Scroll of Psalms and Chants*."

While making no motion to receive the card, the Bride asked, "Bestman Comfy, have you read the other side of the card?"

"No, for neither the card nor anything given to you by the Bridegroom by way of his runners is mine. I do not presume to possess, take or use anything without your permission."

"Well spoken," said the Bride. "What has been revealed to me is not withheld from you. Please read the other side. After you have done so, then I will read it."

> Fear not, mine Bride in white,
> When foes chase in thy sight,
> For wrath is their gift,
> To you I uplift,
> Behold the glow of mine light.

Bestman Comfy examined the card's message. He read it several times, understanding what it meant in general and wondering how it might be accomplished specifically, and when. He handed the card to the Bride and watched her reaction as she read it. She imprinted her thumb on the card and returned it to

59

Elizur the Thirsty. He, in turn, began to deliver the petite iron pot with burning embers into the hand of the Bride. With a wave of her hand she indicated it was to be given to Bestman Comfy. Her voice accompanied her desire, "Please give the iron pot to the Bridegroom's bestman."

Elizur the Thirsty ignored her direction and extended the petite iron pot with burning embers closer to the Bride. She understood that the runner was under specific orders. The gift belonged to her, not to the bestman or to anyone else. The runner would give the gift to her alone. With a tired smile she received the gift from him. Despite the fiery coals inside, the petite iron pot remained cool in her hands.

Before the runner could salute and depart, the Bride spoke, "Bestman Comfy, I entrust the petit iron pot with burning embers to your stewardship. Use it in the service of the Bridegroom and for the welfare of his Bride and her children."

She turned back to Elizur the Thirsty, allowing full attention for his salute. After receiving acknowledgement of his salute, the runner scrambled to the top of the trench. He surveyed the panorama and motioned all within the trench to follow him.

Bestman Comfy opened the hinged door to the small wooden box at the one end of his chain and carefully placed the petite iron pot inside. He picked up the chain stole and placed it upon his shoulders. The children helped the anxious Bride and the old bestman up the trench while Elizur the Thirsty waited.

When all were on the plain, the runner repeated his motion for them to follow. He ran in the lead and they attempted to stay with him. The effort was futile. Within five minutes everyone had lost sight of him.

The troop slowed to a walking pace. They were confused about what to do and where to run. One of the children spoke, "I was so fascinated with the runner, I never removed my eyes from him. When he ran, I noticed that he was heading to that bright star on the horizon to the west. He never really veered from it during the time he remained in my sight. Do you think that we should run straight for that horizon star?"

"Yes," agreed the Bride.

"Very good," announced Bestman Comfy, "yes, very good indeed. Let's go."

CHAPTER 8

LIFTED UP AND LET DOWN

The flight from the enemy and to Logos proceeded at a slow and encumbered pace. As if under the direction of a sinister force, the underbrush thickened to obstruct their escape. Stands of devil's walking stick answered the evil call to eclipse the guiding star on the horizon. Thick masses of conjured clouds blew across the night sky as the moon was hindered from shedding any precious light on their path. The raking fingers of briars entangled them. Barbed cheat grass penetrated clothing and plagued the host. Stinging nettles and poison oak dispensed venom to those making contact. The dark wind blew against the eight and carried their scent to the Nephilim. In unending waves, pollen and dust assaulted the eyes, attacked the sinuses and stifled the lungs.

Remaining together became the greatest difficulty for the Bride, her few children and Bestman Comfy. The trenches deepened, resulting in longer falls and more demanding climbs. The agile, older children ran the fastest and climbed the quickest. Bestman Comfy, slowed by age, hindered by a lack of stamina and troubled with failing eyesight, began to trail the others.

Had any of the fleeing congregation stopped to listen, the dark adversaries would have been heard in the distance. While hindered by the same obstacles the small congregation faced, the enemy forces were compelled to ignore the irritating seeds of cheat grass and to drive through flesh-tearing thorns. Madness, fueled by a blood-frenzy, threw them into trenches with abandon. Several of the fallen ones broke bones as they plunged to the bottom of the deep ditches and as they fell upon one another. They ignored the injuries and continued to be driven.

Though the forces of darkness worked to delay its advent and prevent its brightness, the gray dawn of a new day mercifully arrived. Bestman Comfy, breathless after climbing out of a deep trench, gazed back as he gathered his wind. The pursuing enemy's host had just ascended from the previous trench. Further back, the pale beast pulled the black net of death. The tired bestman turned to continue his flight. A minute ahead of him, he saw the white-cloaked Bride running. She had the hand of her youngest child, a daughter. That sight of their love for one another provided a spurt of untapped energy within the bestman.

After climbing out of the next trench, Bestman Comfy surveyed the scene behind him once more. The enemy had cut the distance to him nearly in half. Having raked his foot with a length of bone-dry briar, Bestman Comfy asked himself what he was doing and how much farther he could run and when he should quit. Mixed thoughts swirled in his head. Was the Bridegroom aware of their situation? Should he try to protect the Bride and her children by fleeing in a different direction? Didn't the Bridegroom care? Should he stay and fight, giving the Bride a few more seconds to run?

The questions received no answers. Actually, no decision now needed to be made by the bestman. Ahead, the Bride and her children stood huddled. Fear froze them in place and despair paled their faces. They stood near the edge of a cliff, their location being a point which jutted out the farthest. The plain abruptly ended. There was nowhere to go and the landscape at the cliff's edge contained little vegetation; that too, an apparent conspiracy to provide no further cover.

Bestman Comfy arrived to behold, up close and with minute detail, the faces of utter anguish and consuming terror. He approached the cliff and inched his head over the ledge looking for an escape route. The sheer cliff bore witness against any hope of eluding the enemy.

On the other side of the wide chasm, the donkey and the servant stood. Though they were only one hundred feet apart, there was no way to get to them. A chasm separated them. The servant's face was determined and stern. Bestman Comfy quickly checked the pursuit. In two or three minutes, their foes would overtake them.

The bestman removed the chain from his shoulders and spread the gapped circle on a patch of barren ground. He motioned the Bride and her children to enter quickly. They did so, ignoring the traditional procession through the gap. The children sat near their mother and all stared back at the approaching foe.

The Bride closed her eyes and recalled the words on the card. She spoke aloud, *"Fear not, mine Bride in white, When foes chase in thy sight."* She hesitated and Bestman Comfy continued, *"For wrath is their gift, To you I uplift."*

At fifty feet the forces of the enemy halted. Every way of escape was blocked and the satisfying of their hunger for despair, and particularly, the feeding of their lust for the kill would not be rushed. A line of Nephilim formed as the file extended in a half-circle around the captives. From the cliff edge on the left to the one on the right, the enemy line was reinforced, their ranks filling to a depth of three or more warriors. Silence descended momentarily as the enemy eyed the eight huddled in the tiny circle.

The hostile brutes emitted a low, guttural hum and slowly began building volume. When the awful drone ascended to the height of a lusting frenzy, an attacking shout would sound forth as the annihilation of the remnant commenced. Just before the shout to initiate the slaughter of the eight was released, a great cracking noise interrupted the Nephilim's crescendo. Instant bewilderment invaded the enemy and all mouths were stopped. Each descendant of Lo-Beni crouched to the ground as it shook violently.

Forty feet in front of the encircled Bride, the earth cracked open. Vibrations from the deep echoed and intensified as they surfaced on the face of the land. From the abyss behind the bestman, raging winds billowed dust clouds. A deep grating, so low it was felt rather than heard, caused everyone, the octet included, to embrace the ground. No step, in any direction or for any reason, could be taken. The grating intensified and the cracking crevasse opened wider. There was now a four foot open trench between the Nephilim and the encircled eight. Had any of them been able to peer into the crack, they would not have seen the bottom.

The Bride screamed. She had been gazing over Bestman Comfy's shoulder, not concentrating on anything but only looking at Logos. Bestman Comfy held up his wool robe made from the black sheep and protected his face from the blasting wind. He turned his head to see what caused her horrifying scream. The donkey and the servant, both there an instant earlier, were gone. Only the flat slab of gray ground where they had been standing was visible. Death clouds of darkened earth boiled as lightning bolts slashed the rock beneath them and sent a chorus of booming thunder-echoes in the depths below.

"They ... they stepped to the edge ... and then leaped ... into the abyss," the Bride shouted in gulping spurts which were barely heard by those near her.

"Look," yelled one of her children, pointing to the line of the Nephilim. Their pursuers had not only fallen to the ground, but were slowly sinking as the grinding sound intensified. The entire land beyond the great crevasse was submerging into a sea of fuming, churning clouds of choking dust. Occasionally, but only for a second or part thereof, a high-pitched scream reached the ears of the troop.

Finally, the howling winds subsided and the clouds appeared to settle. The awe-full, violent shaking caused by the great earthquake ended. However, the deep, grinding tone and the low vibrations continued. Somewhat calmed, those huddled in the gapped circle sat up and examined the horizon. Their world was now a mere seventy-five feet at its widest point and 450 feet long.

One of the Bride's children spoke, "Everything has settled around us."

Another asked, "How do you know it has settled?"

"What do you mean? Didn't you watch the ground under the feet of our enemy sink below the dark clouds? Didn't you see it?"

Bestman Comfy said, "The card from the runner said the Bride would be uplifted."

As the Bride opened her mouth to speak, the deep sound of grinding stopped. After a moment of silence, she spoke, "From our point of view, everything sunk around us. But it is possible that this whole piece of the land lifted up. From our point of view would we be able to tell whether everything else was sinking or we were being raised?"

Several of her children added in a chorus, "No."

The youngest child, a red-haired girl with green eyes and a blue, children's cloak, added with a certain air of spunk, "Maybe both took place!"

Bestman Comfy chuckled as he grabbed the little girl and said, "Yes, little one, maybe you are more correct than we imagine. The enemy was lowered to the deep places of the earth while we were all being lifted up to the heights of heaven."

More evidence was being experienced that the red-haired girl might be right. The clouds, now far below, were turning a soft, fluffy white as the morning sun began to brighten the day. The pure air of the upper atmosphere reached deeply into their lungs and refreshed them with new life.

The Bride laughed too, but tempered it when she remembered the pair descending into the abyss. She said, "Bestman Comfy, we no longer have Logos to be our guide."

"Possibly true," he said, "but what we do have is the word of the Bridegroom. We are to partake of what he has sent to us by his runners."

"Yes," the children called out, "please, we are hungry. Feed us, Bestman Comfy."

He smiled and began by putting the petite iron pot of burning embers in the center of the circle. Water, wine and bread were brought to their places and served to the Bride and her children. The bestman read to them from scroll and volume, tome and the writings. Bestman Comfy led the Bride in the Great Dance. With both body and soul fed, the divine service ended with a solemn speaking of *The Psalm of the White Horse*, the *Children's Chant* and all whispering the *ah yes*.

With the Bride and her children escorted from the gapped circle and the sacred items returned to the shiny wooden box, Bestman Comfy put the chain around his neck. Huddled together and holding hands, the eight toured the perimeter of their tiny, isolated world. White clouds surrounded the rock pinnacle and blocked any view of the world below.

Months passed. The Bride spent time with her children. Bestman Comfy continued to lead the Bride in the Great Dance. Each day they gathered for the *Divine Service of Reading and Feeding*. The bestman, inspired by Ruach, wrote of the events. He assembled the writings and bound them in a book. He entitled it, *The Album, Scripting of the Great Comedy*.

On the 150th day, the low, grinding sound began once again, though the sound was much softer than before. It continued forty days and during that time, the eight noticed the clouds rising slowly to engulf them. The red-haired girl told them their stone tower was being lowered into the sea of clouds. No one disagreed with her.

Late one afternoon, as Bestman Comfy led the Bride in the Great Dance, the orange-colored clouds engulfed the stone tower. Bestman Comfy, the Bride and her six children were baptized into the cloud. For many days, fog obscured the sun as the grinding sound continued. A morning dawned when a gentle wind arose and cleared the clouds away. The dingy sky became bright and blue as their small world reflected pure color once more. Having carefully approached the edge, they discovered they were still a hundred feet or more above the rest of the world below. The land appeared clean and inviting.

Several days later they awoke to silence, stillness and the realization that their world and the world below were one and the same. Bestman Comfy gapped the circle and led them in *Morning Worship with Individual Absolution*. Having been sufficiently fed, the eight stepped forth from the circle. Ever since their eyes beheld the refreshed land below the clouds, they had scanned it for signs of the Nephilim. Neither in person nor in sign had they seen anyone or anything associated with the fallen ones.

As the mass emerged from the circle, the red-haired girl suddenly spoke, "They're back."

All turned in fear, expecting to see several Nephilim. No Nephilim remained. Their fear did. A glance cast to the side beheld Thanatos and the pale horse waiting for them. The black net, still filled with the bodies of the dead and now three times longer than before, stretched out behind Thanatos.

Thus life and death began once more on the plain. A few years passed and one of the Bride's children, now a young man said after awakening one morning, "Was the stone tower a dream? Did any of that really happen to us?"

Shortly after this, Bestman Comfy died and was gathered, his body into the net and his spirit into the paradise of the Bridegroom. Century upon century passed and the black net lengthened. The Bride placed the chain stole upon man after man. Each bestman lead her in the practicing of the Great Dance. Each one grew old and each one died. The Bride, now a mature woman, begat many more children. Sadly, most left the circle, while joyfully, some stayed gathered unto her. Whether they stayed or not, each one died, some of disease, some of war and a few, of old age. The black net extended by three times as the face of the earth was covered with people who lived in a land of thorns, thistles and trenches.

When the earth filled once more, people who did not know the Bride congregated. The newly-fallen bowed down to living creatures: beasts, birds, trees, reptiles and people. They traded the truth for a lie and venerated non-living things. From the rocks and the earth oozed a legion of fashionable things. Those whose hands formed such, bowed down to them. From the mind seeped a host of invoked things. Those whose imagination called such into being, served them.

The Bride was concerned. She had good reason.

CHAPTER 9

REBELLION

During the next forty generations, scattered pockets of people congregated and developed into large towns separated by great distances. The vast lands between the small cities hosted farmers, wood cutters, nomadic families and roving bands of opportunistic raiders. The peoples paid homage to a legion of deities. Some of the divinities had life, like *The Sacred,* the *Night Cat of the South* and the *Python.* Individuals rose up and were idolized by the masses, among them a notorious woman known only as *The Princess* as well as a mighty warrior and able leader named *Progenitor.* Shrines hosted lifeless idols like the *Celestial Jewel.*

The greatest of the deities, however, came neither from human hands nor creatures of this world, but originated from a vile undertone calling from the dark shadows of a decaying earth. The seductive voice, undetectable by human ear or conscious mind, spoke directly to and through the evil imaginations of the heart. A morning arrived when the peoples of the land awoke and certain men and women in sundry places had a strange word on their lips. They spoke the name, *Ophis.* The name was powerful and many invoked it.

The land to the south came under the spell of Ophis. The disciples of Ophis controlled the southern governments while the clerics of Ophis made rules about worship and sacrifice. The people hearkened to the teachings of Ophis, especially the doctrine permitting them to have other deities. The only restriction was that the people had to say that Ophis was above all the other deities. The people were willing to do this because they could keep their other personal deities.

Some of the Bride's children heard of the foreign teachings and fell under the influence of Ophis. At first, they pleaded with the Bride to move their tents to the southern land. Following the advice of Bestman Frank, the Bride refused to go. Children became discontented and muttered words to each other against both Bestman Frank and the Bride. Rebellion fermented among the children, ready to erupt. Though they continued to enter the gapped circle, they did so with disjointed spirits. Though these defiant, fallen children of the Bride participated in the rehearsals of the Great Dance, they loathed each step.

One of the rebellious children invoked the name of Ophis, asking to be shown a way to move the Bride to the southern land. On a night when many strong winds blew against the tents, a strange voice whispered into the heart of this child and the prayer was answered. The next morning the plan was shared with other children of like mind. Rather than convincing the Bride to move directly to the southern land in one sudden relocation, the journey would be accomplished gradually. The movement south would take decades and not be noticed.

The rebellious children marveled at the patience of Ophis as they carried out the plan. For every two movements in a generally southern direction, one was made to the north.

A strange man arrived in camp as the edge of the earth engulfed the sun. His advent caused no small stir among the children. As he focused his eyes on the Bride and moved straight in her direction, the Bride smiled, knowing a runner was coming after so many years with no word from the Bridegroom. He bowed his head and presented her with a card.

I am Elishaphat the Merciful,
a runner from the ancient village of
Benedicamus at the base of High Mountain.

(Please imprint your right thumb on the other
side of this card and return it to me.)

The Bride spoke, "It has been many years since a runner has brought us word from the Bridegroom. The last time was just before the uplifting of the stone and our baptism in the cloud. Please, sir, tell me how he is."

Elishaphat the Merciful did not reply. Instead, he directed his concern to the card, never letting it pass from sight. The Bride did not force further attempts at conversation. She read the other side of the card and a look of fear descended upon her. Her eyes scanned the camp from one end to the other and filled with tears. She motioned Bestman Frank to read it with her.

> Some ears of thy seed now enfold,
> The voice of thy foe from of old,
> Beware of these weeds,
> Their words and their deeds,
> With abyss-mal success they grow bold.

Upon receiving the thumb-impressed card, Elishaphat the Merciful conducted a brief, but complete inspection. Satisfied, he saluted the Bride and ran to the north. A hundred younger children attempted to follow the Bridegroom's runner, but could not keep the pace. Within minutes Elishaphat the Merciful vanished into the nearby hills.

Bestman Frank gapped the circle that evening with many thoughts occupying his mind. The chained stole covered a span of two hundred feet at the center when all the Bride's children assembled within the circle. He doubled the readings from the words entrusted to his care, mostly from the *Tome of Odes* and the *Volume of Consequences*. The pauses between the readings were longer than usual, giving greater time for personal reflection. After nurturing the body with the bread, Bestman Frank fed the souls of all with the wine and the chanting of *The Psalm of the Wedding Hall*. He took the Bride in his arms, leading her and her children in the Great Dance. The bestman's steps were forced, the Bride tense and her children nervous. As the children left through the gap that evening, Bestman Frank made an effort to look into the eyes of each. Many avoided his eyes as they departed.

Clumps of quiet discussions seeped from the dark corners of the camp that evening. The Bride listened late into the night, hearing the conversation but not well enough to understand the words. She said to Bestman Frank, "This is not good."

"You are right. I fear that I have failed in my duties as bestman. I should have known what was taking place among the children."

"There is blame enough for all to share in the guilt, Bestman Frank."

"True, but there is only one bestman. I've grown old and am weary. I don't see and think as clearly as in previous years. I'm glad my understudy has been in training for many years. He's ready, you know."

"That may be," said the Bride, "but you have many years of wise service left. At this point, don't you think we should concentrate on what we should do tomorrow rather than what we did not do yesterday?"

Bestman Frank laughed and answered, "The children of this camp have a wise mother." His face changed as he continued in a determined tone, "Since reading the card brought to us by Elishaphat the Merciful, I've thought much on what we should do. For several years now, we have drifted closer to the southern lands."

The Bride asked, "Should we confront the defiant children and head straight north immediately, or drift back to the north with the hope of not alienating too many of them?"

"What would the Bridegroom do?"

She replied, "That is difficult to say. Back in the beginning, judgment came quickly. At the same time, he was patient with me and Bestman Dusty. I do not know how to answer your question."

He said, "Nor do I. As I've read the writings, I know what is his will and what is not. The application of his word is always the difficult part. Perhaps we should wait a day or two before deciding."

"To find out how extensive the corruption is?"

"Yes."

In another part of the camp several rebellious children spoke in hushed voices.

"... and take the initiative before there is time for them to react. Look, it must become public sooner or later."

"She's right, but do we have a majority?"

"Don't need one. We only need the appearance of a majority. Dispersion and sporadic proclamations work the crowd in our favor."

"A voice spoke through my heart last night. We're to wait until Bestman Frank tries to divert us from drifting further to the south. When he does, we move to take immediate control. In the meantime, there is much persuading to be done among the others. Keep talking about the futility of following the Bridegroom. Say he never was, or, if he was, he is no more."

"But I think we already have a majority on our side. There are only a few handfuls of supporters who will resist us."

"Let's ask around as we go about our work."

"I too, have heard a voice and part of our work is to discredit Bestman Frank. A voice tells me that he speaks too forthrightly and clearly, but that he is also old."

"The voice of Ophis has just spoken to me, and rather than leading an open revolt at this time, we're to take the temperature of the others."

"What does Ophis mean by this?"

"Tomorrow we disperse throughout the sections of the camp and begin talking about not being a part of the gapped circle this evening. We tell the others that many are unhappy with the leadership of Bestman Frank and, as a passive demonstration, many children are not going to enter the gap until he is replaced."

"This plan will work, for it is not an open revolt but a silent complaint. It is a gauging of the people which will tell us how many others are sympathetic to our cause."

The next day, Bestman Frank announced they would not pull up their tent pegs and move. Rather, they would remain in the area for a day or two. This fit into the plan that the rebellious children had. They sowed disgruntled seeds about how desirable the south was and how Bestman Frank was forcing his will on the Bride's children.

Throughout that day, the word of discontent spread and grew. When twilight came and Bestman Frank gapped the circle, only thirty-four children entered the gap. Hundreds remained in their tents, most not wanting to rebel openly, but desiring to be defiant, wanting change and demanding it. Fear fell on the remnant in the circle. The Bride gasped at how few of her children remained with her.

The voice of Ophis spoke loudly in the ears of a few that night, "Go, my children! Do it this night! Go now!"

The Bride woke with a start and an immediate dread and feeling of loss. When she whispered for Bestman Frank there was no answer. She called for a light and received none. One of her younger children came to her crying. The Bride held the sobbing girl who spoke of her nightmare. The girl fell back to sleep in the arms of her mother who held her close, not only to comfort the child, but to be comforted by the little girl's presence.

The morning light arrived and Bestman Frank was no longer in the camp. During the night, several of those who heard the voice of Ophis, gagged Bestman Frank and took him away from the Bride. The black robe was taken from him and a strong man began wearing it. The chain stole was removed from Bestman Frank and was used to hang him on a tree outside of camp. Unable to cut the chain after he was dead, the strong man severed his head with a sword. Bestman Frank's body fell to the

ground. Two rebellious children untangled the chain and placed
it on the shoulders of the strong man.

Thanatos netted both head and body of Bestman Frank.
The pale horse continued to stand ready for a greater pull.

The Bride did not sleep that night, waiting in tears and
great fear for the dawn of a new day. The same little girl, once
again asleep in the arms of her mother, was taken by the forces of
the strong man and killed. Four others who attempted to aid their
mother were killed as well. The ashen beast dragged the net to
the place of death and Thanatos threw their bodies into the
meshed receptacle. The black net, filled with the dead, snaked
behind Thanatos for six hundred miles.

"I am Bestman Intrepid. Pull up your tent pegs. We're
going south."

"No," replied the Bride in a firm voice, "you are not the
bestman. I appoint the bestman and I do not choose you."

Instantly enraged, he shrieked in her face, "Silence,
woman!"

Calmly she queried, "What have you done with Bestman
Frank? The Bridegroom is not pleased with all this business."

Several mocked her in succession, "Oh, he's not pleased;
oh, what shall we ever do?" "I know I am scared!" "I'm terrified."

Bestman Intrepid fumed, "The Bridegroom is dead and we
are leaving this land. We go to the lands and deities to the south."

He tried to gap the circle but the chain did not grow in
length. When Bestman Intrepid attempted to open the small
wooden box with the hinged door, he could not do it. After a
furious outburst, he calmed and spoke to the people, "This box
and its contents are of no use to us. To symbolize our new life, I
retain the black robe but give an order to hide the chain in the
rocky hills to the east.

A fierce man with a sinister grin stepped forward to take
the chain and hide it. When he received the chain stole and
indicated he would take it to the remote hills, the Bride shouted,

"No, you can not do this wickedness. That chain and everything in the ironwood box are gifts from the Bridegroom."

Bestman Intrepid said, "I won't if you answer one question. What is at the other end of the chain?"

"I do not know," said the Bride.

"Then off to the hills with the chain."

"I forbid it!"

Bestman Intrepid, with a seething look of hatred, ordered in a sharp voice, "Gag that woman. I grow weary of her talk." As his attendants did this, a grin formed on his face and he continued, speaking in a slow, fiendish manner, "Wait. Remove the white cloak from her and dispose of it with the chain."

The Bride's eyes widened. No one in the camp made a move. Bestman Intrepid shot a glance at those near the woman and barked, "Do it!"

This they did and the nakedness of their mother was seen by everyone. The Bridegroom's Bride was now exposed to all. A collective gasp sounded from the camp. While a thousand turned in shame, only a hundred wept tears of remorse.

CHAPTER 10

REPULSIVE

In the following days, Bestman Intrepid solidified his domination over the Bride and his death grip on the children, both the rebellious who strongly supported him and the Bride's faithful remnant who hid in fear. He force-marched the entire group to the south and told them they were no longer under the dominion of the Bridegroom. Rather, as he explained, everyone would pay homage to Ophis who reigned above all and thank Ophis for being so generous. Ophis permitted the children to have lesser deities, ones fashioned by wood carvers, shaped by stone sculptors and/or conjured by local sorcerers. Free to choose personal deities, the majority of the children thanked Ophis and sampled the field.

In addition to the shame and hurt experienced within, the Bride's body suffered as her exposed, tender skin became red and burnt by the desert sun. With her hands tied together in front of her, she attempted to hide her nakedness with her arms and hands. Not permitting her even this modesty, the fallen children whom she begat noticed her attempt to cover herself and tied her hands behind her back. Their mother hung her head in shame and a dreadful, piercing hurt penetrated to her very being. Abused by her mocking children, her reddened skin formed blisters on her back, shoulders, arms and legs. Her face and throat were spared these blisters only because she hung her head so low, shielding them from the sun.

The Bride was paraded through the marketplaces of towns and exhibited by ones who had once heard the many psalms with her and learned the Great Dance in the gapped circle. Her hair became matted and stringy, falling to the side of her face. The men of the marketplace, idle in their days, whistled at and taunted the Bride as they shouted advice to the rebellious children.

"Ya must be giving her away. Surely ya don't expect us to purchase time with 'er." Base shouts of approval followed.

A coarse fellow suggested, "Hey, if ya gonna sell 'er, ya better put some paint on 'er, or bring strong drinks to dull our eyes!" A great laughter arose from the crowd.

The rebellious children, led by Bestman Intrepid and stung by the jeers from the base fellows, acted upon two of their suggestions. They jerked the Bride to the edge of the marketplace, and in one of the alleys, they made her ready for rental. Scarlet juice from pomegranates was forced on her lips and cheek bones. Uneven blue smears from crushed desert blossoms adorned her eyelids and navel. The Bride, sufficiently painted with the gaudy makeup, was led to the auction block and rented to the highest bidder.

At night the Bride wept. Rivulets cascaded from her eyes, leaving behind dusty creek beds along her cheeks when she could tear no more.

The few children who loved their mother and remained faithful to the Bridegroom, did so in hiding. Ophis decreed that any of the children who would not ridicule the Bride's nakedness and renounce the Bridegroom were to be sacrificed. Suspected of being sympathetic to their mother, two of the Bride's children were brought before her. One was a man of twenty-four and the other a young woman of sixteen. They were forced to look at their mother and instead of mocking her, they wept. The disciples of Ophis, inflamed by the couple's unwillingness to refute, rebuke and deny their mother, pressed them further. The disciples of Ophis asked them if they renounced the Bridegroom. Neither would and both were slaughtered in the presence of the Bride.

As their bodies were being gathered by Thanatos, the Bride shouted, "All my faithful children, you will die. I will live. Run! Flee to the hills this night and hide among the rocks. Do not forget me; I do not forget-."

Before she could finish her words, the Bride was struck in the mouth with a blow that caused the loss of two lower teeth. The clout drove her to the dusty earth. Unable to cushion her fall with either arms or hands, one of her tear-stained cheeks became imbedded with sand. The people were silent as they eyed each other. No one moved.

The man wearing the wool robe from the black sheep bellowed his command, "Watch your neighbors this night. If anyone - man, woman or child - if anyone acts strangely this night, bring him to me."

While the many night fires caused dancing shadows in the camp, turmoil and confusion reigned; brother rose up against brother, sister accused sister, brother betrayed sister, and sister reported brother. Those overcome by others were prepared for appearance in the morning court. When the daylight hours arrived, those bound and gagged were brought before Bestman Intrepid.

The great priest of Ophis told Bestman Intrepid how to carry out the proceedings. Ophis ordered the judge to announce that each of the accused would determine his personal innocence or individual guilt.

The bestman announced, "You are brought before me this day. The court is merciful and fair and just. It may be that you have been falsely accused of being a faithful child of the Bride. Neither Ophis nor I have any desire to punish anyone who is not guilty. In the presence of all assembled here this day, each one of the accused will be brought before me. Each one, in turn, will be given the opportunity to state the truth by answering two questions. The first question is, 'Do you, this day, renounce the Bridegroom and the Bride?' The second is, 'Do you, this day, acknowledge and worship Ophis?' If the answers are *yes*, then

81

6

you will be untied and freed. If the answers are *no*, then the sentence will be carried out immediately. The sentence is death."

He turned aside and whispered to the great priest of Ophis, "I want to begin with three whom you believe will answer *no* to the questions, followed by two whom you know will answer *yes*. Do you understand?"

The great priest of Ophis nodded his agreement.

Three women and two men were led before the bestman in the sight of all the children of the camp. Tethered with a rough cord, the Bride stood between the bestman and the great priest. With a demeanor of sadness, she gazed upon the five children before the judge. The oldest daughter's eyes twinkled as she stared at her mother. A determined resoluteness exuded from the child. The younger son strained to avoid the Bride's eyes. The older son set his jaw and lifted his chin in obvious defiance of the proceedings, the judge and the great priest of Ophis. The youngest daughter showed fear, while the other was shaking in terror.

"Present the first," ordered the bestman.

The great priest of Ophis motioned for his two attendants to bring the older son forward. The judge spoke to the gagged man, "When the gag is removed from you, one word will be permitted from your mouth, either *yes* or *no*. The one word is your answer to the two questions. Do you, this day, renounce the Bridegroom and the Bride? Secondly, do you, this day, acknowledge and worship Ophis? If you say anything other or anything more than your one-word answer, a sentence of death will be carried out immediately by one of the purgers in the Order of Ophis. Remove his gag."

The instant his mouth became unleashed, the man declared loudly, "You are a fraud and have disgraced the wool robe of the black sheep. I renounce you, Ophis and any and every other deity. There is only the one and I follow the Bridegr-"

The last part of his confession was not heard in this fallen world. One of the purgers stopped his heart with a precise thrusting of Nagad's Dagger. Those within the camp gasped, but remained in place as the pale rider nudged the beast forward to collect the mortal remains.

"Present the second," commanded the judge.

The youngest of the three women was positioned in front of the judge. Still showing more of the girl she was than the woman she might become, she stood small and appeared spindly before her oppressors and guards. Bestman Intrepid spoke firmly, "Only one word. Do you renounce the Bridegroom and the Bride, and do you acknowledge and worship Ophis? One word."

He motioned to the two purgers. With her tongue loosed, she stared with resolute determination into the eyes of the man wearing the black robe. The girl defied his authority and loathed him with her eyes. The woman's silence, while lasting only brief seconds, created tension and uneasiness. Her failure to answer temporarily immobilized her guards. When she sensed this, the girl, destined never to be a woman, blurted out in a rapid fashion, "I'm a child of the Bride and the Bridegroom is the only-"

After her life ended and her body was netted, the great priest of Ophis leaned across the Bride and whispered into the ear of Bestman Intrepid. The judge smiled and nodded his head.

"Present the third."

The oldest woman stumbled to the front after being pushed by the great priest's henchmen. Her brown eyes sparkled in anticipation and expressed a determination that contained no fear.

"You people," declared the judge, "you people have abused the privilege of speaking and are no longer permitted to voice your answer to the questions. Now you are to remain gagged during these court proceedings. After being asked the questions, you will be required to answer with a nod of the head. If you nod up and down, it will be taken as a *yes* answer and you will be immediately released from your bindings and freed. If you move your head from side to side it will be taken as a *no* answer and your sentence will be carried out at once. If you do not answer, it will be taken as a *no* and the same penalty will be imposed."

Bestman Intrepid redirected his attention to the woman in front of him. "Do you renounce the Bridegroom and the Bride, and do you acknowledge and worship Ophis?"

Though robbed of her final opportunity to speak her confession of faith, the woman turned her head widely from side to side. In doing so, her intense, confident eyes never moved from Bestman Intrepid. As her head turned to the left side for the third time, it stopped in place. She kept her eyes on the judge momentarily and then cast them upon the Bride. Their eyes met, one set glistening with tears, the other set sparkling with joy. An instant later, Nagad's Dagger ended a life in this world.

"Next," ordered the bestman.

The younger man was placed in position. He was terrified and refused to look at the Bride.

"Do you renounce the Bride and the Bridegroom, and do you acknowledge and worship Ophis?"

The young man nodded his head up and down in a rapid fashion.

"Freed," cried Bestman Intrepid. "Remove his bindings and gag. Give him an extra ration of food and return him to his place. Wait! Young man, do you wish to serve Ophis by being a part of my escort?"

"Yes, good sir," the man replied with a stiff jaw.

"Good. You are now Master of the Order of Ophis. All purgers are under your control. Do you want the assignment?"

"Yes," he replied.

The bestman continued, "Then you must spit in the face of the Bride."

The new Master of the Order of Ophis rubbed his wrists as he approached the Bride. With a confidence born of malevolence, he stared directly into the eyes of the Bride and said, "You harlot. I spit in your face."

With the spittle sliding down the inside corner of her eye and approaching her mouth, she spoke, "I pray that the Bridegroom will turn your heart back to him and that you will return to me."

The Master of the Order of Ophis summoned bile into his mouth and spit in her face a second time. With his eyes fixed on the Bride, he ordered over his right shoulder, "Purgers, bring the next prisoner forward to appear before the great, wise and almighty judge, Bestman Intrepid."

The purgers looked to the judge. The impressed ruler grinned as he motioned them to follow the orders of their master.

"Do you renounce the Bride and the Bridegroom, and do you acknowledge and worship Ophis?"

The woman nodded her head in the affirmative.

"Freed. Release her. Do you wish to serve Ophis by attending to my needs?"

"Yes," she replied.

"Then slap the Bride's face."

The woman marched to the Bride and slapped her across the face with her left hand. The blow stunned the Bride and a red hand print appeared immediately on her cheek. Still reeling from the hit, the Bride declared, "Remember my daughter, you may always return to me. The Bridegroom and I love you."

With her momentum shifted to the right after the vicious slap, the woman braced her foot and returned with a powerful backhand slap to the other cheek of the Bride. The blow penetrated to the area where her two teeth had already been knocked out. Pain shot through the Bride's face and she fell to the ground in a kneeling position. The woman placed her foot on the Bride's head and shoved her face into the ground. Sufficiently demonstrating her ability and desiring to prove her loyalty, the woman approached Bestman Intrepid and knelt at his feet. She took one of his feet with her hands and placed it on top of her head, inviting him to do to her what she had done to the Bride. The judge laughed and raised the woman to a standing position.

The judging continued through the morning. Most of those who appeared before Bestman Intrepid denounced the Bridegroom, declared allegiance to Ophis and were freed. The few who remained loyal to the Bridegroom were slain immediately. While the Bride wept at each martyrdom, the tears of sorrow mixed with ones of joy.

CHAPTER 11

REVELATIONS

During the chaos of the previous night, when the sibling betrayals occurred, the majority of the Bride's children fled across the desert to the hill country to the north and east. Secluded groups of the scattered children hid and lived in fear, not knowing of one another's existence. Self-isolation in the wilderness became the only way for these sons and daughters of the Bride to survive. Each group, the largest being no more than thirty, thought it was the only people left from the Bride. In the early years of the wilderness isolation, roving patrols, sent out by the Master of the Order of Ophis, sought to destroy the children of the Bride. However, as Bestman Intrepid led his forced captives farther south and as the scattered remnants of the Bride moved deeper into the wilderness, the roaming gangs of thugs became fewer.

Most of the exiled children of the Bride lived in the deep caves hidden in the barren mountains. A few of the smaller groups lived in tents and moved about with their meager possessions. Water always determined where they lived and how far they traveled. Because the sources of water were rare, the people did not venture far from the known springs and cisterns.

For nearly forty years these children lived detached from their mother with most of them having never seen her. The older children recalled the stories they remembered being told by Bestman Frank and others. The younger children listened carefully and said *oh* and *ah* when they heard an especially exciting part of the account recalled by an old one from the *Volume of Consequences*. The most exciting part for the littlest children came when told of the Bride being led in the Great Dance. The young delighted to learn and sing many of the psalms and chants from the oldest children. These elderly brothers and sisters often sighed with sorrow and slept with tears as they hungered for the bread and wine served by the bestman.

Far to the south, in the land of many deities, the Bride continued to be abused. She was led on a circuit and sold at every opportunity. Night after night others used her for their entertainment, satisfying the base, perverted desires of man. Following the abuse, she was cast into the streets until morning. Now middle-aged, the Bride's face showed the wrinkles of time and the marks of terrible beatings. Her skin, rough to the touch and leathery to the sight due to various exposures, no longer radiated as it once had.

The Bride begat few children during those long years of captivity and every child was taken away from her. Some were offered to the multitude of deities, others were left to die in the desert. When the market was right, many were sold into slavery. When the price for slave children was low, the newly begotten sons and daughters were slaughtered to the deity of choice. The Bride shed many bitter tears for these children. Their sacrifice occurred quickly, usually before a breath of life could be inhaled by their tiny lungs. The Bride called them *Choice Children* and she wept for them because they were no more. Thanatos scooped many of these little ones into the black net.

The Bride was given one favor. She could select any two of her daughters to serve as attendants. The two daughters had to be six years apart in age. Each daughter could serve her no more than twelve years. At the age of twelve, the daughter was taken from her mother. The Bride selected a newly-begotten daughter who was put under the care of the six year-old. The older daughter cared for the younger daughter and taught her how to attend to their mother's needs.

The Bride loved these daughters and, as she had opportunity, secretly taught them the chants and psalms and odes.

From memory, she recited many of the sacred writings and told them the stories of the Bridegroom's love for her and her children. Each time the twelfth year approached, the Bride earnestly told the older daughter never to forget, no matter how badly she was treated and no matter where she went. Just before the twelve year-old girl was taken away by evil men, mother and daughter wept as they embraced for the last time.

Bestman Intrepid died in the eighth year after the captivity of the Bride. Following a power struggle to wear the black robe, Bestman Ribald ruled the woman and continued to market her for another twenty-three years. Her life was bitter under his cruel reign, particularly in his last years. Bestman Ribald, increasingly filled with pain from his diseased and dying body, vented his anger on the Bride. Whenever she came too near him and he was able to grab her, he pulled out tufts of her hair. He died and after his body was netted, Bestman Marquis assumed power. The new bestman exercised his dominion over the Bride with severe physical beatings. He handed her over to others who terrorized her. It was Bestman Marquis who discovered that she could not die. He made her life miserable and inflicted a multitude of pains upon her. She cried out for deliverance.

In the rocky hills to the north lived an eight year-old boy whose spirit was unsettled. Jo dwelt in the caves with other children of the Bride, but he longed to travel to the lands at the edge of his sight. In the morning Jo often sat at the entrance of his cave and viewed the landscape as the sun emerged from the edge of the earth and the dawn winds blew across the desert. Whether originating from within or from somewhere else, Jo felt a beckoning, a yearning for him to explore the mountains to the east. On still nights when the other children slept soundly, the restlessness awakened him. Quietly, Jo left his bed and stood outside, gazing at the stars and longing for his journey to the east.

In the late spring, Jo told the other children of his need to explore the mountains to the east. He said he knew his return would be only after many days and nights had passed. One morning, hours before daylight, Jo started across the desert. The wind carried the sound of a hound's baying as the sun peaked above the distant hills.

The unrelenting sun sapped the boy's strength in a twofold manner, once as it shone from above and again as it reflected off the sand. Half of his five day supply of water was used before the next morning. Four hours after sunrise on the second day, Jo came to the edge of the eastern mountains. Hoping to find shade and water before the end of the day, he began ascending the mountain.

As the boy climbed, the sloping sides of the ravine steepened and appeared to converge, forming a high pass between two peaks. The ascent was slow and offered no shade to the young hiker. Pockets of scrub vegetation suggested a source of water. The boy investigated the possibilities and discovered nothing to help him except a straight stick to aid his climb.

Near the top of the pass and the end of his strength, Jo drank the last of his water and sought a place to spend the night. On the north side, a small opening led through the rock. Hoping to discover some shade, Jo followed the natural pathway to a triangular opening in the rock. The boy scrambled into the hole far enough to be in the shade, but no farther. He sighed at the relief from the unrelenting sun. An attempt to moisten his parched lips with his tongue was unsuccessful. He closed his eyes and slept.

A sound deeper within the cave stirred him. At first, he thought it a dream. The sound was dripping water. Before Jo opened his eyes, he thought it wise to turn his face to the darkness of the cave, thus not ruining his night vision. With the bright light behind him, he saw clearly into the cave. Some fifty feet straight ahead was a pool of water. While fighting the desire to hurry, he also did not hesitate to satisfy his thirst. He passed a shelf in the rock wall to the left without notice. Jo tested the water and was thankful it was suitable for drinking. He drank deeply from the cave's pool and thought it the coolest, most satisfying, thirst-quenching water he ever drank. After eating travel-bread and enjoying a second helping of water, he slept once more.

The Voice appeared to the boy in a dream.

"Jo."

"Sir?"

"Jo."

"Sir, I am here."

"Go to the south and bring my Bride to me."

"Where is she?"

"South."

"Sir, I've never seen her. How will I know her?"

"She knows you."

"I don't know enough to find her."

"You will know."

"Will she come with me?"

"Wear the wool robe from the black sheep."

"Sir, I don't have it. Where is it?"

"Jo, you will have it soon. Wear it."

"If she asks who sent me, what should I say?"

"Give her the white cloak from the snow leopard."

"Sir, I don't have it."

"Jo, you will have it soon."

"Sir, who are you?"

"Jo, I am the Bridegroom."

"Sir, where should I take her?"

"Bring her to me."

"Sir, I don't know if I can do this thing."

"Jo, I am Headbanger."

"But-"

"Jo, I am the White Pair."

"I-"

"Jo, go."

"Please, Bridegroom, I have an important question."

"I know you do."

"Will you answer it?

"Yes, but ask it aloud. You need to hear yourself ask the question. Ask it again."

"Sir, where should I go with the Bride?"

"Listen carefully to the answer, Jo. You are not bringing my Bride to a where; you are bringing her to the when. Now, go."

The boy woke with a start and a maturity beyond his years. For several minutes, he thought about the dream. He knew it was real. While the boy had many questions, he possessed an awareness they need not be answered immediately. He resolved to travel south and return with the Bride.

After eating a meal and replenishing his water supply, Jo left the pool of water to exit the cave. He noticed the shelf of rock to the right and stopped to investigate. A large boulder, most different from the surrounding cave material, rested precariously on the hewn shelf. Jo remembered seeing the rock shelf on the way to the pool and wondered why he hadn't noticed the boulder at that time. He reasoned either he had been more interested in the water and had not noticed it, or, the boulder had not been there when he entered the cave.

Within the boy arose an undeniable desire to touch the boulder. He did and realized it was not rock at all, but a large cloth pack. Jo slid the pack off the shelf, discovering it had considerable bulk. After carrying the pack into the light at the cave's exit, he opened it. Jo discovered a length of chain. At one end was an unknown metal device. At the other end was a small ironwood box with a hinged door. The box puzzled Jo. He understood its workings, but was unable to open its door. After several minutes of investigation, he turned his attention to the other items. From the pack he removed a bulky, white garment. Knowing what it was, he set it aside without unfolding it. Jo reached into the dark pack and grabbed the last item. Even before removing it, he knew it was the wool robe from the black sheep. The boy removed his outer garment and donned the black robe.

CHAPTER 12

REUNIONS

Hours later, Jo was traveling south along the seams where the mountains intersect the desert floor when he met another boy. At first, neither spoke as they looked at and wondered about each other. The other boy was older and bigger than Jo.

"Who are you?"

"I am Jo."

"Are you a scout for the Purgers of Ophis?"

"No."

"Where are you from?"

He pointed west to the mountains and rebuked himself for doing so. He asked the older boy, "Are you a scout for the purgers?"

"No, I am Nathan, one of the sons of the Bride. I live in the mountain valley to the southeast with my brothers and sisters."

Relieved and astonished, Jo said, "I also am a son of the Bride. I am from the western mountains across the desert. My brothers and sisters live there."

Nathan asked, "Why did you come across the desert and what are your intentions?"

Jo answered, "I am going to get the Bride."

Nathan laughed and continued his questioning, "The Bride is held captive to the south. Are you going to rescue her by yourself?"

"I'll do what I was sent to do."

"Who sent you to do this?"

"The Bridegroom," said Jo.

The answer puzzled Nathan in a pleasant way. "You should come with me and speak to our oldest sister. She will know about these matters. Will you come with me?"

Jo thought a moment and replied, "Yes, Nathan, my brother. You live to the southeast and it seems on my way. I will come with you."

The golden sun was being swallowed by the edge of the western mountains when the boys reached the village of Nathan's brothers and sisters. Jo became the center of attention; at first, the object of skeptical stares, and later, when the others were told who he was and what his journey involved, the recipient of curious grins and closer inspections.

Nathan permitted a few delays, but always directed his younger brother to a hut at the eastern edge of the village. An old woman, seated in the front of the hut, tended the dying fire before her. Her glazed eyes stared into a world not seen by any of her younger brothers and sisters.

Nathan asked in a loud voice, "Old Sis, are you awake?"

"Yes, Nathan," she replied. "Who is this one with you? Who is this one causing such chattering among the people?"

"Jo," the younger boy answered, "Jo, a son of the Bride from your sisters and brothers living in the mountains to the northwest."

The woman sharpened her focus. Nathan continued, "Jo, this is Old Sis. She is the oldest of the sisters and brothers living here."

In a maturity recently received and far beyond his years, the eight year-old boy knelt beside the old woman and hugged her. "I am honored to meet you, my beloved older sister."

Old Sis grinned and asked, not expecting an answer, "And why, little brother, are you honored to meet me?"

Jo responded immediately, "I believe I have before me someone who clearly remembers the years of being with the Bride. I am honored, Old Sis."

94

Her attention piqued further, she said, "Your voice is that of a small boy, but you speak sincere words with the language of wisdom. Tell me, Jo, why are you so interested in the Bride? Does your village not have anyone who remembers the days of old?"

"We have two brothers and one sister who recall the Bride, but their memory is limited for they are not as old as you, Old Sis. Besides, when I left my home I was not interested in such things."

Old Sis continued, "And why are you now so greatly interested, Jo?"

The young boy declared, "I am going to get the Bride."

A few of the sisters and brothers snickered, some spoke to each other in hushed words. Old Sis added with increasing interest, "You are a rather strange boy, little brother. I believe your sincerity, ..."

"... but doubt my ability?" added Jo.

The old woman laughed and admitted, "How should I doubt you when such a little brother of mine has crossed the desert and stands before me? How is it that you are going to get the Bride?"

Jo answered, "The Bridegroom has sent me."

Startled, Old Sis barely continued, "How ... uhh, how do you know that he has done this thing?"

"I saw the Voice in a dream I had last night as I slept in a cave. Headbanger directed me to go south and get his Bride."

The old woman was visibly stirred and trembled. She thought a moment and said, "Headbanger. How long has it been since I heard that name?"

Nathan replied, "Doesn't this all seem rather silly? I mean, this eight year-old boy shows up in a black robe, has a dream, speaks about a head banger and travels south to get the Bride. It just-"

"Wait!" interjected Old Sis, "You have not thought things through carefully. Reason says that an eight year-old boy could not cross the desert, but here he is. Logic dictates that this boy should not know such details about the Bridegroom and the old name, Headbanger. But before us is a child who speaks a name I have not heard since I was his age."

"But-"

"Nathan, you said something a moment ago. I know I heard you correctly, but I need to hear it again. Please tell me what our little brother is wearing."

"He wears a black robe," Nathan said.

Old Sis placed her hand to her mouth. "Jo, please come here. I want to smell your robe. May I?"

"Yes," answered Jo, drawing near as he spoke.

The old woman smelled the robe. After the initial sniff, she inhaled deeply and laughed. "Just like Bestman Frank, it smells just like his robe. Instant memories return with the aroma of the black robe."

Jo waited to keep from interrupting the old woman. Finding a suitable moment, he said, "Old Sis, there is a white garment in my pack. I believe it to be the Bride's cloak. But there is another item and I am not familiar with part of it. Perhaps you can tell me what it is and what I am to do with it. Let me show you." Jo thought a moment and paused, "Dear sister, would you please hold the Bride's white cloak while I get the other item out?"

He placed it in her lap without giving her time to answer. Her aged, arthritic hands slid across the snowy surface. Lifting it to her face, she smelled it and permitted her cheek to be touched. Special, unabated tears, held in reserve for a lifetime, flowed forth. She said only one word, over and over she spoke it, "Mother."

Wanting not to interrupt and glad he had given her this one grace, Jo hesitated. The boy of eight looked at Nathan and both grinned. When the woman returned from the ancient childhood she had spent in her mother's lap, Jo removed the length of chain with the two attachments.

The clanging of the links pulled another memory from the old woman. "Bestman. Oh, Bestman Frank. The Great Dance. Oh, to have the bestman gap the circle and for me, once again, to step through the gap and be a part of the Great Dance. Is the wooden box with the hinged door still at one end of the chain?"

"Yes," replied Jo quickly, "but I am not able to get the door open. I have looked at it closely and there is no reason why it will not open. Do you know anything about this, Old Sis?"

"No, but perhaps it is not for you to open, or perhaps it is not the right time. You know, it doesn't really matter, Jo."

Nathan asked, "What do you mean?"

"Only this, little brothers, that everything has been prepared for the right time, for the when. Jo is ready and the Bridegroom speaks to him. Our mother needs to wear the white cloak and it is ready. All things are prepared for their proper purpose and time. The ironwood box with the hinged door is not going to open until the proper time. Don't be concerned about this, Jo. It will open at the time when the Bridegroom desires."

"I understand," he replied and continued to speak, "but if you can, please tell me what this is at the other end of the chain."

Old Sis answered, "I don't know. I remember seeing it and playing with it whenever Bestman Frank permitted. Now that I think about it, I don't believe that either our mother or Bestman Frank knew what it was, ... I mean, what it is."

Nathan spoke, "Evidently not important for them to know then, nor for us now."

"Well spoken," his old sister said with gusto, "very well spoken, Nathan."

Jo laughed in agreement and said, "If I may ask one more question?"

"Please go ahead," said Old Sis.

"In the vision, the Bridegroom told me he was Headbanger. He also said he was the White Pair. Do you know anything about either one of them?"

The old woman answered, "Headbanger I have heard, but I do not know what it means. Whenever I heard Bestman Frank speak the word, Headbanger, it was always connected with suffering and victory. That's all I remember and it's more of a feeling than anything else. As for the name, White Pair, it means nothing to me. I'm sorry I am of no more help, Jo."

"That is fine. You have been very helpful, Old Sis. I must go south now."

The old woman replied, "Not tonight, Jo. Please rest here with your brothers and sisters tonight. You may leave as early as you desire in the morning. We want to fill your pack with food and water."

Early the next day, before the sun had risen, the entire village sent Jo off on his journey.

Nathan smiled and admitted, "Jo, I wish I could go with you to get the Bride."

"I know, Nathan, but an army wouldn't stand a chance of getting near the Bride, ..." He hesitated and finished his declaration, "but an eight year-old boy might!"

"Jo," called out Old Sis, "if it is the Bridegroom's will, please bring the Bride to our village."

After many days of hiking south and hiding often, Jo was halfway to the Bride.

Many more days later, the Bride sat weeping in the dirt of the gutter. The Bride cried for herself and her children. Her personal defilements had increased. Bestman Marquis sold her to any and all. When both men and deities had finished using her, they beat her savagely and always threw her into the dark, filthy gutters of the streets. The cuts on her back and face pained her. The purple bruises about her eyes remained visible and sore until the next blow. Her skin, now leathery from exposure to the sun and wind, cracked. These aches were minor to those felt in her heart.

The Bride wept for her children. Recently she had begotten an infant daughter, a dark-haired girl she would be permitted to keep for twelve years. Tears came to her heart as the Bride thought about the twelve year-old daughter who would now be taken away from her. Her name was Mina and her mother loved her. What made the hurt run deeper was that Mina didn't want to leave. The girl was afraid of what might happen to her and that she would never be able to see her mother again.

Usually there was a week when the Bride had three daughters with her. She longed to keep them all, but evil men were forcing her actions and denying her true desires. The twelve year-old Mina, a beloved daughter, would be gone in four days. The Bride begat Rae only three days earlier. Immediately the Bride put Rae into the arms of Mina. The caring action brought immediate memories to the older girl. Mina remembered how, six years earlier, the Bride begat Anne and placed her into the arms of her older sister, Tara.

At first light the next morning, the Bride slept in the gutter, recovering from her nocturnal abuse by the forces of Ophis and the desires of man. Her left eye, unattended after a severe blow, was swollen shut. A patch of hair above her left ear had been removed to the roots. Her lower lip was cut and had bled periodically through the night.

Mina had taken her two younger sisters for a walk to find food. The early risers of the city were out and already bartering in gossip. One said the talk of the market that day would concern the young stranger who asked the whereabouts of the Bride. No one called her the Bride, only horrid names like the bestman's harlot. The town gossips speculated on why such a fine young man was looking for that wench.

Mina held Rae close and grabbed Anne by the hand. The trio walked quickly back to the Bride and tried to rouse her. The Bride, confused by the effects of a concussion, endeavored to gain consciousness and sit.

"Here comes the young stranger," whispered Anne pointing down the street. "Will he hurt us?"

With the present condition of her eyes, the Bride could not see clearly. She covered her nakedness as best able. As the stranger closed within ten feet of the Bride, he was attacked by several warriors of Bestman Marquis' guard. The weaponless young man surprised his attackers with his speed and strength.

Though he fought off the warriors, the young man was not able to defend himself completely. Finally, he succumbed to their brutal assault. The stranger, pummeled by many fierce blows from blunt weapons, breathed his last. The warriors, several of whom were hurt, left his body in the gutter.

While the death dance between the warriors and the stranger took place, Anne noticed something had fallen from the young man. The six year-old girl scurried to the place where it fell and picked it up. She returned to her mother, giving her the card.

> I am Eliphalet the Pure-Hearted,
> a runner from the ancient village of
> Benedicamus at the base of High Mountain.
>
> (Please imprint your right thumb on the other side
> of this card and return it to me. Do not forget what
> this card promises. Be ready. The advents are soon.)

The Bride gasped as she read the card with her one eye. "A runner. It's been so long. The Bridegroom knows where I am."

"What is it, Mother? Tell us who he was," Mina begged as the pale horse pulled the net into position. The runner's body was unceremoniously dumped into the meshed net by Thanatos.

"My children, something has happened here that has never before occurred. A runner has fallen. Eliphalet the Pure-Hearted is dead."

"What will happen now, Mother?"

Ignoring her daughter's question, the Bride stared at Rae and continued giving voice to her thoughts. "My children, I am not able to think clearly. I fear for what I do not know; I fear the consequences of Eliphalet the Pure-Hearted's death. What happens when one of the Bridegroom's runners has been murdered? But I am filled with joy for what I do know; the Bridegroom knows where I am and has sent a message to me."

Mina's face revealed an impending tear, "But the young runner has been silenced before he could deliver the message."

"No, my daughter. The message is on the other side of this card."

Anne asked, "What does it say, Mother? Please read it."

The Bride did not hear her daughter, but continued to speak her ponderings. "Look at me. I sit in filth and must wash my face with gutter water. I have been unfaithful because I could have resisted more, always could have done more to prevent it from happening again and again. When I passed through the Portal I was young and clean. Look at me now. My stringy hair, matted with dried blood and urine, hangs down my face. I find no relief from my shaming treatment and will the Bridegroom want me if he sees what I look like? Will he want me after what has happened to me? What will he see when his eyes behold what is left of me after being abused by both man and fallen spirits? I feel dirty on the outside and dirtier within. What a wretched sight I must be. Look at me, Mina. What do you see?"

Mina held Rae closer and wept. Anne hugged her mother and told her she loved her. The Bride turned the card over and read it to her children.

> Two in black will engage in the fight,
> Of the silv'ry the green has no fright,
> Aged sage in the young,
> Blest word from his lung,
> Take his hand for the Great Dance in flight.

Mina asked, "Mother, what does it mean?"

The Bride answered, "We should fear, love and trust in the Bridegroom above everything else."

CHAPTER 13

REUNITED

Twenty-two hours later, in the pre-dawn stillness, the Bride slept in the gutter with her three daughters huddled next to her. Only Mina was awake, fearful for what might happen to her shortly, perhaps, she thought, this new day. She held Rae in her right arm, observing her peaceful slumbering. Mina's left hand rested on Anne's shoulder, feeling her sister's small bones through her thin shirt. The oldest of the three children sat with her right elbow supported by the Bride's hip. Late into the night, Mina had listened to her mother's disturbed breathing and troubled sleep-sounds. Now the Bride slept deeply, matching the quietest and coldest part of the day.

Mina neither saw the black shadow slipping between the night shades of the nearby shacks nor heard the padded footsteps on the dirt streets as someone stalked the quartet. Rather, she felt the presence of someone watching and hunting and approaching. Without moving, she trained her eyes to the front and wondered if the stalker was behind her. Minutes passed. She detected nothing. More minutes, and then, a hint of movement in the dirt alley to the right caught her eye. The shadow passed before she could focus on it. Seconds later a dark form eased along the front of the long building directly in front of her. Mina perceived enough detail to determine the stalker was alone. The pre-dawn light began to dissolve many of the shadowy hiding places.

Now no more than thirty feet away, the dark figure of the stalker was plainly seen against the light gray shadow of a shack.

Mina watched intently and knew the stalker stared at her. Oddly, she no longer felt a great fear, no doubt due to the stalker's willingness to be seen and lack of imposing size. Mina could see the small pursuer carried only a stick and a pack. She did, however, exhale a sigh of relief when he slowly raised his hand and signaled a stunted, childlike wave.

Darting across the alley and following the footing line of the shack to their position, Jo motioned for Mina to remain quiet and still. He crouched near her as she whispered. "Who are you?"

"I am Jo," he answered. Pointing to the others, he continued, "Who are these?"

Nodding to the infant she replied, "This is Rae." Moving her arm she said, "This is Anna. I am Mina. Why are you here?"

Answering her question and indicating his own by pointing to the girls' mother, Jo spoke, "The Bride?"

"Yes."

"We must get away from this open street. Wake this girl and all of you move to the dark alley to the left. I will awaken the Bride and bring her."

It took Mina several moments to rouse Anne and get her and the baby to the alley, doing so without either of them crying. When they were safely in the shadows, Jo touched the shoulder of the Bride and spoke in her ear, "Mother."

The soft touch and the distinctive voice instantly summoned the Bride from her slumber.

"Who are you?"

"The Bridegroom sent me, Mother. I am Jo."

"But you are a boy," she declared, covering her nakedness by keeping her back to him.

"I'm only doing what I was sent to do," replied Jo. He took the white cloak from his pack. Placing it over her shoulders and back, he continued, "Please put this on quickly and get into the shadows with the others."

The Bride gasped in shock and amazement, followed with an immediate breath of delight and disbelief. She sighed and hugged the white cloak made from the snow leopard.

"Please, you must hurry," urged Jo.

The Bride followed the boy's directions, moving to the shadows as he guided her elbow. Jo, disturbed by the visibility of the Bride's white cloak but not hosting the possibility of its removal, directed the group deeper into the alley. He planned to leave the city to the west, travel north into the desert for half a day and journey in an arc to the northeast. Once in the mountains, he thought they would be safe.

The five fled along streets and alleys, preferring the latter for isolation. Whenever a route allowed a westward jaunt, the group took it. Rae began to cry and Mina failed to keep her silent. The Bride took the baby under her cloak and fed her, maintaining the quiet needed to escape.

Shouts sounded from the direction they came. The commotion increased as guards alerted others that the Bride was gone, either fleeing on her own or taken by someone. Cries reverberated through the alleys as four guards were slain for losing the Bride. Angry shouts caused the fleeing five to increase the pace. Waves of warriors radiated from the center in an ever-expanding circle. Light filtered into the city. The dawn, combined with the shouts, brought many people into the streets. To keep from looking suspicious, the Bride and her children were forced to walk. Whenever someone asked them what the trouble was, either Jo or Mina pointed back and said, "The noise is coming from the center of the city."

The warriors closed the distance and one of them, from the far end of a street, spotted the Bride's white cloak. Jo directed them into a narrow pathway leading past a bakery and the city's Temple of Ophis. Around the next corner their escape route was blocked by the pathway's end at a tannery. Knowing they could not stop, Jo led them under the floor of the tannery. The drippings from hides and curing agents gave off a putrid stench that caused them to gag. Climbing out the other side of the crawl space, they continued to flee, but only for a moment.

As Jo led them around a corner to the west, a lone warrior stood blocking their escape. Stopped in front of the enemy, the five stared at him. Though he had heard the shouts from the street area, the warrior was clearly startled. Inhaling and parting his lips, he turned as if to shout the announcement of their capture. The intended declaration was never uttered as his sorrowful eyes never left the Bride.

"This way," he whispered with certainty.

The Bride offered her hand. He took it and, by her hushed absolution, was acknowledged as one of her returning sons. He led them to the end of the alley and across two dirt streets as the escape continued.

"Well, what do we have here?"

The Bride and her five children did not respond to the leader of the squad standing with weapon at the ready. Jo and Mina started to retrace their steps, but upon turning, were confronted by four armed warriors.

The squad leader motioned his men to restrain the fugitives and continued, "Looks like we have a traitor among us."

The Bride spoke quickly and sharply, "Would a traitor have led us to you?"

"Silence, wench, or I'll add my mark to your ugly, pocked face."

The newly returned son summoned a guttural from the deeps of his belly and forced it through a set jaw and clenched teeth. He pushed his mother behind him with his left hand and prepared for the fight. The battle never began. Leaving his left side vulnerable when he moved the Bride, the new son was momentarily defenseless. The squad leader swung his weapon, breaking the protector's jaw and caving-in the bones on the right side of his face. The next blow ended his life.

The Bride gasped in horror as she stared at her son's lifeless body. The squad leader collared her and motioned his men to bring the others.

Still in shock as she was being led down the path, the Bride said, "I did not even know his name. Who was he? Did he have a family?"

"One more word, woman, and you'll be swallowing the few teeth you have left in your head," threatened the leader.

Jo stared intently at the leader and said to the Bride, "The Bridegroom knows your son's name. He has him now. The best thing to have ever happened to that son of yours was to be standing here when you came by. He might have lived his life and died without ever having the occasion to know the Bridegroom or you, his mother." Jo continued to examine the leader and said, "In fact, Bride, this squad leader here; this other fallen son knows this is his opportunity to return to you. However, he is afraid."

Fuming with anger, the leader halted the group and bent down into the face of Jo. "Be quiet, you arrogant, golden-tongued runt or I'll make you wish you never drew the breath of life."

Neglecting his advice, Jo continued, "Dear Bride, yes, I understand the situation with him. This man's dilemma is that there are men here who will report him if he does what he really would like to do. He truly wants to be with you. He is one of your sons, but he is afraid of what his men will do if he helps you escape."

"Shut your mouth," the leader roared.

Jo continued, "See, he threatens with his mouth but does not want to follow through on his warnings. He fears for what his life would be like if he goes with us. But he is one of your sons, and for what he is doing, the Bridegroom forgives him."

The leader back-handed the boy, sending him to the ground and cutting his lip. "Will the Bridegroom still forgive me, boy?"

"Yes."

Flustered and with a hint of fear, the leader grasped the elbow of the Bride. With a wavering voice he commanded his men to follow him. As the small troop rounded the corner to enter the street and proceed to the marketplace, the Bride glanced over her shoulder. Thanatos and the pale horse were drawing near the body of her recently received son.

Word spread that the woman, her attendants and a young boy in a black robe had been captured. Bestman Marquis issued an order for them to be brought before him at the marketplace. There, in the presence of all the people, court would be held and the anticipated sentences immediately carried out. Unusually crowded at this time of the morning, the raucous marketplace buzzed as Bestman Marquis, with pompous swaggering and great ceremony, ascended the platform to take his place at the Chair of Judgment.

Bestman Marquis, dressed in his usual black robe, motioned for the guilty to be brought before him. While he was taken back by the white-cloaked Bride, Bestman Marquis was clearly astonished to see the boy in the black robe.

After recovering his composure, he guffawed and declared, "Let the trial begin. Among those assembled here as witnesses to this trial, are the guilty present?"

The court announcer stepped forward to begin the trial. He did so by stating the obligatory answer of *yes*. Before he said the word, Jo marched to the place where the announcer intended to be. He was now a mere twenty feet from Bestman Marquis. Jo held the pack with his left hand and carried the walking stick in his right. When several laughs came from the crowd, Jo turned in the direction of the laughs and pointed his walking stick at the people.

"Yes," Jo answered. "The guilty one is here. There are two in the city who are wearing the black robe. There is only one who is guilty here today, and that one is wearing a black robe."

The crowd, taking its cue from the mocking snicker of Bestman Marquis, roared with laughter. Jo, with his face to the judge and his back to the crowd, raised his walking stick. The good humor of Bestman Marquis ended abruptly. He fumed and raised his hand for silence.

The Bride seized the opportunity. As the crowd's noise began to diminish, she handed Rae to Anne and moved in the direction of the judge's chair. In the dazzling white of the snow leopard cloak, the Bride stepped between the two wearing black robes. Turning her back to the Chair of Judgment, she faced the crowd and raised her arms for silence. Bestman Marquis threw his head back in another robust guffaw.

No one in the crowd laughed.

The Bride spoke.

CHAPTER 14

REVOLTING

"Every one of you gathered here this day should feel honored."

Several in the crowd responded with jeers. The Bride waited for them to quiet before continuing.

"You will be spectators of a competition that will be told for generations to come."

Stunned at the Bride's boldness, Jo could only listen and watch. Bestman Marquis, furious at the proceedings, stood and shouted at the woman only ten feet from him, "Competition? This is no competition! You are guilty and on trial."

"No," said the Bride, now facing the Chair of Judgment, "I am to be under the care of the bestman."

"I am the bestman. Woman, you are under my care," he shrieked.

Calmly the Bride responded, "My eyes behold two present who wear the black robe." She turned to the crowd as she asked with feigned uncertainty, "How many men do you see wearing the black robe?"

The crowd, now caught up in the hilarity of the event, shouted in cadence, "Two! Two! Two!"

Jo's lips parted as his lower jaw fell. His mind whirled in confusion. The Bride persisted. With courage she asked a wise question, "Should I not be under the care of the bestman and should you not be allowed to witness the competition between Jo and Marquis?"

Each of the people, assured of remaining anonymous in the crowd, began to chant, "Yes! Yes!"

Marquis demanded quiet and did not receive it. He shouted to no avail, "I am the bestman."

The Bride raised her hands and the crowds stilled. "Marquis believes that he is the bestman. I believe that Jo is the bestman. You see, Jo here is stronger, wiser and certainly more clever than Marquis."

Laughing agreement spread throughout the people and the woman in white spoke once more, "How many of you believe that Jo is the better man than Marquis?"

The crowd roared its vote of agreement.

She asked one more question, "When should the competition begin?"

The crowd chanted, "Now! Now! Now!"

"Silence," Marquis demanded in vain.

An abrupt change flowed through Jo. He stepped to the Bride, placed the walking stick in his left hand with the pack and extended his right hand to the Bride. She accepted his hand and he escorted her to the side. The assembly quieted as Jo resumed his confrontational position before the astonished and fuming Marquis. The boy placed the pack on the platform and removed the chain with the unknown object on one end and the small box with the hinged door on the other. He hung it upon his shoulders and the Bride's eyes teared for what she had not seen for many years. Gasps of amazement mixed with the sighs of delight uttered by a few old children.

"Marquis," Jo said in a voice that carried to the multitudes, "the Bride is right. I'm stronger than you are. I'm wiser than you. And, I'm certainly more clever than you. In saying this, I also confess that none of my strength, wisdom or cleverness comes from me. All glory belongs to the Bridegroom, for he is the source of all these things. So, Marquis, are you willing to concede victory to me now?"

With a seething rage, he answered, "Never, fool!"

Jo remained calm and spoke to the crowd, "See, his answer reveals his stupidity and my wisdom."

Laughter erupted from the people.

The boy issued the challenge, "Marquis, if you are the bestman, put your sword inside this small wooden box with the hinged door. If you are able to do this, you are the bestman. If you are not able, then I will put my walking stick inside the box, thereby demonstrating that I am the bestman and, as a result, the Bride is under my care."

Jo turned his head and asked, "Agreed?"

The crowd shouted, "Yes! Do it!"

Jo's challenging eyes returned to Marquis, who replied, "You fool. That box is too small. My sword is nearly four feet long."

"Do you give up so easily, Marquis? Perhaps this is much too difficult for you. Let's take this in two steps. First, you open the hinged door on the wooden box. Then, if indeed you accomplish the first step and you are able to open the door, you must put your sword inside the box. Are you wise enough to understand? But of course, if you are not able to do these things and want to acknowledge me as bestman, then I will open the door and put my five foot long walking stick inside. You decide. Are you strong enough to open the door?"

Jo lifted the box from the end of the chain and held it in his hand, taunting his opponent. Marquis, seething in his hatred of the boy, pulled his lower lip into his mouth and clenched it with his teeth. His fiery eyes never left Jo. The silence of the multitude weighed heavily on Marquis and compelled him to the contest. He approached the boy and took the box in his hands. Rather than attempting to open the hinged door, Marquis slowly examined every surface of the box and tried to determine the difficulty in opening the hinged door.

Moments passed without a word. A voice among the people was heard in sarcastic proclamation, "He's finally found the door!" The multitudes broke out in mass laughter.

Stung by the ridicule, Marquis tilted the box, twisted the small knob and pulled at the hinged door. Nothing happened. He jerked at the door, increasing his exertion as he vented his frustration. Alternately he shook the box in anger and worked the knob in every way possible. He twisted, pulled, pushed, cranked, jiggled, jostled and attempted to slide the small, serrated knob. Nothing worked and the door remained closed.

Marquis threw the box into Jo's chest. A corner of the box hit the boy on the breastbone. Only resolute determination enabled him to show no effect. Instead, Jo held the box so all could watch, also holding back tears from the sharp blow to his chest.

"Now, Marquis, I will demonstrate that I am stronger than you, and yet not I, but the Bridegroom."

Jo held the small box with the hinged door in his left hand so all could see. With the index finger and thumb of his right hand he lightly gripped the knob. Leaving the door stationary, Jo rotated the box on the small hinges. He was the first one to look inside the box for decades. What he saw amazed him. The interior was larger than the outside of the box and there were many items inside. Jo saw the scroll and chalice, petite iron pot and white quill, tome and volume, as well as the script and other writings. Everything was properly placed inside and without damage. It took a moment, but Jo understood what to do.

"People of this city, now we determine which of us is wiser. But Marquis, before you are given the opportunity to show your wisdom, you must demonstrate that you are strong enough to open the little door of this small box. As for me, let my wisdom be manifest now, yet not mine but the Bridegroom's."

The young boy took his long walking stick and slowly placed it in the box. A collective sigh of amazement issued from the crowd. Jo shut the hinged door and offered the box to Marquis.

Jeered on by the heckling mass, Marquis grabbed the box and pulled it to himself until the chain jerked the boy's neck.

Marquis examined the box and attempted to open the box as Jo had done, by holding the door and turning the rest of the box. It remained closed. He tried to use a gentle touch with forefinger and thumb in turning the serrated knob. He not only succeeded in looking foolish before the people, he was also unable to open the door by mimicking Jo's actions. Marquis resorted to random movements, wild shaking and forceful prying to gain entry.

Jo taunted him, "Perhaps you need to say a special word. Do you remember if I used a word when I opened the box? Certainly the bestman would be able to recall if a word was spoken. If I did, do you remember the word? Oh, sir, you are failing miserably!"

Marquis spit vindictive words at the box and shot venomous, obscene phrases at Jo. He thrust the box back to Jo who was prepared to catch it.

The boy in the black robe opened the box as before and removed his walking stick. He smiled as he asked the other in black, "Do you concede that I am the bestman?"

"Never! You stand there with a stick. On either side of me are my armed attendants who will be on you the instant I command it. You don't seem so clever, boy. You with your tricky little box while I am here with a sword that will slit your throat in a flash."

"Not a wise move," the boy said, "no, not wise at all."

Jo turned to the people and asked, "Is Marquis the bestman?"

A roar resounded across the marketplace, "No!"

Jo faced Marquis and said, "You say that I am not so very clever. Perhaps you are right; perhaps you are not. But this I do know. When you came here this morning, you ruled all these people. Now you don't. With one voice, they have renounced you as bestman."

Jo looked to the Bride and asked her, "Am I the bestman?"

She voiced a loud, firm, "Yes!"

He faced the people, "Am I the bestman?"

113

The marketplace shouted as one, "Yes!"

"Marquis, it would appear that you have only two who are on your side right now, and I wonder just how loyal they are to you. They have heard the multitudes and they know that if they attack me they are dead men. Do you dare to try? Go ahead, order them to attack me. See if you have even two who call you the bestman."

Marquis didn't hesitate, "Run him through."

Neither of the armed attendants moved.

"Didn't you hear me," he bellowed. "Kill him! Has this imposter, this runt bewitched you with his magic box? I order you to run him through. Do it now!"

Again, there was no movement from either of them.

When he felt their hesitation, Marquis raised his sword and shouted, "I'll do it myself."

Marquis moved; Jo remained in place; and the armed attendants pounced on the older man in black. After taking his weapon away, the guards jerked the bestman to his feet.

A wide grin formed on his face and Jo whispered to his opponent, "Clever, wouldn't you say?"

He motioned to the armed attendants and ordered, "Take him away." The boy's command was obeyed.

The boy stepped to the front of the platform to address the people. He desperately wanted to get the Bride away from the city and to the mountains with the rest of her children. That was his task and he continued to accomplish it.

"This day you have voiced your desire for a new life. My reign as bestman here will not be like what you have just experienced, unless that be your desire. If you want me to be like Marquis, then please say so this minute."

Not a sound came from the marketplace.

"My first desire is to grant you freedom from the reign and rule of any bestman. Do you want freedom?"

The platform vibrated with their answer, "Yes!"

"Before I declare your freedom, several other matters must be the subject of your attention and must receive your approval. The woman in white has not been free for four decades. Like you, she has been bound and oppressed and used and abused. Like you, the woman in the white cloak deserves to be free; to come and go as she pleases. Will you grant this to her?"

"Yes," declared the voice of the multitude.

"If the woman in white desires to leave your city, will you stop her?"

The crowd responded with an emphatic, "No!"

The Bride motioned for Jo to come near her. He did, listening to her for a moment. He nodded his head in agreement and returned to the people.

"The woman in the white cloak will be leaving within the hour. She wants those of her children who desire to go with her to be able to do so. All of her sons and daughters, no matter what age and no matter how long they have been away from her and no matter what they may have done, are invited to return to her and go with her. They must understand that they will be leaving their lands and houses and businesses for those who remain. If some choose to leave with the Bride, and if they leave all their possessions here for you, will you permit this?"

"Yes!"

"Those of you who are not her children but desire to become one of her children are invited to accompany her. You will be leaving all of your lands and houses and businesses behind for others. Will the rest of you permit everyone who wants to go with her, to do so? Property and possessions will be left here. Will you permit it?"

"Yes!"

"The woman in the white cloak will be leaving in one hour. Those accompanying her are to be at the north gate. She will depart with her children, old and young, old and new. In just a moment, as the bestman, I am going to declare you free from the reign and rule of any bestman. Do not let yourselves become involved with another bestman or ruler or king like Marquis. How you decide to govern yourselves will be left entirely to you. Do you understand this?"

The multitude answered with a shout, "Yes."

Jo concluded his speech to the people, "I, Bestman Jo, wearer of the black robe, bearer of the chain and its end-items, turner of the ironwood box, and caretaker of the Bride -- I declare you free from any bestman, and announce that this city is a free city, and proclaim all of you to be free people. It is done!"

A huge roar erupted from the multitude.

"Quickly, we must leave," Jo said with an intense degree of urgency.

He grasped the Bride's arm and led her away from the marketplace and into the alley. Mina, now carrying Rae in one arm and guiding Anne's shoulder with her free hand, followed the Bride.

CHAPTER 15

REASSEMBLING

From the alley, the Bride directed Jo and her daughters to the street leading to the north gate. As they hurried along, Mina noticed others following them. She brought it to the attention of Jo, but the Bride told her everything was as it should be.

In half an hour the five arrived at the north gate and waited. The several people following said nothing as they sat beside the Bride. She welcomed them and called them children. Tears streamed down the face of one old man.

Jo removed the chain stole and began to place it in the pack. The Bride noticed and spoke to him in private.

"Listen to me carefully. What has happened here today was not something temporary. You have not played a part. You may not go back to your old way of life."

Jo stopped and gazed quizzically at her, "What do you mean?"

"Bestman Jo," she called firmly and distinctly.

"What?"

She continued, "Today I called you to be the Bridegroom's bestman. This was done not only to rescue me from this place. I have called you, bestman and it is most certainly true that you are his bestman. You are Bestman Jo, and I am under your care."

"How can this be? The Bridegroom sent me to rescue you. That's what I'm doing. Nothing more."

"And nothing less, Bestman Jo. If the Bridegroom did not want you to be his bestman, why did he give you the robe from the black sheep? And why does it fit so well? Why did the length of the chain stole adjust to hang properly on your shoulders? Why did the small ironwood box with the hinged door open for you and for you alone, Bestman Jo?"

"But please, Bride, I am no more than one of your young children."

"Do not say, 'I am only a child.'"

"But you don't understand."

"I do understand. Bestman Jo, think about what has happened today. Could you have said or done what you just said and did using only your own knowledge and will?"

"No."

"Take a look at those around you here."

He did. In addition to the three daughters who attended to the Bride, others had quietly drawn near and knelt waiting. The old man who had wept earlier sat with an expression of repentant joy and gladness. Fifteen others huddled in silence, anticipating an imminent departure with the Bride. Even as he surveyed those waiting nearby, others stood in the foreground.

The Bride continued, "They are here because of you, Bestman Jo. They are afraid and they wonder if they have done the right thing. They hope and dream and pray. These are my sons and daughters, Bestman Jo. You are their leader and I am their mother. Right now, at this instant, their eyes are fixed on us. If you take off the chain stole or hesitate or doubt, they will waver and might be lost."

Bestman Jo, resigned to his call, spoke quietly, "I don't know what to do. I thought my task would be complete with your rescue. What does it mean to be the bestman? What do I do? How am I able to lead all these people and take care of you? I am certainly unable to do this great work."

"Your words are beautiful, Bestman Jo. They indicate the heart of a bestman." She smiled at him and continued, "Each day, read from one of the writings in the small box with the hinged door. You will learn what it means to be the bestman and how such a great thing is to be done. Talk to the Bridegroom and let him speak to you by means of his words."

Bestman Jo whispered as he adjusted the ends of the chain stole, "Bride?"

"Yes," she answered with a smile of approval.

"Is my appearance as it should be for being the bestman?"

"Yes," she repeated.

Bestman Jo directed his attention to the scattered pockets of people and announced, "Please, my dear brothers and sisters, please stand and gather before your loving and caring mother."

As they congregated, Bestman Jo spoke to the Bride and she answered with an affirmative action of her head. He spoke once more and she replied.

"Many of you are aware that there is a pool of water to the northwest. We will go there first and get a full supply of water. From the pool we will travel north across the desert and northeast to the mountains. In the mountains, we will be joined by more of your brothers and sisters. First to the pool."

When the company arrived at the water hole, Bestman Jo counted fifty-eight people, excluding himself and the Bride. Both of them circulated among the children. Though Bestman Jo greeted them, the majority wanted to speak to the Bride. She heard their words of guilt and sorrow mixed with expressions of joy and thanksgiving. This was especially true when she personally acknowledged each of them as her daughter or son. People from the city drew near and waited on the outskirts of the area. The Bride greeted them and welcomed them. Before the large family left the pool, the number of sons and daughters increased by nine.

One of this number was a warrior named, Dynamis. He was the squad leader who captured the Bride and led her to the marketplace. The Bride approached the warrior and his head lowered for the shame he felt. She lifted his chin with her hand and spoke, "Son, back in the city you were weak with fear. Now you are strong with power. The power of Ruach has delivered you. I am filled with gladness that you, my son, are here. Come with me and meet your brothers and sisters."

Bestman Jo led the Bride and her children across the hot desert floor for several days. One early evening, just after the edge of the earth swallowed the sun, and for as long as the remaining light permitted, Bestman Jo read from the writings in the small wooden box with the hinged door. Some of the writings frightened him, especially those written in *The Volume of Consequences*. Gladness permeated him and made goose bumps rise on his arms when he read *The Psalm of the Bridegroom*. There were stories in the writings that created both fear and joy for Bestman Jo, especially the account of the Bride being lifted up and let down during the days of Bestman Comfy. Bestman Jo asked the Bride if these stories were true. She said that all things in the writings were events that either have happened, or are happening, or will happen.

Bestman Jo read, with great care and personal wonder, the sections about gapping the circle and leading the Bride in the Great Dance. He asked the Bride about the Great Dance and she told him it was time for him to welcome her children into the gapped circle and lead as the bestman was called. He was reluctant and offered the Bride many logical reasons why he should not do this thing. She gave him the look; the look that shut the boy's mouth and opened the bestman's heart.

Several nights after reading and studying, Bestman Jo assembled the children of the Bride in the gapped circle. He began by telling them that the Bridegroom was preparing the Wedding Hall, making preparations for the banquet and would soon be coming for his Bride. The Bride's children were to be found faithful and that meant trusting in Headbanger and being fed the gifts he has given to his Bride. Bestman Jo told them that whenever they gathered in the gapped circle, they were participating in a rehearsal for the Great Wedding. The rehearsal, however, was not merely a game of practice in which the children of the Bride were going through the motions. The things they thought, said and did meant something and availed much.

The service that evening, and for many that followed, was clumsy and stilted. Bestman Jo had to refer to the writings often and think about what came next. The events seemed out of order and Bestman Jo knew it as he led the service. When leading the Bride in the Great Dance, he watched his feet. After the first service, when all the children left through the gap, Bestman Jo apologized to the Bride and asked her to forgive him for the obvious awkwardness of the service. A solemn expression appeared on her face.

"Bestman Jo, please listen to me quite carefully. If you have been faithful in your service, then never apologize for having fed my children and having led me in the Great Dance. The Bridegroom does not require you to be anything other than faithful. Believe me when I say that I would rather have my daughters and sons fed by a clumsy, stuttering bestman who is faithful to the Bridegroom than by a deceiver who leads them away from the coming wedding. As for the forgiveness you ask, please remember that you are one of my children too. The essential theme in the writings you read and the message you speak and the Great Dance that you lead is intended for you as well as for the others."

Bestman Jo did not respond in words. He listened to the Bride and thought about what she said. He loved the Bride and the Bridegroom more than ever.

She continued, "Tonight, for the first time in decades, my children gathered with me in the circle of worship. Most of them had never done so before. As I looked at them, wonder and amazement filled their eyes. The faces of the youngest children radiated happiness and joy. Bestman Jo, I watched the older daughters and sons who last stepped through the gap more than forty years ago. Their faces expressed gratitude, devotion, love and respect. As for me, well, let me say that I have always been loved by the Bridegroom. His love has always been mine. I have

121

not, however, always been loved and cared for by the bestmen. Now I am cared for once again and for that I am thankful."

The following day Bestman Jo led the Bride and her children to the northeast. Traveling at the same rate, the company would reach the mountains by evening of the next day. Just before stopping at the hottest part of the day, Dynamis reported to Bestman Jo that two people were approaching. The bestman ordered the Bride and her children to rest and eat while the two people came to them.

Less than an hour later, the two arrived. They were out of breath, exhausted and nearly overcome with thirst. The others attempted to give them some water, but the couple refused, instead desperately desiring to speak.

With gasps of breath, the woman spoke first, "They are coming ... run ... fly to the mountains!"

The man continued, "We have no time ... flee ... we must get away."

Bestman Jo asked, "Who is after us?"

"Marquis and his entire army of warriors," the woman answered.

"Marquis?"

"Yes," said the man, "after you left there was a trial for Marquis. He talked his way out and returned to power."

"We left to warn you," continued the woman. "They will be upon us in less than a day."

Bestman Jo issued orders. "We will neither panic nor delay. Give water to this woman and the man. We will travel quickly, but we will not run. Dynamis, you lead the company. Take us straight to the mountains. The Bride will be in the midst of her children. Care for one another and help each other as we quicken our pace. Do not run. I will be at the back of the company. Dynamis, get to the front and get us going!"

The children of the Bride followed the powerful warrior's lead and fled to the mountains. Bestman Jo stood and waited until all the people had gone by him. He looked back and thought he saw a dust cloud on the desert floor. With walking stick in hand and chain stole hung on his shoulders, he fled with the Bride and her children.

The evening approached and Bestman Jo stopped the company to speak with them.

"Do not sit down. It will only make you more tired. We stand and eat because we are in a great hurry. Therefore, take out a little food and eat. Do it now. Drink half of the water you have. We must keep fleeing through the night. The enemy is closing on us, even at the fast pace we are traveling. The dust cloud grows as they approach. In four hours they will be here where we are standing. Help each other and stay close together in the dark of this night that is ahead. Keep your eyes on Dynamis. Let's go."

The Bride and her children fled that night, aided by the light from the full moon. But what gave help to them also aided Marquis' army. Before the morning light, the children reached the base of the mountains. The pursuing army was only a half hour behind them and closing fast as they sensed the kill.

That morning, an uncharacteristic, massive, dense blanket of fog rolled down from the mountain heights, enveloping the sloped terrain. When the cascading cloud of thick water vapor reached the bottom of the gorge, it spread across and covered the desert floor.

The Bride and her children formed a human chain, Dynamis being the first link and Bestman Jo the last. They fled up the mountain, following a dry streambed. The advancing army was now several minutes from them. Though unseen, the army's movements could be heard as it started up the mountain. Twenty minutes later, Bestman Jo heard the voices of individual warriors behind him.

Suddenly, a violent shaking of the earth began, a heaving so turbulent no one could move. The crashing sound of boulders and rocks permeated the thick fog. Bestman Jo, the Bride and her children fell to the ground and covered their heads with their arms. Everyone, each one, was alone in a sightless world, surrounded by dense clouds and thunderous racket and commotion. After what seemed an eternity in each one's mind, there was lonely silence. Minutes later, a gentle wind descended from the upper slopes of the high mountain and slowly cleared the thick fog. Light from the sun exposed the mountain and a new day dawned with blue sky.

Bestman Jo stood and gazed down the mountain. The gorge below them, which they ascended, was filled with rock from the high ridges on both sides. Marquis' army had been buried alive. Every warrior was now in the grave. Not a single child of the Bride's was lost or even hurt.

"Look," cried Anne, "one of the warriors is still alive. He's coming after us!"

And indeed, far below, across the top of the rock rubble, someone was coming at them.

CHAPTER 16

RECOILING

The man who survived the rock avalanche continued to work his way through the rubble. Dynamis left his forward position and ran at double-speed to the place where Bestman Jo and Anne stood. The warrior had a difficult time stopping when Bestman Jo indicated with his arm that Dynamis should descend no farther, but remain with them.

"He has no weapon," Bestman Jo observed, thus justifying his restraint of Dynamis. "Certainly, if that man is a weaponless enemy warrior, you will be able to subdue him before he hurts any of us."

"Yes, Bestman Jo, you may depend on it," replied Dynamis.

"Besides," added the Bride, "he may be another of my children who wants to be with us."

"True," agreed Bestman Jo.

The man continued to make his way up the broken terrain, obviously hurrying. A couple times, he stumbled, causing small rock slides and suffering bruises to his knees and shins. When clear of the rubble beneath him, he began running at full speed. Dynamis lowered his weapon and braced himself.

The Bride commanded Dynamis, "Wait! I know who the man is. Let him proceed."

The man approached the company of people and ran directly to the Bride. He bowed and handed her a card.

I am Eliab the Peacemaker,
a runner from the ancient village of
Benedicamus at the base of High Mountain.

(Please imprint your right thumb on the
other side of this card and return it to me.)

The Bride spoke as she prepared to turn the card over. "I am glad the Bridegroom still sends his runners to me. Mina, do you remember what happened to Eliphalet the Pure-Hearted?"

"Yes, Mother, he was beaten to death," she said.

The Bride, desiring to get some reaction from the runner, noted none as Mina answered her question. The Bride continued, hoping the runner might convey some message to the Bridegroom, "I love the Bridegroom for his undeserved love for us."

Eliab the Peacemaker listened, but neither spoke nor gave any hint about his thoughts. His eyes, however, never left the card in the Bride's hand.

"Bestman Jo," she said, "please read the words on the other side of this card. They are important and you will need to memorize them."

"Certainly," he responded as the Bride shared the card with Bestman Jo.

The Headbanger is coming as said,
'Tis the first step to stand in thy stead,
The word's not forgott'n,
Beget the begott'n,
He'll appear at the Small House of Bread.

"I really don't understand all of this," admitted Bestman Jo.

The Bride said, "You do not need to understand all of it right now. Please memorize it."

The bestman read it aloud twice. He closed his eyes and attempted to repeat it, stumbling in a couple of places. Each time one of the Bride's children added the word needed. He read it aloud once more and had it memorized. The Bride pressed her thumb on the card and returned it to Eliab the Peacemaker. He examined the card and began running up the mountain.

"Strange," the Bride mumbled.

Bestman Jo inquired, "What's strange?"

"That is the first time a runner has not returned in the same direction whence he came."

Everyone stared at Eliab the Peacemaker as he ran up the mountain. After Mina turned to speak to Bestman Jo, she gasped and said, "Oh how horrible! What is happening?"

The others turned and in glancing looks were able to view Thanatos and the pale horse. Thanatos pulled the bodies from the rock and tossed them into the black net. The ashen beast trudged up the slope as the harvest of the dead commenced.

The Bride had known of this from the beginning, but she was not prepared for what she saw that morning from the mountain height. The black net, filled with the bodies of all who had ever died, extended across the tan desert floor. It stretched for a thousand miles and more, slithering through busy city streets and across abandoned fields where one army annihilated another. The dark tube of death slid through silent lands of past plagues and through troubled waters of seas and rivers. Nothing stopped death's duet. They worked day and night. The trailing end of the black net, stuffed with the body of Lo-Eli, was far beyond the horizon. No eye could see it, even from the top of the mountains.

Several days later, the Bride welcomed Old Sis, Nathan and the other children of the mountains. The circle was gapped, the chain once again lengthening to include the increase in the number of the Bride's children. Here it was that Bestman Jo and

127

the Bride asked Nathan to write down all the events that had taken place. The white quill from the high-soaring eagle and the golden chalice with the ink of blood were used as Bestman Jo dictated to Nathan. He was also to take all of the writings, copy them and put them into one large book to be used during the times of the gapped circle. Nathan was told to title the work, *The Book of Ancient Promises Given*. Nathan agreed to this vocation and solemnly pledged to accomplish his work. A proclamation went forth among the children that he would no longer be called Nathan, but Nathaniel the Inscriber.

In the months that followed, Bestman Jo led the Bride and her children throughout the mountain region gathering those who had been scattered. Most rejoiced and were glad when she arrived. Some, however, had taken other deities and refused to give them up. Such a stir arose among the people that Bestman Jo made a declaration permitting no personal deities. The Bride had only one to whom she was faithful, the Bridegroom. He would not share her or her children with any other object of worship, whether real or imaginary. Bestman Jo announced that anyone serving any other deity may no longer enter the gapped circle and participate in the Great Dance. The people who no longer were sheltered by the white cloak left and this was a source of more sorrow to the Bride, Bestman Jo and the others under the cloak's absolution.

Thirteen years later, the mountains to the north had been searched. The dispersed children of the Bride who wanted to be found, were found; those who did not, were not. Those abiding with the Bride lived and grew older with the certain hope of meeting the Bridegroom one day soon. The oldest daughter of the Bride did so near the end of the thirteenth year. Old Sis died in her sleep before dawn one morning. Though her body was snatched by Thanatos, the essence of Old Sis went through the Portal to the good land.

The Bride begat many other sons and daughters during this time in the mountains. The circle grew and all within were filled with joy. Bestman Jo read of the old promises for the Bride and her children. He grew in his understanding of what it meant to be the bestman of the Bridegroom. Not all of his questions were answered, but he continued to do what he was called to do. He wondered what the item was at the other end of the chain stole. He thought about the meaning of *Small House of Bread* and pondered the reality of the one named *Footstomper*.

One morning Bestman Jo awoke realizing that the Bridegroom had communicated to him in a dream. The Bride and her children were to journey across the high plateaus to the southwest. The long trek was to begin immediately, though Bestman Jo did not know the precise reason for such haste. The Bridegroom had communicated to him that the time was being fulfilled and the hour was drawing near.

Three days later the Bride and her children left the high mountains. Dynamis, now much older and losing the sight of one eye, resumed his forward position in the advancing column. A young warrior-in-training stood at his side. The Bride remained in the middle surrounded by her children, most of whom were thrilled at the adventure ahead. Bestman Jo and Nathaniel the Inscriber were the last two to step from the mountains and onto the high plateaus.

Being on the open plains made the Bride, the leaders and the older children nervous. The mountains provided bountiful opportunities for escape and hiding. The wide plateaus left everyone vulnerable and on guard. The eye of Dynamis scanned the horizon for trouble, and not trusting himself, he often asked his understudy to survey the landscape ahead. Bestman Jo checked the rear often. The only pursuers he saw, when he cast a glancing look, were Thanatos and the pale horse.

For weeks the direction of travel was southwest, following a curious groove in the earth. Dynamis tried to depart from its line but Bestman Jo told him to continue following the skid marks on the flat terrain.

129

On the fortieth day of the journey, a runner approached from the southwest. As usual, he bowed to the Bride and presented the card.

> I am Elijah the Persecuted,
> a runner from the ancient village of
> Benedicamus at the base of High Mountain.
>
> (Please imprint your right thumb on the other side
> of this card and return it to me.
> I am the last of the nine. The forerunner is next.)

The Bride made no attempt to speak to Elijah the Persecuted. Instead, she motioned Bestman Jo to read the back of the card with her. He memorized it without her having to ask.

> A week and a day first blood's shed,
> A score and a half first born's dead,
> So lift up thy face,
> He's taken thy place,
> A-rose and a wedding's ahead.

With thumb printed in place and verified by Elijah the Persecuted, the runner returned in a southwesterly direction that paralleled the groove. Seven of the Bride's sons and four of her daughters tried to keep pace with the runner. The runner's head looked neither to the left nor to the right as the others sprinted ahead of him slightly. They stayed ahead of him only a short while. In turn, each of the tagalongs fell back, doubling over and gulping the desert air in exhaustion.

The Bride asked Bestman Jo, "I know we are not able to comprehend the entire meaning of the card, but what do you understand of it?"

He replied, "There are three certain things in the future. First, there is suffering and more death ahead." He directed the Bride's attention to Thanatos and the pale horse following at the ever steady pace. Bestman Jo soberly continued, "Not only ahead, but behind us, much suffering and death."

She noted the ever present pair and asked, "Do you mean the part about *first blood shed* and *first born's dead*?"

"Yes, but the second part about *taken thy place* is also difficult to understand. Has it already happened? If so, who has taken the place of whom? Or is it a future event? Who does *thy* refer to; to you as the Bride, or to me as the bestman, or to all of us?"

"I believe I know. Bestman Jo, study the *Volume of Consequences* once more."

"Certainly."

"What was the third thing that you understood from the card that was ahead for us?"

Bestman Jo answered as he watched the runner, "A wedding?"

"Yes," she agreed, "you perceived that too. So, no matter what may happen, my Bridegroom will come and take us to the Great Wedding. He has promised it."

"By the way, did the card say *a rose* or *arose*?"

"I don't recall. No doubt we will find out."

"No doubt."

As Elijah the Persecuted disappeared into the horizon, the Bride focused her eyes carefully. Just to the left of the point where the runner vanished, a dark spot appeared. In order to better examine the dark spot, the Bride stopped walking. Bestman Jo noticed her hesitation and did so himself.

She asked, "Is that a dark spot on the horizon?"

"Yes, it is at the end of the groove."

"Any idea what it is?"

"No," he replied, "but I'm certain of one thing."

"What is that?"

"We are going to find out."

Each day the spot became larger as they traveled. After the sixth day, they overtook the dark spot. The Bride and her children were horrified and shocked to discover that it was the end of the black net being pulled by the pale horse. The black net, containing all the dead, now circled the world. The net slid across the land at half the pace of Thanatos and its horse. Weighed down by the mortal remains of humanity, the meshed tubing slid across the land and grooved the earth. Though the Bride passed by the net, the black snake now slithered along at their left side.

CHAPTER 17

THREE THRONGS AND A FEW BABIES

Three groups formed within the children of the Bride during the next four centuries. Each became a powerful force, working together to accomplish their mutual purposes and to achieve their individual goals. The Bride, able neither to prevent the groups from existing nor to protect her children from their diverting influences, remained docile during these years, preferring to occupy herself with the faithful children.

The Coterie of Inscribers claimed its origins from Nathaniel the Inscriber. Membership into the coterie consisted of three requirements. Based upon the nine runners delivering cards to the Bride, the seeking candidate was required to receive nine epistles of recommendation from present members of The Coterie of Inscribers. Once received and approved, the seeking candidate sought to find a mentor among those members who did not provide an epistle of recommendation. If such a member was found and agreed to be the mentor, the working candidate was required to copy *The Book of Ancient Promises Given*. The copy was made available for inspection by the members of the coterie for the period of one year. Any copying errors discovered rendered the entire manuscript worthless. If the copying work contained no errors, the manuscript was declared clean and the candidate was received in the membership of The Coterie of Inscribers. A proclamation was made among the children of the Bride and the newest member of the coterie was permitted to carry his copy of *The Book of Ancient Promises Given* wherever he went. Thus, the inscribers boldly decorated the covers of their manuscripts and walked about proudly displaying the evidence of their membership in the coterie.

The *Corps of Escort Sentinels* was charged with the physical protection of the Bride and her children. The captain of the corps stood in a succession of soldiers that was traced to the mighty war veteran and leader, Dynamis. A legend was told that Dynamis decided to wield his sword against the black net of death and, as he was purported to have said, "cut the cursed snake in two." Having slit a hole in the net, he entered among the bodies. Rather than returning, he stayed to free the dead. He remains within the net to this day, searching among the bodies for children of the Bride who are worthy of being released. That was the legend. Had the truth been known, the account would be told of the aged, one-eyed warrior seeking solitary relief one morning, wandering too close to the edge of a precipice and stumbling over the edge. His demise was never discovered by the children of the Bride.

The Corps of Escort Sentinels numbered thirty-nine plus the captain who commanded them. To become a sentinel in the corps a man had to be a skilled wrestler, be a long distance runner and be proficient with pike, sword, spear and mace.

Each year, the captain led all who desired membership in the corps on a forced march for a distance of one day's travel away from the Bride. A race started at dawn the next day. The runners ran to the Bride and back, each racer having to record his name in the Bride's book. The first 128 finishing the race entered a double elimination wrestling tournament. The top sixteen wrestlers squared off against each other with pikes being the weapon for the first round of competition. The second round was fought with swords, the third with spears. The weapons were blunted and none of these rounds was to the death. The winners were seldom decided by the sentinels' decision. The two fighting in the fourth round were given maces and they fought to the death.

The champion was escorted to the Bride and her children. He then challenged one member of the Corps of Escort Sentinels. The challenged sentinel picked the battle weapon and, a week later, they fought to the death. If the challenger was successful, then after seven more days, he received one whip lashing from each of the thirty-nine members of the corps. If he did not survive the scourging, the original competition began again with the winner not challenging a sentinel but receiving the thirty-nine lashes from the whip.

Such initiation rites into the Corps of Escort Sentinels insured the quality of the guards. These brutal men were feared by everyone, whether children of the Bride or those remaining outside the gapped circle. The Bride despised these rites and mourned over the senseless loss of life among her children. She was, however, powerless to stop them.

The third group to rise up among the children of the Bride was the *Cadre of the Seventy Groomsmen*. Bestman Jo had been killed at the age of thirty-nine when a king from an enemy army faced him on a high plateau. Devastated with the loss, the Bride was not able to select another bestman for several weeks. With noble intentions, the new bestman, Bestman Cho, discussed with the Bride the possibility of having one young man who would begin reading *The Book of Ancient Promises Given*. This man, selected by the Bride, would study under the bestman and be prepared to step forward when needed. The Bride asked Bestman Cho if the Bridegroom included anything in *The Book* which prevented such an understudy or even hinted that it might be displeasing. Bestman Cho stated that he had already done this and that it was one of the many adiaphora.

The practice, once in place, began to change. More young men were added to the number. As the bestmen grew older, so did the men who coveted the office of bestman. Soon, only old men were waiting to be selected as bestman. A hundred years later, an announcement was made that no more than seventy men would make up the cadre and the men would be referred to as groomsmen. After another century, the right to select the new bestman was taken away from the Bride and given to the Cadre of the Seventy Groomsmen. When one of the groomsmen died and a replacement was needed, the process of naming a successor began. In the final analysis, entry into the cadre was made based upon social position and economic compensation, the latter being given the greater weight.

As the cadre sought to solidify its position and secure its future, not only against outsiders, but especially against the corps and the inscribers, it enacted legislation. The rules tended to cause four effects, two of which were unintentional.

The first intentional result forced consolidation of political and economic power around the bestman. The declared reasoning was that Bestman Jo had called both Nathaniel and Dynamis to assist him in caring for the Bride. In the beginning, the Bride agreed with the forefathers of the cadre who pushed for this position of power. Neither the corps nor the inscribers could argue against the original appointments, especially when it was supported by the Bride. They attempted to argue that differing conditions now existed. However, when pointed out to them that their respective groups may then be declared obsolete, they backed down and retained what power they could.

The corps presented fewer threats. To ward off any risk, the cadre assigned itself the primary responsibility of paying all the wages of the corps. Rumors periodically circulated about the cadre having a spy or two among the corps' ranks. The distinct possibility of unknown internal observation, together with the economic stability of the corps dependent upon the cadre, minimized any threat from the corps. These actions reduced to near zero any chance for a threat to the cadre from within.

The second result of the cadre's power was the need for peaceful alliances with foreign controllers. The Bride and her children were neither large in number nor powerful as a united people. More often than not, she found herself under the control of other powers or governments. Usually a local ruler was assigned to care for the affairs of the Bride and her children. As long as the Bride, including all her daughters and sons were cooperative and obeyed the laws imposed on them by the foreign rulers, the cadre was permitted to tend to its own affairs. Thus, it behooved both the cadre and the Bride to have envoys representing them with the various foreign nations. This offered an opportunity, if the cadre exercised wisdom and discernment in its dealings, to keep foreign rulers away from the reign and rule of the bestman.

These two intentional posturings by the cadre resulted in a shift of power from the Bride to the bestman as well as a loss of authority by the Bride. All decisions were made for the Bride, as the cadre declared, "to spare the Bride from the cumbersome and laborious duties which only take away the quality time she has with her beloved children."

In addition, the Cadre of the Seventy Groomsmen, led by the bestman, began to dictate the words and actions of the Bride's children. This legislation occurred not only in the daily lives of the children outside the gapped circle, but also within. The Great Dance, rather than being a blessing centered on the promises of the Bridegroom, became a recitation of rules and litany of laws.

Inscribers decorated their manuscript covers with brightly colored plumes and dazzling bits of crystal. The members of the cadre competed with one another for the flashiest tassels hanging from their royal robe hems and sleeves. The sentinels, stoically presented in full dress, marched through the gap with polished weapons at the ready. Only the bestman appeared in the Bridegroom's black robe. However, the bestman's attitude was one of a pompous snob who wearied at the boredom of having to put up with these inferior children of that old hag. Usually the bestman was simply going through the motions of reading and leading. There were times when the Bride wondered why the Bridegroom allowed the small, polished, ironwood box with the hinged door to be opened in such blatant attempts to draw attention to those entering the gapped circle.

Many of her daughters and sons mirrored the arrogant attitude of the ostentatious inscribers, the gaudy groomsmen, the dispassionate sentinels or the detached bestman. Many children resorted to comparing the spiritual worthiness of each another by the success of their businesses, the deeds done in the sight of others, the brightness of their clothing or any number of outward signs. Those children who did not, could not or had no desire to keep up such pretenses, were characterized as second class children, the worst being called illegitimate.

The Bride, frustrated and unable to resist the posturing of groups and the politicking of the factions among her children, focused her attention on those outcast children, especially those who were either hurting, sick, mourning or babies. These children encouraged, prayed for and helped one another. If a son or daughter was dying, the Bride and her faithful children sang the old psalms and spoke of the Bridegroom and his wedding celebration that was ready and waiting. The Bride recited parts of the *Divine Service of Reading and Feeding* as her dying son or daughter left this life. While bitter tears welled up in her eyes when she saw the pale horse pull up and Thanatos continue working, she mixed them with tears of joy that another guest was being seated at the banquet table of the Bridegroom.

She went wherever she was forced to travel, from town to city, from marketplace to farm, across hot deserts and through lonely areas. In each place, the Bride begat many daughters and sons.

She begat one such son in the city. From the very first, he began to cry. He cried so loudly and so much of the time that the Bride was told by some of the city people that if he did not stop crying, he would be taken out to the desert and exposed. She did not want her son to die, and still, he would not stop crying. In order to save his life, the Bride asked one of her daughters, a girl named Lizzie who was begotten more than a decade earlier, to take her new son out into the desert and raise him. She was to bring him back when her son stopped crying. Lizzie, who loved her mother dearly, gladly obeyed.

Three months later, in a little town outside the big city, the Bride begat several other daughters and sons. One son stood out among the rest of the children and excelled at whatever he undertook to do. His older brothers and sisters were well-pleased with him and named him, Sonodad. The Bride, while not caring for the name, also did not voice her protest. Rather, she remained silent, pondering in her heart what sort of son he might be. Other children begotten in that little town were Maria, Soloman and a set of twins named, Nellie and Nels.

CHAPTER 18

THE TENTH RUNNER AND THE LAST CARD

Alarming accounts had been received for nearly a week and, rather than having to deal with the incessant complaints, Bestman Rancor resolved to end the matter. While two sentinels could have handled the annoyance, Bestman Rancor decided against the military solution. Sending two such warriors on assignment might be noticed by the governing authorities. Therefore, he sent three groomsmen to the river to investigate the disturbance.

The field trip completed, one of the groomsmen gave the report to Bestman Rancor. He reported this was only another demented man gone berserk and drawing a crowd. Such deranged men surfaced among the peoples at various times and places. They were usually driven from the cities and forced to live in the badlands, graveyards or wastelands.

The groomsman indicated this one came from the desert and was particularly hostile to people in positions of authority. The groomsman and his two companions were the object of the wild man's loud, verbal assault. When asked who he was, he bellowed that he was a son of the Bride. When asked why he yelled so much, he declared loudly that he had a wilderness cry and needed to be heard all the way into the city where the bestman lived.

Bestman Rancor, with sarcasm and no semblance of a smile, indicated he heard no unusually loud sounds coming from the direction of the stream bed. He shortened the groomsman's report and ordered one of the sentinels be sent undercover to monitor and record the activities of the madman. The sentinels disliked going undercover. They were not seen by others and were not given the recognition that fed their self-righteousness.

The Bride's thoughts carried her to the ancient Portal as she sat with two daughters. One had recently turned three years old and lived in the warmth of her mother's care and love. The other daughter neared her eightieth year. Her mother thought about this elderly daughter's passage through the Portal to the good land. The Bride wondered whether that was a trip to the distant past or a journey into the future. She admonished herself for such useless speculations.

The three year-old giggled during a game and the Bride chuckled upon hearing such unblemished laughter. Her attention sufficiently diverted, the Bride did not see the strange man who ran to her. She was startled, not only at the suddenness of his advent, but also by the apparel of the wild man. She drew the little girl to herself. The strange man was a runner who immediately saluted the Bride and presented her with a card.

> The nine have come, who'll meet on the mount,
> One more must precede, and complete is the count.
> The Bridegroom is near, that promise disperser,
> His advent's fulfilled, when you've met the precursor.

The Bride turned the card over and read the other side.

> I am Precursor,
> the forerunner of the Bridegroom.
>
> (I was raised by Lizzie in the desert.
> You may keep this card.)

The woman in the white cloak was startled. Her puzzled demeanor did not go unnoticed.

Precursor asked in a booming voice, "Is there a problem, Mother?"

Stumbling in her reply, the Bride said, "Ah, well, yes. I was startled by your voice."

"I am loud. I have a wilderness cry, you know."

"Yes, but it is not so much the loudness of your voice, though I do confess, you command attention, Precursor. Really, I am amazed that you spoke at all."

"Why?"

"Rarely has a runner spoken."

"No doubt, very true, Mother," Precursor agreed, "but I am the forerunner."

"Please, Precursor, answer me this one important question. Is the Bridegroom coming?"

"No, he is not coming."

The Bride, bitterly disappointed, argued, "But the other side of this card says that he is near and that he is coming."

"Mother," Precursor smiled, "read that side again and then read the back side once more."

The Bride did so, this time being more careful in her reading. After realizing what the implication was on the back side of the card in light of the front side, tears welled up. She studied Precursor's face for any indication she had made an error in her reasoning. She saw none.

"Do you mean," she began but could not finish.

"Yes, Mother," he concluded for her, "the Bridegroom is here."

"When will I get to see him and talk with him and be with him? Where is he now?"

Precursor said, "You have already seen him. He has been here for three decades now."

A shade of fear cast itself across her face, "What? I have seen him! And I did not recognize him? Oh, how he must be grieved and disappointed in me!"

"Please, do not concern yourself. He is well pleased with you and will be making himself known to you and to your children soon, very soon."

"Oh my, what must he think of me?"

"Listen to me carefully and understand. He is well pleased with you, Mother. All things are as they have been known and as either planned or permitted. He has his reasons why you have not recognized him. Patience and strength are called for now, more than you have ever had to muster before."

The Bride asked, "Why, what is going to happen?"

The forerunner replied, "For as much as any of us are entitled to know, the answers have been given to us in the ancient writings."

She remained in thought for a few moments and said, "Thirty years?"

Precursor smiled, "Yes, about thirty years."

The Bride fingered the card in her hands, "You do not want this card back, do you?"

"No," he replied, "and you know the reason, do you not?"

"Yes. Since he is here, you do not need my thumb print to verify that I received the card. Your work in bringing this message to me is done, correct?"

Precursor's countenance changed as he considered the answer to the Bride's question. "Yes, perhaps in more ways than we both might be able to imagine or want at this point."

She noticed his tone and said, "You are one of my sons and if you need anything that I am able to provide, Precursor, you need only voice it."

"Ah," he sighed with great admiration, "you have given me so much as it is. You begat me and after that, you saved my life. What more could a son ask for?"

144

"You ... you are the one, Precursor, ... long ago ... I sent you into the wilderness."

"Yes, the Bridegroom had a reason for my going out there and though it was not easy, it was his reason. If he uses me as a small means to accomplish his purpose then my life is fulfilled and satisfying in a way beyond my dreams. Besides," he snickered loudly, "I prefer your sending me out to the desert to be raised than the alternative you had at that time, dear Mother. Lizzie spoke of the love you had for me."

"The great act of love for you must be attributed to Lizzie, not me. How is she?"

"Better than she has ever been in all her life."

The Bride caught the way Precursor answered her question and said, "Do you mean--"

"Yes," he interrupted.

Deep in contemplation for several minutes, the Bride revealed her thoughts, "So much was placed on her when I asked her to take you away and raise you by herself. Also, too much was taken away from Lizzie for the same reason."

"Mother, just as the Bridegroom had a purpose for me that necessitated me being taken into the desert and raised, so you had a purpose for Lizzie that compelled you to send her out there to do what needed to be done. I do not find fault with the Bridegroom for what he had to do. Rather, I am honored to serve him as I am. Likewise, Lizzie did not find fault with you for what you had to do. It was her privilege to serve you as you needed."

She continued, "True, but she would not have ever chosen such a way to expend her life."

He replied, "Possibly true. However, she would have never known this purpose for her life had you not called her and given her the task."

"True again, forerunner, had she been given the opportunity; but would she have ever chosen it?"

"Left to ourselves, not one of us would likely choose the difficult path, especially if we think we are deciding the matter

145

alone. But if she knew that you wanted her to take on the task, she would have volunteered and felt honored to have been accepted. In reality, she was given the opportunity to decline your request. She needed only tell you *no* or abandon me in the desert. In the beginning and in the end, Lizzie truly wanted to do this thing because you desired it."

"You speak wise words, my son."

"I speak the words of Lizzie, Mother."

Precursor and the Bride spoke for nearly an hour before their conversation ended abruptly. The interruption came when one of the groomsmen directed three heavily armed sentinels to restrain Precursor and take him to the lower cell in the jail.

Precursor offered no resistance, but spoke the message he was sent to deliver. The Bride attempted to plead with the sentinels but the booming voice of the forerunner muted her.

"Groomsman! You are heading straight for a date with the second death," his voice thundered. Numerous by-standers stopped and listened as he was taken away. He continued to rail, "Groomsman! You are ready to fall right now. How much time do you have left? I will answer it. You have a lifetime. Now you answer the next question. How long is your lifetime?"

The groomsman, unnerved by the commotion, tried to hurry the sentinels. A gathering, such as was quickly taking place, might be reported to the governing authorities and become an embarrassment to Bestman Rancor. The forerunner's loud voice, blasting away at the groomsman with righteous indignation, made the three sentinels uneasy. Even though the accusations had been directed against the groomsman, each one of the three sentinels felt the sting of words had been intended for him.

Another of the sentinels, a savage sort of beast in both mind and body, spit in Precursor's face and asked in a mocking, vile manner, "And us, loud mouth, what are we poor warriors to do?"

146

The contrite sentinel used the occasion for adding his voice to the question, but doing so in a sincere way, "Yes, what of us? What are we, as sentinels, to do?"

The forerunner perceived the intent and answered him, "Look to the Bridegroom and do your duty. As long as you have life, look to the Bridegroom. As long as you are able, do your duty."

CHAPTER 19

TWO RESOLUTIONS AND ONE SPEECH

Sonodad viewed the great city from a grassy hillside. Early morning provided the quiet atmosphere for deep thinking. At the dawn of a new day, he considered the pressures surfacing in the city, the personal crises encountered in the lives of the people and the great difficulties the Bride and her children faced.

While not under the same direct siege faced by the northern city-states for the last six years, the city below was part of the spoils of war. When the northern city-states fell, so did the great city he beheld. The emperor appointed viziers to be "goodwill ambassadors assisting the local officials in the administration of the city for the benefit of all the people." To show the great concern the emperor had for all the people under his rule, each vizier carried the title, *guide*.

From his viewpoint on this small mountain, Sonodad remained aloof. Whoever ruled the city was of no particular concern to him from here. When it was a free city-state, he paid his tax and did his duty as all law-abiding citizens did. In so far as his good conscience permitted, he assisted in the defense of the city-state. And yet, when it fell and when JeJune, from the Sutnopian region to the north, was appointed guide, Sonodad did not openly oppose him. As long as the city gates remained open and the people within were not oppressed, he would not rise up against Guide JeJune.

The city's ruler promised equity and fairness. While that was the theory, the practice was much different. From the start,

Guide JeJune sensed and responded to the defiance of the city and the hatred of the people. Once, in retribution for an ambush that killed three of his soldiers, Guide JeJune picked nine men and women for execution. He announced that if the murderers did not come forth and confess, the nine would be executed Sutnopian style. This method of capital punishment was particularly effective as a deterrent since death did not occur immediately and the event was public. No confessions were made and nine executions took place. Five days later the last of those executed died.

With the morning breeze in his face as he sat on the high hill, Sonodad understood how people might gaze on this city and believe everything fine within its walls. The shrieking screams and the grinding moans from those nine never carried to this height. From here, people couldn't see the little boy searching the garbage in the street for a bit of food to eat. Ears couldn't hear the old woman weeping in the night because of the arthritis in her knees and the leg cramps which kept her awake. From here only a deity might know of the teenager being abused by others who controlled her life. The old man, coughing up blood as he summoned his final breaths, remained hidden from the eyes, ears and hearts of people who sat on the mountain. In his own way, Sonodad viewed those sights and heard those sounds. His heart surged with compassion and he resolved to go down there on a sacrificial mission.

But before descending, he listened once more and looked again. The unjust oppressor raised an iron rod and shouted words of hatred, but people on the mountain never heard the voice. The prescriber of toxins dispensed the poison and spoke the subtle instructions necessary to discharge the growth within a woman's womb. No one sitting on the mountain would ever hear the silent scream from the depths below. Acts of tyranny mixed with words of malevolence were seen and heard by the eyes and ears of Sonodad. His heart surged with fury and he resolved to go down there in measured wrath.

What intensified Sonodad's righteous anger to the boiling point and his compassionate, sacrificial love to the empathetic level was the fact that all this was also happening among the children of the Bride. He loved his mother dearly and was willing to die for her. Oppression, tyranny and vile words among the peoples not of the Bride were common to the point of expectation. But these abuses, and more, were happening among, within and between the children of the Bride. Sonodad resolved to go down and help the hurting. He further swore, by whispering an oath on the basis of his very being, that the acts of malice and the words of abuse would not go unpunished. If it meant challenging those in authority, either within the city or among the leaders of the Bride's children, it would be done. He pledged to do everything needed and to die if necessary to accomplish it and set things right again.

Sonodad returned to break the fast with his sisters and brothers. As he entered the house, he nearly stumbled into Juan, his younger brother by almost a decade. Juan ate as he walked about the room and placed a few items in a cloth bag.

"Where are you going today, little brother?"

Before Juan could answer, Maria, his older sister answered for him, "Oh, he worked all night and he's probably going to get another peek at Bestman Rancor's house."

"Not a wise move," Sonodad said sourly, but added, "However, it's a great move if you position yourself to become an infiltrator. Would that be right, do you think, to do such a thing as spying on the bestman?"

Sonodad often made a statement, declared its opposite and then asked a question about a certain aspect of the topic. There seemed to be more behind his words than what he spoke. The others, rather used to his lofty discussions, tended to ignore him.

"I'm not a spy," stated Juan. "I've no interest in doing that. You're all being quite silly. If the truth be known, I've never spoken with Bestman Rancor. One of his servants is a friend of mine and I am able to help him clean the bestman's house."

"So, you're not a spy," Sonodad observed, "rather, you are a snoop. What, if anything, is the difference between a spy and a snoop?"

Juan, doing his best to ignore the grilling said, "It's really interesting to see what he has, especially in the room where he studies. One day I was close enough to his chain stole that I could have touched it. He also has many books and letters."

"Maybe Juan's studying to be a groomsman," joked Nels.

"He's smart enough," admitted Nellie.

Soloman added in a positive tone, "I have no problem seeing Juan wearing the black robe."

Only Maria and the twins laughed. Dark furrows formed on the forehead of Sonodad. He said, "He will never be the bestman. Not only that, I don't believe Juan will ever get to be a groomsman. No matter how intelligent he is, our brother doesn't have enough money to purchase his way into the Cadre of Seventy Groomsmen." The laughter ceased among the family members and he continued, "He also needs prominent political contacts among the elite children of the Bride."

Then a twinkle formed in his eye and he spoke directly to Juan, "Little brother, if your goal is to attain to the office, then you must rely either on the social status and economic position of your sisters and brothers, or on the recommendation of Bestman Rancor's servant. My advice for you little brother, the one whom I love dearly, is to hurry out this door and help your friend clean the bestman's house."

The others laughed as the youngest left the house.

"The twins and I must leave for the fields," Maria admitted as she assembled a number of items.

Nels feigned ignorance, "Sonodad, should we guess where you are going this morning?"

His sister joined in, "Hmmm. Would I guess correctly if I said that you will be with your followers out on the hill again?"

151

Sonodad received their jesting with brotherly affection, "You would be wrong, Nellie. We are not meeting out on the hill. Rather, we have agreed to meet in a house near the north wall."

Maria replied, "You are gathering too large a crowd when you meet in a public place, aren't you? When you want to teach the inner circle of your followers some of the secret things, you are unable. So, today must be an inner circle teaching day."

"You know too much," Sonodad bantered. "Not much gets by your watchful and intelligent eye."

Soloman asked, "May I come with you this morning?"

Sonodad sighed and answered, "Dear brother, it is best for you not to know so much. There are things which must be done my way. Those things are contrary to your gracious, humble disposition. For now, the less you know, the better it is for you. When the critical time comes, you will know and understand."

"Critical time?"

"Soloman, please. After the seventh hour, I will approach the central marketplace from the north gate. We will meet along that way somewhere. ... I must go now and go quickly."

"Yes," Maria interjected, "because if you don't hurry, a crowd of people will follow you to your secret meeting."

Sonodad wore the weary face of resignation, not because she was testing his patience, but rather, because she was correct.

"Too late," Nellie announced and pointed to the front of the house. "Behold, your congregation awaits you."

Maria handed Sonodad a different head covering and said, "If you leave by the back window, you might get away without them recognizing you."

With exaggerated head movements, Nels exhaled deeply and complained, "It's so very difficult being a leader of people when they keep following you."

In the end, Sonodad left by the door and spoke briefly with the thirty people assembled outside. As usual, Guide JeJune's soldier stood at the perimeter and listened. Sonodad studied the people, discerning four were spies hiding among his true followers. The two groomsmen and the sentinel were not unexpected. The inscriber was unusual and indicated that his activities were being noticed by more than the common folk.

He stared in the direction of the two groomsmen and began to speak, "You get angry at the way you are treated by the rulers of this city, and you are ready to take matters into your own hands. Do you have any idea of what the Bridegroom feels and what he will do to those who mistreat the Bride?"

He shifted his eyes to Guide JeJune's soldier and continued in a moderate tone of voice, "Now, I am certainly not advocating any revolt or violence against or within the city at this time. However, this I do know, only the Bridegroom can fight the battles for his Bride and only he can win the war for her. Therefore that war is not ours to fight. So, my dear friends, and any of you others who may have gathered among them, if you've got ears attached to the sides of your head, use them."

The groomsmen smiled, the soldier's demeanor stiffened, the inscriber looked around, the sentinel's gaze remained unchanged and Sonodad walked through the crowd, disappearing in the maze of alleys. He had a secret meeting to attend.

CHAPTER 20

TOO LATE AND ONE DECISION

Teaching his followers and answering their many questions in the private meeting delayed Sonodad's arrival at the central marketplace until well past the ninth hour. The crowded area did not lend itself to much searching, particularly for someone whose face was recognized and whose reputation was spreading. Though he looked as he hurried, he did not see Soloman either on the way to or within the marketplace.

Once at the central marketplace, the word of his presence spread quickly. The gathering of people around him not only prevented him from any further search for his brother, but also placed him in a position of having to field questions. While he did not mind responding to the inquiries, he was aware there were spies in the crowd who sought to hear him say something that could be used against him. In the events that were soon to be taking place, timing was critical. If others entered the flow of history, a diversion could occur that would upset the crucial timing. Sonodad took great care in what he said and whether he spoke at all.

He stood on a vendor's fruit cart and motioned the people to be silent while he spoke. Before he could begin, a voice from the crowd shouted, "Have you come to bring peace?"

Sonodad smiled as he thought for a moment. Then he answered, carefully speaking only the truth, "Your question leads us by the nose. Your guide wants to tickle your ears. As for me, well, I only want to address your hearts. Have I come to bring peace? You, the one who asked the question, you don't believe we have peace, do you? Sir, you look around and though there are no enemies outside the gates of our city, you still feel under siege don't you?"

He anticipated his question being unanswered. Instead, the man shouted, "Yes, our enemies have moved inside the walls of the city!"

The crowd snickered and nodded in agreement.

"So," continued Sonodad, "you feel no peace even if there are no enemies attacking you. Perhaps they are attacking, but now use weapons and tactics you don't recognize."

The stir of the people ceased. Then Sonodad pointed in the direction of two men, both of whom were immediately recognized as Guide JeJune's soldiers.

"But what, dear people, as we behold these two peace-keepers, ... what do we do if the weapons used against us are the spear of suspicion, the sword of intimidation or the axe of threat? Well, what do we do? What you do, of course, will depend on whether you believe that we have peace or not. If you believe there to be peace, then why not eat, drink, marry and give in marriage? Let all things be as they have always been. But, if you don't believe there is peace, then you have no alternative. You can't believe one way and act the other, else you become like those groomsmen who stand and pray on the corners of our streets. You must act the way you believe. If not, you are neither true to your confessed creed, nor true to yourself, nor to your neighbor to whom you bear witness by your life."

The lone voice cried out, "Have you risen to your position of fame for the purposes of bringing us peace or taking up the sword?"

Sonodad replied, "Dear people, there can be no peace without death."

Another man shouted, "Ha! You begin to sound like Guide JeJune's publicity men! Which is it, peace or sword?"

The magnetic speaker inhaled deeply and uttered his answer, "I have not come to bring peace, but a sword."

His words echoed across the silent marketplace as the people stood motionless. He glanced over to see the reaction of JeJune's soldiers. They were gone. Sonodad, longing for the upcoming events to be finished, closed his eyes momentarily.

An instant later, he clicked them open in stolid determination and begged, "Please do not misinterpret what I have said. The way is different than what you imagine and the time is not now as you might hope. Later, you will understand everything. Please, dear people, wait until the right time. Will you wait?"

Though most people indicated their reluctant approval through a verbal "yes" or a nodding of the head, a few walked away giving no response.

A huge voice bellowed out a lone, "Hosanna!"

Sonodad, his head jerking instantly in the direction of the cry, screamed, "No!" He jumped down from the fruit cart and left the people via the nearest alley.

Two months later Nels viewed the last brilliant colors at the end of the day from the threshold of the house. He stepped inside to the light of the oil lamp and asked, "How long is all of this going to continue to take place?"

Without looking up, Maria replied, "Your question is worthy of an answer, brother. I only wish I were able to answer it."

Nels picked up again, not really having heard his sister's response, "We have people at our front door when we go to sleep at night. They, or others, are there when we wake up in the morning. Don't these people have anything to do other than stand around waiting to hear a few words of wisdom from Sonodad?"

"What bothers me," admitted Maria, "are not the crowds of people out front and their curious stares, but what all this is doing to Soloman. He still isn't home."

Sonodad, who listened to the conversation from the back room, entered the front room. "Where is Soloman?"

"We don't know," said Maria speaking for her sister and brother, "but I have a good idea."

"What do you mean?"

"Look, Sonodad, he is only doing, in his own way, what you are doing. He sees you being a leader and having people follow you, and he wants to imitate you. So, he pretends to be a leader and begins talking to people in the streets. He's been doing it for weeks now."

Nellie spoke intensely, "He frightened us today, Sonodad, and we don't know what to do."

"What happened?"

She continued, "This morning when he left, we followed him in secret. He went to the north gate and said something to a man. The man agreed to something and they left together, proceeding to the mounded pasture east of the marketplace. He began by speaking to nine people. Soon others came and listened to what he was saying. In a little while, Soloman had a crowd of forty to fifty people listening to him. We moved in closer. Sonodad, our brother was talking crazy!"

"We tried to get him to stop and come with us," Nels said. "He wouldn't listen to us, and suddenly, he claimed that we were not part of his family."

"What was he saying?"

Maria answered, "Just the same things you have been saying. I told you he's copying you. But someone is going to hurt him because he doesn't know when to stop. You are wise and careful with your words, he isn't. Today, he began hurling remarks aimed at the groomsmen and inscribers. As Nels said, he was talking like a crazy man and we couldn't get him to stop and come with us."

Sonodad thought for a few minutes while his sisters and brothers waited. Finally, he said, "There is much danger in leveling an attack against either the cadre or the coterie. They have powers and influence that cause their enemies to disappear in the night, never to be seen again. I believe I know a way to help Soloman. It will involve a diversion to redirect the attention from him to me."

While he thought in silence for several moments, Soloman stood in the darkness of the doorway and began to listen. Sonodad said, "Listen to me carefully. Tomorrow I must do something I don't want any of you to know about. However, after I do it, I will not be able to return to live here anymore."

Nellie interjected with surprise and concern, "Sonodad, you're not going to do anything illegal, are you?"

"Please, dear sister, don't pursue this. I just won't be able to live here any longer. That day was coming soon anyway."

Soloman stepped in from the shadows and announced, "Good evening. I have come to announce to you that I will no longer be able to live here as a guest in this house. You have been gracious in permitting me to stay with you. I will be leading a few of my followers to some of the small towns in the surrounding areas. I love all of you. Good evening."

Soloman returned to the shadows of the doorway and disappeared into the night. The two nearest the door hurried outside but were unable to see him.

"There you have it," Maria said. "He heard what you said and is copying you before you can even do it!"

Nels inquired, "Will this change what you were going to do tomorrow?"

"No," replied Sonodad, deep in his thoughts. "It actually assists in the diversion."

CHAPTER 21

WON DECISION AND TWO WARRANTS

Sonodad recognized the risk involved in the next step of his work. He needed to win the hearts, not only of the people in the city, but of those among the children of the Bride. Now, it was not that Sonodad needed this himself. He was free. Rather, the people for whom he had conceived the plan and was now carrying out, needed his person and work. Even his closest and most trusted followers did not know of this next phase. Here he was very much alone.

The charismatic leader waited until the Corps of Escort Sentinels gathered in full session for their monthly meeting. With the forty congregated, Sonodad confidently marched past them and positioned himself directly in front of the captain. He turned his back to the captain and made a bold declaration to the others.

"I am Sonodad, defender of the poor, summoner of the outcast and contender for the common."

The sentinels derided him with jeers and yelled for him to go away.

"I have invaded the meeting of the Bride's great escort and do you attempt to get rid of me with only words? Have the Bride's sentinels lost their heart and stomach for fighting? I challenge any one of you!"

The captain roared back, "Step aside, fool! If you want to challenge, then go through the procedures and win the right."

The corps affirmed its captain's advice with an ovation of voice and applause.

Sonodad raised his hand to quiet the warriors and said, "The corps no longer understands the purpose for which it was formed. Each of you now thinks only of the challenger event. The Corps of Escort Sentinels was formed to defend and lead, not wait until a yearly event came around to find out which one of you will be challenged. What a sorry, sickening bunch of lingerers you are."

Growls and jeers came from many of them.

"Silence! Would Dynamis approve of what you have become? Would he approve of someone like myself, with no weapon in hand, coming in here without at least being stopped? If he were here this day, he'd be ashamed of every single one of you. If he were in this place today, he would either carry me out with a pike hooked in my ribs, or fall in the attempt to defend his name and protect the Bride. But look at you! Isn't there at least one of you with the courage to answer the challenge of the unarmed, unprotected man who is insulting you this day?"

Inflamed with anger and seething to avenge their individual and corporate honor, all members of the corps volunteered with shouts of derision. Several promised that Sonodad would experience a slow, excruciating, painful death.

Sonodad raised his hands once more and waited until they quieted. "I will wear no protection and the challenger you choose will select the weapon. I am waiting and I grow weary of your failure to accept my challenge."

After a moment of complete cacophony, the corps' champion stepped forward to the chant of "Levi! Levi! Levi!" The groomsman strode forward with two spears in hand and confidence in his gait. Standing in full armor, Sentinel Levi towered over Sonodad by more than two hands.

With no discernable exertion, Levi pitched one of the seven foot spears sideways to the infiltrator. Sonodad caught it with both hands and felt the momentum of Levi's throw. Levi brought the killing end of the spear to bear and began circling to his right. Sonodad assumed his position as well.

"So, you now take up a defensive posture," noted Levi. "Good, you will find me to be most offensive. I will need to restrain myself in order not to finish you too quickly. My brothers call for me to make you suffer and beg me to prolong your death. I will attempt to accommodate their desires."

"Fool!" cried Sonodad, "When you fight, don't change from the way you have been trained. You had better engage me as you have practiced. If you don't, you will pay a huge price."

Levi responded, "You have done nothing except talk since you came here. The time for tongue-wagging is over."

Before he finished the last word, Levi feigned a spear thrust and swung the other end around to strike the side of his opponent's head. Sonodad slipped under the arc and parried to the side. Back and forth they moved, shifting in split seconds from offensive moves to defensive positions. The shouts and commotion of the remaining members of the corps cramped the fighting arena for both combatants.

After fifteen minutes of fighting, Levi was still breathing through his nose. He arced his spear like a long pole and lunged to the right, catching Sonodad's spear and turning him. Keeping his motion in the same direction, Levi permitted the momentum of his spear to continue and he caned his opponent on the back. An instant red lump, over a foot long, formed on the bare back.

Sonodad rolled with the caning and hooked his spear under Levi's. The blunt end opened Levi's lip. The warriors separated. Levi's blood enraged him and he whirled his spear and sliced at Sonodad's exposed chest. The slice missed but the following spear thrust penetrated the skin over the heart. Sonodad would have been slain had not his rib stopped the spear point, thus preventing a lethal plunge.

Levi felt the spear hit its target and saw Sonodad slump over. While the latter did not feign the pain, he did use it to propel his opponent into a killing attack. This move to end the fight by Levi left him open and the instant he moved, Sonodad countered by raising the middle of the spear shaft with both hands and catching Levi under the chin. Levi lost consciousness and his spear was kicked aside. Sonodad positioned himself over his

161

opponent. Deftly with the tip of his spear, he lifted the bottom edge of Levi's breastplate and placed the point on the flesh between two ribs.

He waited until Levi regained his senses. A moment later Levi jerked in a reflex grab for his spear. His empty hand and a touch of added pressure on his bare breast from the spear tip settled him immediately. His comrades fell silent. Levi curled his upper lip in a final gesture of defiance, desiring to die the death of a warrior.

Sonodad did not budge as he spoke, "Why? Why would we want this warrior to die at the hands of one of his brothers? Here we are, sons of the Bride and brothers to one another, fighting amongst ourselves with the distinct possibility of killing one or the other."

He eased back slightly on the spear tip and said, "Aren't we under the restraint and control and power of a foreign governor? If one of you warriors should have to die, wouldn't you want it to be for something worthwhile?"

He looked at Levi and said, "You know that today is as good a day as any to die, but not in this way -- not at the hands of your brother. I certainly want my death to count for something. I am willing to die for everyone of you -- for the Bride and all her children. Levi, do you want to die right now, like this?"

"No."

"How many of you would like to die here, like this?"

No one responded.

"Levi, if you had to die today, wouldn't you want it to be as you were fighting against your oppressors?"

"Yes."

"How many of you would like to breathe your last in the midst of a battle where many of Guide JeJune's soldiers are at your feet, having felt the deadly bite of your sword and the sting of your spear?"

Several sentinels shouted aloud, "Me" or "I would" as others raised the arm of might high into the air.

Sonodad stood up and extended his wrist to Levi. Levi accepted and was pulled to his feet. Sonodad walked over to Levi's spear, picked it up and handed it to him. Admiration, respect and thanks shone from his face as he stared at Sonodad.

"I am not asking you to renounce your membership in the Corps of Escort Sentinels. I am asking you to be ready to come to the defense of the Bride, her children and this city when summoned to do so. I am not asking you to come under my command; you have a most capable captain to obey. I am asking you to move against our enemies if your captain so commands."

He stopped and faced the captain.

"Good sir, are you opposed to anything I have said here?"

"No," he replied.

"Are you willing to lead the corps into battle should you, personally, be convinced of the need to defend the Bride, her children and this city?"

"Yes."

"I do not wish to speak to the brave men under your authority any longer. However captain, sir, I would like to know if I may count on the support of your men should the need arise. Captain, would you please ask them?"

The captain asked and received unanimous support.

"Thank you, captain, and please thank the corps for me. I take leave now."

Sonodad left and went to one of his secret places. His gamble had paid off and he now had the support of the Corps of Escort Sentinels. However, the episode was not without its costs for Sonodad. Later that evening, when the corps had been dismissed, one of the men hurried to Guide JeJune's headquarters. The entire incident was reported to the guide.

The next morning two warrants from two different jurisdictions were issued and proclaimed throughout the city. One of the warrants was for Sonodad. The person turning him over to Guide JeJune's soldiers would receive a sum of silver as a reward.

CHAPTER 22

TWO ARRESTED AND ONE RELEASED

For weeks, Sonodad was able to hide within the city. The crowds protected him from those among the people who sought to arrest him. While he stayed with trusted followers and moved from place to place attempting to remain hidden, the wanted man knew he was being pursued. His plan, once begun, required public appearances. As the leader of a resistance movement, he had to maintain momentum. At the same time, being a public figure put him at risk.

Sonodad attempted to be in control of his public appearances. His arrival to and departure from such appearances were sudden and involved intricate movements. He would quickly appear in and to a bustling crowd, spend no more than ten minutes teaching the people and telling them what needed to be done and then leave, by either blending into the crowd or disappearing in a series of buildings. The escape routes were well researched and his followers assisted in these operations.

When he sensed himself establishing a pattern of either times or places, he changed his itinerary and locale. The weakness in this mode of operation was his need to rely upon and put his trust in others. Those who wanted to arrest him, had opportunities to do so, but Sonodad's popularity with the people prevented this from happening in public. His enemies were patient, however, and began to take note of those whom Sonodad trusted. Those seeking his arrest studied the actions and habits of his followers. As Sonodad's popularity increased, more people were entrusted with his public appearances and subsequent escapes.

Near the end of his speech in the central marketplace one afternoon, Sonodad sensed the presence of many within the crowd who sought his arrest. His followers, planted among the people, watched as the spies moved to position themselves at places where the wanted man might have an escape route.

The signal was given for Sonodad to leave immediately and he did so jumping from the fruit cart and stepping into a small shop on the edge of the open marketplace. Within the shop, a man handed him headwear of a different style and color. He made the exchange and moved through the shop to an adjacent building. Sonodad climbed through a window and entered the alley where a cart with two men waited. As one man placed a shoulder shawl on him and helped him onto the cart, the driver urged the animal to move. The wanted man joined the driver in hunching his shoulders, appearing to be an old man. The driver moved through the alley to a specific location where Sonodad was to get out and go into one of the secret locations until evening.

Neither man spoke as the animal plodded along the back streets and alleys. The driver drew back the reins when they came to a certain house. A hooded man stepped out and extended his hand to the disguised leader, indicating that he should get inside quickly. Following the directive, Sonodad stepped down from the cart and into the house.

Once inside, his head wear was removed by the swift movement of one man's hand and a gag was slipped over his mouth by another. Two more soldiers restrained Sonodad who, upon recognizing the well-planned ambush, did not resist.

The captured leader surveyed the seven men in the house with him. Five soldiers and their commanding officer were from the ranks of Guide JeJune's militia. The other man, known to Sonodad, stood next to the commanding officer. Sentinel Levi Athan's eyes remained fixed on the gagged man. Levi's face showed neither remorse nor satisfaction at his action of betrayal. As he continued to stare at the prisoner, Levi slowly extended his left hand, palm up, to the commanding officer. The man in charge

165

dropped a pouch of silver into it. Levi received the money and left.

Sonodad was immediately taken to the inner prison at Guide JeJune's headquarters. He remained there four days, unable to receive visitors. Word was sent to him that he had been found guilty of twenty-three counts of promoting rebellion, twenty-three counts of unlawful gathering and a number of counts associated with insurrection. His execution would be in two days and he would be permitted neither counsel nor visitors. Since his crimes were ones conducted by his mouth, Sonodad would remain gagged until his death. The guard removed the gag only once a day, and then only long enough for the prisoner to drink a cup of water.

The day of the public executions came and it was obvious the report had spread concerning Sonodad's capture and sentence. A large, boisterous crowd assembled, including several sentinels. Since another arrest had been made and another trial was now taking place, Sonodad was being held outside the sight of the fickle people. He could, however, hear the proceedings taking place at Guide JeJune's courtyard.

The Bride also heard what was being said. Word had gotten to her that the Bridegroom had been arrested and was to be sentenced this day. She ran the entire way to the court yard. All along she asked herself, "How had I missed him? Why had I not seen him? Is it really him? This can not be true that he has been arrested, can it? The Bridegroom would never permit such a thing, would he?"

Guide JeJune spoke to the crowd, "At the direction of Bestman Rancor, a warrant was issued for this man's arrest. The warrant was served and the arrest was made by several of your sentinels last night. The request has been received that he be executed this morning. However, after having sufficiently questioned him, I do not find him guilty of any crimes, let alone ones worthy of execution."

Several members of the crowd shouted, "He claims to be the Bridegroom."

The Bride's mouth hung open as she thought, "Can this be? I need time to think. Can it be him? I need more time. The promises. The cards from the runners. It does make sense, but can this man be him?"

Guide JeJune snapped back, "What is that to me?"

One of Guide JeJune's attendants spoke to him for a moment. Guide JeJune turned red with anger and lashed out, "You are ignorant people. Don't you know that the Bridegroom, or whatever you call him, means nothing to me. Being the Bridegroom is not something against my law."

A chant began, "Execute him! Execute him!"

"No!" screamed the Bride, but her voice was consumed by the juggernaut opposing the word.

"Silence," Guide JeJune commanded. "It is the time of the year to enact the *Rite of Release* and I choose this man, the one whom you call, Bridegroom, to be released."

A voice rang out, "We don't call him, Bridegroom. He calls himself the Bridegroom."

"No, he is the Bridegroom," said the Bride. Her confession resulted in her being pushed to the ground.

"No matter," said Guide JeJune, "whatever he is called and whoever he is, I choose him to be the one who gains the Rite of Release."

"Yes," the Bride said to herself. "What mercy!"

"Dear Guide JeJune, I am Bestman Rancor, and I believe there is a slight misunderstanding here. You, most beloved lord and wise ruler, you said it is the time for the Rite of Release to be undertaken?"

"Yes."

"That is fine, and your loyal subjects, indeed, thank you, most magnificent guide, for this great sign of your mercy and good will. Is it true you wish to enact the Rite of Release this very day?"

"Yes."

"That is fine. It shall be done, oh benevolent one.
However, according to your own edict, oh great ruler and leader
of the city, the person named in the Rite of Release is to be
declared by the people, not by you. It would be better for the
people to decide which of the prisoners is to be released."

Bestman Rancor, was lifted onto the shoulders of two
sentinels. He turned his head and asked, "Well, people of this city,
name the person you choose for release. Who is it?"

The crowd burst forth with a mighty shout, "Barabbas!"

The Bride tried to cry out the Bridegroom's name, but was
knocked to the ground again.

Guide JeJune silenced the crowd and asked, "Who?"

The name sounded forth in a unified voice once more,
"Barabbas!"

The Bride, being kicked by scuffling feet and with tears
moving down her cheeks, shouted in vain, "Wait! I understand.
Please, listen to me. I finally understand. We must stop. Wait!"

Bewilderment covered Guide JeJune's face and he turned
to his attendant. "Who is Barabbas?"

The attendant answered, "That is how the people say his
name in their own tongue. To us, his name is Sonodad."

Guide JeJune was livid and turned to the crowd in spiteful
anger, "No! You will not be receiving that insurrectionist back at
all. If you want anyone released today, you better take your
Bridegroom."

Bestman Rancor stepped forward again and spoke, "Oh
most gracious and kind lord, perhaps the beloved guide of this fair
city will want to reconsider his decision in light of the Emperor's
edict concerning the non-disruption policy of any and all local
traditions approved by the local guide. In your most generous
mercy, you have done this every year and I am certain that the
Emperor would not be pleased to receive a letter from some
disgruntled person pointing out your failure to abide by empirical
policy. In addition, you have already received the notice from the

Emperor on corruption by locally appointed guides. There's been so much of that taking place among the appointees that the Emperor has stressed the need for integrity in the words and actions of local guides. Again, I don't believe the Emperor would receive news that you have gone back on your word favorably, do you, Guide JeJune?"

The crowd was quiet as the guide considered the weight of Bestman Rancor's threat.

Finally, he spoke bitterly and with an obvious sense of frustration, "Release Sonodad."

Sonodad's heart spiked with joy. He exclaimed a shout of exaltation through the gag. The people cheered wildly and Bestman Rancor smiled with an equally obvious sense of accomplishment. Guide JeJune waited until the people quieted and then directed a bitter question to the mass, "What do you want me to do with the one who calls himself the Bridegroom?"

"Execute him," they roared as one.

Guide JeJune demanded, "Why? What has he done? Why do you seek the blood of this poor man? Will this beggar's death be of any benefit to you?"

The crowd ignored his questions. "Execute him!"

"No!" shouted the Bride timing her reply in order to be heard. An unseen fist slammed into her mouth and she was knocked to the ground.

"Actually, I think not," stated Guide JeJune with forced smugness, "I believe I will release him as well."

The Bride looked up with a glimmer of hope in her wet eyes.

"Execute him! Execute him!"

Bestman Rancor motioned for quiet and spoke, "Dear Guide JeJune, perhaps I did not make myself clear on this matter earlier. The Emperor does not want to hear about his local officials asking the people what they want and then, when they tell him what they want, the local ruler, in an obvious attempt to inflame the people to take up arms in rebellion, denies them what he had promised them. You really ought to reconsider your release of this man who calls himself the Bridegroom, or have I failed to perceive that you were playing a small joke on us?"

Beyond anger and desiring to be done with the whole process, Guide JeJune saved face as best he could by saying, "It was a joke." He turned to his soldiers and gave the order, "Execute him."

A consuming cheer erupted from the people, not only because of his command, but because at that instant, Sonodad stepped into the presence of the assembly. He was no longer bound and gagged. In tears, the Bride was buffeted and forced to the edge of the people. Sonodad raised his arms in triumph and joy. He moved across the court to be with the people when he saw the one condemned to death in his place and now under the guide's order of execution.

He saw no one save Soloman.

CHAPTER 23

TWO DIED AND ONE WON

The iron instrument for the Bridegroom's execution became a heavy burden hoisted onto his shoulders. The soldiers force-marched Soloman to the place on the rise of land outside the north gate. From centuries past, the place had been named, *The Ground that Drinks Cursed Blood*. More recently, under the heavy hand of Guide JeJune, it became known as *The Place of the Snare*. That hill of prolonged death, slightly higher than the surrounding area, provided suitable public viewing of executions.

The mob, moving from the court scene to follow the condemned, left several people alone at the court yard. Sonodad stood stunned, his mind swimming with confusion and contradiction. Not only was there no one left to condemn him, there was no one left to follow him. The mob and its leaders were now only interested in Soloman's death. Confused by his accusing and excusing thoughts, Sonodad disappeared into the alley.

The Bride remained on the ground, having been knocked down by several, walked on by a few and kicked by many. One of the blows struck her in the side. The kick took away her breath and left her gasping for air. As she tried to inhale, her eyes attempted to follow the Bridegroom. She could not see him because of the great horde dogging him. She bent her head down, the strands of her hair touching the ground while tears from her eyes moistened it.

Juan stepped near and knelt beside the Bride. He placed his hand on her shoulder. She turned to see her comforter and covered his hand with hers.

"Where would you like to go? I'll help you."

"To the Bridegroom," she replied.

"Are you sure?"

"Yes. I need to be there for him, for me and for my children. Please help me get there."

Juan lifted her to a standing position and walked with her. Neither spoke until the half hour journey neared completion.

"Perhaps something will stop the execution. Maybe someone will do something to bring a halt to this awful miscarriage of justice," Juan muttered to himself.

"No," the Bride countered. "Only the Bridegroom has the power to stop it, and I know he won't."

"I don't understand," Juan confessed.

"This is the Bridegroom's promise from before the beginning. He knew of it when he sent us through the Portal. I knew this day would come and he will not stop it. Today, your eyes will behold just how much the Bridegroom loves us and wants the Great Wedding to take place. Stay with me, Juan."

"I don't understand all of what you say. However, I will do what you ask."

When they arrived, the iron instrument had been removed from the Bridegroom's shoulder. The metal mechanism was staked securely to the ground. The soldiers now cranked the heavy, metal jaws open. The Bride covered her mouth and silenced a horrified scream. She saw, for the first time, what the metal item was at the other end of the bestman's chain stole.

She asked, "It is horrid. Juan, what is it?"

"It's a man-trap."

"Tell me what will happen," she commanded in a determined voice.

Juan objected, "No, it is best that you not know."

"Tell me. I need to know."

Perceiving her determination and strength, Juan told her. "The iron jaws are cranked to the open position, the tension increasing as it is done. The trigger is set and the iron jaws are released, remaining in place only by the slightest thread. The victim is seated on a pallet above the trap. His left leg is bent while the right leg extends horizontally. The height of the victim is adjusted so that the heel of his foot is just above a wire that leads to the trigger mechanism. When the victim is no longer able to hold his leg straight out, his heel touches the wire and trips the trigger. The jaws slam shut, catching and crushing the victim's foot or lower leg."

The Bride, dismayed and repulsed by the devious nature of the ghastly instrument of death, asked once again, "How long before the victim is finally able to die?"

Juan waited a moment. "Hours if the jaws clamp and cut an artery, enabling the victim's blood to flow freely. Days if they only crush bones, muscle and sever no large artery. Please don't ask me any more about this."

The Bride remained silent. The two of them stood forty feet from the Bridegroom. With everything in place, Guide JeJune's soldiers removed the support. The Bridegroom was seated on the pallet over the trap. His right leg, hovered horizontally less than an inch above the trip wire.

Then something happened that no one else could see or hear except the Bridegroom. From everywhere and from nowhere, Footstomper appeared on the opposite side of the trap. It carried a huge book.

"You have come, Footstomper."

"I was never far away."

"I know. Why do you not use my name?"

"Mere preference."

"No. You are not able to deceive me, Footstomper. Using my name is the admission of your defeat. You may not, even now, make such a confession of the truth."

"I disagree with you, ..., I may say your name! ... uhh, er, I oppose you, ... Achhh! You are ..."

"I said that you may not use my name. You had then, and you have now, neither power nor permission to utter my name,

173

Footstomper. You are able neither to resist me nor to overcome me. What power and permission you have, you have because I grant it to you, Footstomper. I am Headbanger."

When the Bridegroom said *Headbanger*, a violent earthquake shook the heavens and the earth. The only thing in all creation that did not shake was Soloman's leg, the man-trap and its hair trigger. Footstomper fell to the ground, clinging to its book. It could neither move nor speak.

An hour later, the Bridegroom spoke, "Footstomper, you may speak once again."

Footstomper, with a pressurized build-up of words inside, exploded, "icansayyournamebutwillnot"

"Footstomper, you speak without spaces between your words. Proceed"

"I will begin," Footstomper declared.

"You are permitted," Headbanger announced. "Also, you may stand."

Footstomper regained its ancient position and composure, but remained silent for a moment. With a vindictive spray of spittle, it erupted, "You're preventing me from beginning, ..."

"Yes, Footstomper, I am. During this proceeding you will tell the truth. There will be no holding back and no deception. You are bound. I know your very thoughts. You are bound. Begin with me and then proceed to all those who have died the first death."

Footstomper squirmed as a spiteful, malicious, vindictive, hateful, malevolent, rancorous countenance surfaced in its face.

The Bridegroom roared, "Begin! You are permitted."

The accuser read one name from the book and stopped, "Soloman."

"Continue!"

"Soloman. Not sinful and no sins."

"Proceed!"

"Dusty. Day one. Sin one. Dusty despised your word when he failed to speak to your Bride."

"Put that sin on my foot. It is now mine."

Instantly, the sin disappeared from Footstomper's book and appeared on Headbanger's foot.

"Proceed."

"Dusty. Day one. Sin two. Dusty did not to look to you after he failed to speak your word to your Bride."

"Put that sin on my foot. It is now mine."

It was done and Headbanger ordered Footstomper to proceed.

"Dusty. Day 1,530. Sin 144,001. Dusty was angry with one of the children who asked him for a drink of water."

"Put that sin on my foot. It is now mine."

For four hours Footstomper listed the sins of Dusty and, for four hours, Headbanger ordered them placed on his foot. Thousands of sins per minute were listed and placed. Then Footstomper stopped.

"You have stopped. But you hide nothing from me. You have left gaps in the numbering and not spoken a complete listing of some of Dusty's sins. Declare all of his sins. Proceed!"

Nearly two hours later, Footstomper stopped again.

Headbanger demanded, "Are there any more of Dusty's sins that you have not declared?"

"No."

"Are you certain? Check again."

Unable to do otherwise, Footstomper examined the huge book and responded bitterly, "There is not one sin left here."

"Have all of Dusty's sins been placed on my foot?"

"Yes."

"Proceed."

"Eli. Day one. Sin one. Eli's original sin."

"Put that sin on my foot. It is now mine."

For nearly six hours, all of Eli's sins were declared and transferred.

"Are there any of Eli's sins that you have not declared?"

"No."

"Have all of Eli's sins been placed on my foot?"

"Yes."

"Proceed."

"Lo-Eli. Day One. Sin One. Lo-Eli's original sin."

Thus the proceedings continued for everyone who had ever lived. Six hours were spent for each person. The declaration and transfer of all sins, no matter how many or few, no matter how large or small, no matter how great or minor, were declared and transferred. Sins of commission, omission, weakness and will were stated and transferred. The Bridegroom remained resolute as the sins were heaped onto his burdened foot.

"Comfy. Day 11,847. Sin 102,373. Comfy became angry at the Bridegroom for making him the bestman as he momentarily progressed from questioning to doubting to despair while reading *The Volume of Consequences*."

"Put that sin on my foot. It is now mine."

So they continued through the people - each one of the Nephilim, The Princess, Frank, Intrepid, Ribald, Marquis, Jo, Old Sis, Mina, Rae, Anne, Tara, Dynamis and all those who had ever lived. The Bridegroom's foot trembled above the trip wire.

"Clang!" The sound of iron jaws slamming shut on a trap cracked across the valley, followed by a scream of excruciating pain. Everyone standing at The Place of the Snare jumped in response. The hair trigger on the trap next to the Bridegroom's trap had been tripped. The victim next to the Bridegroom was now being executed.

The Bridegroom spoke, "Footstomper, proceed with all people who are now living."

"Levi Athan. Day one. Sin one. Levi Athan's original sin."

"Put that sin on my foot. It is now mine."

"Levi Athan. Day 9,296. Sin 108,627. Murdered Petros the Zealot in order to become a sentinel.

"Put that sin on my foot. It is now mine."

After more than five hours, all the sins that Levi Athan had committed and would commit had been read and transferred.

"Are there any of Levi Athan's sins you have not declared?"

"No."

"Have all of Levi Athan's sins been placed on my foot?"

"Yes."

"Proceed with the next name."

Footstomper asked, "There is a person who holds a book in hand, whose eyes are focusing on these words I speak, and who is reading this book about you, me, the bestman, the Bride and her children. Am I to list every one of that person's sins too?"

"Yes. Call that person, Reader."

"Reader. Day one. Sin one. Reader's original sin."

"Put that sin on my foot. It is now mine."

"Reader. Day 318. Sin 596. Became angry at a parent when hungry and was not fed immediately."

"Put that sin on my foot. It is now mine."

"Reader. Day 1,520. Sin 5,047. Lied to a friend."

"Put that sin on my foot. It is now mine."

"Reader. Day 9,133. Sin 93,455. Forgot to pray today."

"Put that sin on my foot. It is now mine."

"Reader. Day 13,007. Sin 164,908. Cursed the Bridegroom."

"Put that sin on my foot. It is now mine."

At the six hour mark, all the sins that Reader had committed and would ever commit had been declared and transferred to the Bridegroom's foot.

"Are there any of Reader's sins you have not declared?"

"No."

"Have all of Reader's sins been placed on my foot?"

"Yes."

"Proceed with the next name."

Footstomper asked, "There is a person who is listening to the words of this book being read by another. That person hears

177

12

these very words I speak and is listening to this story about you, me, the bestman, the Bride and her children. Am I to list every one of that person's sins too?"

"Yes. Call that person, Hearer."

"Hearer. Day one. Sin one. Hearer's original sin."

"Put that sin on my foot. It is now mine."

"Hearer. Day 248. Sin 402. Had a temper tantrum,"

"Put that sin on my foot. It is now mine."

"Hearer. Day 2,152. Sin 7,234. Coveted."

"Put that sin on my foot. It is now mine."

"Hearer. Day 7,921. Sin 81,729. Did not respect the governing authority."

"Put that sin on my foot. It is now mine."

"Hearer. Day 12,648. Sin 108,222. Doubted the Bridegroom's ability to hear and answer prayer."

"Put that sin on my foot. It is now mine."

At the six hour mark, all the sins that Hearer had committed and would ever commit had been declared and transferred to the Bridegroom's foot.

"Are there any of Hearer's sins you have not declared?"

"No."

"Have all of Hearer's sins been placed on my foot?"

"Yes."

"Proceed."

In the same manner, the past and future sins of all those presently living were declared before the Bridegroom and added unto him. The load of sins piled onto his extended leg reached the clouds. His foot, straining under the heavy burden, shook from the tension.

"Clank!" The trigger tripped on the second victim to be executed. A heart-rending, collective gasp from those watching was overshadowed by the cry of the woman whose leg was now being crushed and held by the jaws of the trap.

"Continue, Footstomper. Declare all the sins of those who will live but who are not yet alive."

The listing began and finally Footstomper said, "Harold. Day 6,935. Sin 58,666. Harold told the Bride that he didn't think the Bridegroom would make it in time."

"Put that sin on my foot. It is now mine."

"Are there any of Harold's sins that you have not declared?"

"No."

"Have all of Harold's sins been placed on my foot?"

"Yes."

"Proceed."

"There are no more sins to declare," Footstomper grudgingly confessed.

"Check once again," the Bridegroom commanded, his leg muscle now shaking with the strain of the load.

Though fuming with anger, Footstomper examined the book and admitted, "There are no more sins listed. The book is blank."

"Where are they?"

The accuser foamed, squirmed and spit through clenched teeth, "You have taken everyone of them on yourself."

"Do you have any more that you can recall?"

Nearly exploding with rage, Footstomper blurted out, "therearenomoresins."

The burden on the Bridegroom's foot was now larger than the entire earth. His quivering leg muscle was cramping. His over-stretched tendons were near the tensile breaking point. With a touch lighter than a hair, like a spring breath singing over a spider thread, the Bridegroom's straining, shaking heel kissed the hair trigger of the trap.

"Behold, Footstomper, I bear the burden though I have not been trapped. My leg holds all sins and the trap has not been sprung. I am Headbanger!"

"Youcantbearitanddefeatmeatthesametime!"

The Bride and Juan continued to view the tragic events unfold before them. The first victim had only been able to hold his leg out for six minutes. The second had withstood the pain in her leg for seven minutes. Amazingly, the Bridegroom was still holding his leg above the trip wire for a full ten minutes.

With her hands wringing, the Bride said, "He will not be able to hold out much longer. Look, Juan, his heel is beginning to touch the trap's hair trigger."

At the same instant, Footstomper appeared. Though no one else saw the accuser, the Bride and Juan did. They did not know, however, whether it appeared out of the air or surfaced from the depths of the earth.

Stunned, Juan mumbled, "What's that?"

The Bride answered in fear and shock, "Footstomper!"

Bursting forth with a devilish shriek, Footstomper bit into the heel of the Bridegroom, pulled the heel down and made it touch the hair trigger on the deadly trap. The ancient jaws closed at once, binding and smashing both the heel of the Bridegroom and the head of the ancient accuser. The head of the deceiver was caught between the metal jaws of the man-trap and the foot of Soloman. The accuser struggled to remove its head from the jagged clamps but could not do so. It had imbedded its teeth into the Bridegroom's heel and the only way to be set free was for the Bridegroom to remove his heel first. The Bridegroom would not and could not do this.

The Bridegroom declared from the death trap, "I am Headbanger! You are Footstomper! You have bruised my heel and I have crushed your head. This death-trap that you have sprung for me in time is the same trap I set for you in eternity, before I placed the foundations of the universe. Footstomper, I bear all sins and you are defeated!"

Footstomper twisted its limbless body in six complete turns but could not free its head from the trap of justice or the heel of the Bridegroom. It wanted to speak but could only moan as it choked on Soloman's heel.

"Footstomper, I know what you are thinking. Do not think that death will defeat me. I am bearing all the sins of all

180

people and you are defeated. Now, I will conquer death for I have promised it in eternity and I have declared it in time. My word is truth. You, however, will remain in the jaws of this trap until the end. You are mortally wounded forever. It is finished!"

A deep, guttural sound emanated from the bowels of Footstomper and its resonance caused the earth to quake. Onto the same soil the blood of the Bridegroom flowed freely from an artery severed by the jaws of the death-trap.

Six hours later, the end came. Only a few of the crowd remained, along with the soldiers on duty. The Bride and Juan had moved closer, now a mere ten feet from the death-trap. They lifted their red eyes and beheld him seated on the pallet, his leg still clamped by the saw-toothed iron jaws. The Bridegroom's parched and blanched lips revealed his loss of blood and the shock to his body. He struggled within as he reached for each breath. He looked down from the grisly jaws of his just death.

The Bridegroom uttered a few last words when he saw his Bride and Juan standing nearby. The Bridegroom said to her, "Woman, behold your son!" Headbanger looked at Juan and spoke, "Behold, your Mother!"

Only moments later, the Bridegroom breathed his last. The Bride and Juan wept. The two attending soldiers moved closer to the trap.

"He didn't last very long," noted one soldier.

"No. That's as quick as it ever happens," agreed the other.

"He sure didn't suffer much."

"No, not much at all. He got off easy."

"What was that one word he said? *Tetelestai*?"

"Whatever."

The pale horse moved into position. The Bridegroom's body, still in the trap, was netted by Thanatos.

The Bride, now an aged woman, felt much older than she was.

CHAPTER 24

FIRST FRUIT AND SECOND GENESIS

From deep within the farthest recesses of the black net that coiled the earth, a still, small voice whispered a message sending a shock wave to both ends of the net.

"The last foe is defeated."

The hushed proclamation jolted the foundations of the earth and the ebony constrictor mewled at the sweet sentence.

"I am Headbanger and I live!"

Aghhh.

"Yes, Footstomper, I do hear your thoughts. You are permitted to communicate to me by your thoughts."

The deceiver smoldered, *I may not be able to speak, but I will create and give birth.*

"No. You will neither create nor give birth. All I will permit is for you to practice a dark magic and conjure from your mortal head wound."

Twins will come forth from me and destroy your precious Bride and her basta-.

"Footstomper, you are not permitted to communicate such a thought. The coming forth which you describe will only be a vomiting of the darkest bile from within you."

If I could only free myself from the jaws of this ancient trap.

"You are entrapped until the end, Footstomper. The jaws of the trap remain, and will always remain. Footstomper, yours is a mortal wound and you die forever. I live and I leave. I go to

182

my Bride and to the Wedding Hall. My Bride comes to me and to the Great Wedding. Because I live and prepare the Feast, all her children will be my wedding guests. My Bride, her children and I will dance the Great Dance. Footstomper, you and your offspring will forever die the second death."

Aghhhhhhhhhhhhhhhhhhhhhhhh.

"I am Headbanger! I live and I leave!"

The Bride and Juan ate the evening meal together, each silently reflecting on the events of the previous two days The Bride pondered conflicting thoughts; regret for not having understood sooner and resignation because the events unfolded as planned from eternity. She thought to herself, "The Bridegroom has died, but that is not the end of it. Something or someone is restraining Footstomper even now. If it were not so, chaos would be the order of this day and anarchy would rule." She commanded herself to be patient and wait.

Juan wondered about the future, whether to remain here, or to take the Bride and begin a new life away from all the reminders of the tragedy and its accompanying heartaches. There had been such hope and promise in discovering that the Bridegroom had come and lived among them. Juan thought back over the times when he treated Soloman shamefully. He attempted to haze the guilt with the conclusion that the Bridegroom did not manifest himself as expected. But even these perspectives evaporated. Time and again, Juan came back to reality. The Bridegroom was now dead. Juan could have been more supportive, but the Bridegroom would not be swayed from his course, and now, he was dead. What was to be done? The Bridegroom called him to care for the Bride, but to what end? The Bride never died. Juan would. The Bridegroom was dead and with his passing, Juan thought the Bride would begin to die.

As the edge of the earth was swallowing the sun, the Bride and Juan walked. Neither made a conscious decision to go outside and meander along the dirt road to the west. With heads down they kept the blazing, orange globe from burning their red, weepy eyes. The two strolled aimlessly along the dusty road.

Ahead of them a figure blocked their way. Holding their hands to shield them from the blinding sun, they could only make out a dark figure in front of them. They stopped.

"Where are you going?"

Juan answered in a resigned manner, "Nowhere in particular; just walking."

"Do not just walk. You should always be going somewhere in particular."

"Sir," the Bride said, "our wondering thoughts have provoked wandering directions."

"Repent."

Startled, Juan asked, "What?"

"Repent. Have a complete change of mind."

The Bride listened carefully while Juan kept speaking, "I'm not following you."

"I know. Repent. Do an about-face."

"Please," said the Bride, but did not finish.

"Turn around, both of you. Face the other direction." After having literally turned around, the next command was issued, "Describe what you see."

Juan began, "There are a few houses at the edge of the city. They give way to the shops along the roadway leading to the center. The evening light gives them a certain glow-"

"No, Juan," interrupted the Bride and directing her question to the other man, "You are the Bridegroom, aren't you?"

The answer came from over her shoulder, "Yes."

Juan started to turn but was stopped. "Not yet, Juan," the Bridegroom added formally. "You have not described what is in front of you."

Juan began telling about the city and the late afternoon light. The Bride interrupted him, "Juan, do you see Thanatos and the pale horse?"

"No, I have conditioned myself to ignore them."

The Bride directed him, "Glance back and forth. When you catch a glimpse, do not focus on it. Look to the side. You will see them."

Juan's eyes flitted about and in a moment, he responded, "Achh! There they are. Why would I want to look at them? They are horrible."

The Bridegroom prompted them, "What do you see?"

"I see Thanatos," said the Bride. "It has netted every one of my children as well as all the others who ever have lived and died."

Juan picked up the description, "I see the pale beast. Its massive shoulders are powerful and the horse stands tall."

"Continue," invited the Bridegroom. "What else do your eyes see?"

Juan asked, "Do you want us to describe the horse and rider in greater detail?"

"No."

"Then," he went on, "there is only the net. It is twice as high as the horse. It appears to be made of black, meshed netting. Through it the dark outlines of bodies can be seen, especially through the torn area several feet behind the-."

The Bride interrupted and blurted, "The torn area! There has never, ever been a tear in the fabric of that dark tubing. But there is a large rip in it now."

Juan inquired of the Bridegroom, "Sir, what does this mean?"

"I am the Bridegroom! I am Headbanger! I am, I died and I live again. Death could not hold me. I have ripped open the net of death and will die no more. Those who are mine, though their bodies are in that net now, will not die the second death."

He stopped speaking and the Bride asked, "The sight of the ripped net is a great sight and we will never forget it. But please, may we turn away from the pale pair and look at you?"

"Yes."

The Bride and Juan turned. His outline was clearly seen, but the glow of the sun behind him prevented them from making out his face and front clearly.

"Juan, why are you trying to look at my heel? You do not quite believe what you know to be true, do you?"

"Sir,-"

"Both of you, circle me. Please, walk around me. You will be able to see that I am. Juan, be sure to look at my heel."

They walked behind him and saw him clearly with the light at their backs. Juan cast his eyes down at the heel. The deep wound marks of the trap were visible, yet he bled no more.

"Sir, you are the Bridegroom. This I confess."

"Do you confess because you have seen? Blessed are the many who have not seen me as you have and yet confess me as you do." He directed a question to the Bride, "And what, my beloved lady, do your eyes now behold?"

In admiration and love, she only looked at him.

"Well thought," He replied.

Juan remained silent until he perceived it fitting to remark, "Sir, I see something else."

"Indeed, you do. Say it aloud so my Bride may hear what your confessional eyes now behold."

"Sir, standing here, on this side of you, I see you between us and Thanatos."

The Bride smiled.

"Well spoken, Juan. You will continue to tell the Bride and her children of such things. You are now the bestman."

"But-"

Before Juan uttered another syllable, he was wearing the wool robe from the black sheep. The chain stole hung over his young shoulders.

The Bride, somber and reserved, spoke softly, "The time for the Wedding is not now, is it?"

"No," the Bridegroom replied, "but it is not as far to the *when* as it once was. You have a long journey ahead and you are to be fruitful. Bestman Juan, when Ruach brings all the events to your remembrance, write them. Do not fear what happens. Bride, recall the wise words of Bestman Juan. I am always between you and Thanatos. I died and I am alive. I am with you always."

"How long will-"

"My dear Bride, until ... just until. Fear no one but me. You will be assailed by two opposites that have the same father. One is able to kill the bodies of your children, but not their souls. The other, while not able to kill either body or soul, does inject deadly soul venom. Their attacks are waged from the expected and the unexpected places of the earth. Behold, even now Rancor is searching for the wool robe from the black sheep. He is pursuing you. This night make plans for you and your children to leave in the morning."

"But where am I to escort the Bride?"

The Bridegroom motioned for the Bride to answer him. She said, "Not to *a where*, but to *the when*."

"I do not understand," Bestman Juan confessed.

The Bride smiled at the Bridegroom and said to Bestman Juan, "Read."

CHAPTER 25

THE CITY OF THE LIONS

It. It was conjured by the evil will. It simmered and bubbled within the foulest recesses of Footstomper. It fed on the bile and the grit, on the acids and the hair of its host. It enlarged and demanded to be cast forth upon the earth. It was duplicity.

When the time had fully come, Footstomper wrenched and strained before disgorging the offspring. Because the trap still held the accuser's head and mouth firmly and rigidly in place, the two hatchlings spurted from the sides of Footstomper's mouth. The name of the one spewed to the right was Opacus. The one to the left has a name which no one on earth knows. Opacus expanded rapidly while the other one uncoiled slowly. Opacus consumed its young and grew larger, over-shadowing its prey. Opacus sought to own the soul by threatening the body with suffering, pain and death. The nameless one differed, remaining small, producing Assassins and sending them to pierce the soul with contaminated and befouled darts, doing so quietly and without apparent harm to the body.

The Bride, her children and Bestman Juan, foregoing sleep, prepared to depart at first light. To avoid suspicion, the message circulated among the children to leave their homes quietly and meet at the west gate while it was still dark. The directions included an order to travel light, bringing only the essentials.

Children of all ages assembled on the dewy earth outside the west gate, some sitting on their haunches and others standing in silence, their eyes cast to the ground in quiet thought. The troop, smaller than the white-cloaked Bride hoped, gathered about her just before day's dawn.

In a subdued voice, carrying no farther than the children around her, she began, "My heart is filled with joy to behold your faces this new day. Please be still and listen to Bestman Juan."

The Bride sat with some of her children and smiled as her eyes beheld a bestman who, once again, cared for her and her children.

Bestman Juan spoke in a loud whisper, "Fear not what this day brings. The Bridegroom, though gone to make preparations for the Great Wedding, is truly with us. We must travel quietly the first hour. Rancor will soon discover the Bride and her children have fled the city. He will send forth the Corps of Escort Sentinels to hunt us down and return the Bride. Fear not, dear children of the Bride. Do not forget, the Bridegroom is with us right now, just as much as he's on the other side of the Portal."

Bestman Juan ceased speaking and began whispering *The Psalm of the Good Shepherd.* Before he finished, the entire congregation whispered it with him. They arose and left.

The colorful pink sky that morning revealed three sentinels, two groomsmen and three inscribers walking among the children. The tension increased as some of the others cast glances of anxiety, concern and even anger over the presence of these men. Bestman Juan traveled and whispered with each of them during the first hour. When the Bride and her children had walked for an hour and entered the lonely wilderness, Bestman Juan announced in a loud voice that the inscribers, sentinels and groomsmen traveling with them, were children of the Bride and no longer under Rancor's reign and rule. A collective affirmation rose from the Bride's children in the sound of a long sigh, accompanied by smiles and gestures of welcome.

The western trek turned to the north and continued across the dry wilderness for years. The parching desert wind callused the aging Bride's face and sapped the strength of her children. Ruach blew where he willed and Bestman Juan wrote down the exhilarating words and bound them in *The Book of Ancient Promises Fulfilled*. The only items discovered by Bestman Juan in the modest wooden box with the hinged door were the two books, the white quill from the high-soaring eagle, the golden chalice with the ink of blood, the cruse of water, the flask of wine and the loaf of bread.

Amazingly, the Bride begat many daughters and sons during these difficult years. It was during this time that the begotten brothers and sisters appeared quite different from one another physically. Sometimes these siblings, whose facial features and skin tones varied, stared at one another with puzzling looks. The Bride, however, smiled with joy at her beloved children whether they were red or yellow, black or white.

Each new daughter or son was marked with the water when first entering the gapped circle. Bestman Juan read from both books, distributed the sacred meal to the children and told them of the Bridegroom's love for their mother whom the bestman called the Elect Lady. He described the wedding and led the Bride in the Great Dance. The younger children often gathered around the bestman to examine the metal trap at the one end of his chain stole. Bestman Juan never tired of showing it to them and telling them how it called them to remember the Bridegroom's sacrificial love and their inheritance. Although her old knees often ached with arthritis, the Bride never complained at the opportunity to rehearse for the Wedding.

The ever present three always cast a sobering pall upon the Bride and her children. The black, meshed net, with its grisly contents, stayed to the left of the traveling assembly. For years, Bestman Juan and the Bride veered to the right and remained distant from the dark border. When the net was no longer in sight, it was never completely removed from their thoughts. Thanatos and the pale horse dogged the Bride and frightened her children, especially when one among them died.

In the 103rd year since the night at the Small House of Bread, Bestman Juan died. His soul passed through the Portal and his body was gathered by Thanatos. The Bride and her children mourned for forty days. After the days were fulfilled, the Bride chose another man and placed him in the office. When Bestman Clemence opened the modest wooden box with the hinged door, the quill and the chalice were no longer inside. That evening, when the circle was gapped, he proclaimed the closing of the two books. From that day on, *The Book of Ancient Promises Given* and *The Book of Ancient Promises Fulfilled* were bound together and were simply referred to as *The Book*.

In the 108th year since the night at the Small House of Bread, the Bride and her children approached an ancient city. Blasted by years of wind-driven sand, an archaic sign on a hill near the outskirts of the city informed passersby of the city's name and foundational decree.

The City of the Lions
Public allegiance to the Liege
is required by order of Opacus.

They moved their eyes from a reading of the sign to a scanning of the horizon. The Bride and her children had no alternative but to enter The City of the Lions. The meshed net of death ran along the western edge of the city. A deep canyon over the edge of steep, sheer cliffs prevented any diverted travel around the eastern edge of the city. At a great distance to the northeast, on the far side of the city, a small dark object was barely visible.

"Going through this city will not be easy. Even thinking of it is difficult," Bestman Clemence admitted while sinking deeper in thought.

The Bride noted his reflection and asked, "We have no choice, do we?"

"No," he answered, his eyes focused on something seen only by his mind. "How long do you think it'll take us to get to the other side of the city?"

192

"A half century or more, I imagine," she answered.

"Then I will die in The City of the Lions," he noted, "and that is not a pleasant thought."

Tears welled up in the Bride's eyes as her glance captured both the bestman and the waiting pale pair. "That will be true for many of my children. Bestman, before we enter the city, may we gather for the divine service of the Bridegroom?"

The Bride's request jolted Bestman Clemence back to his immediate responsibilities. "Yes. I believe there is a need for us to remain here for a few days in order to prepare ourselves. Does that meet with your approval?"

"Yes."

Later that day, Bestman Clemence gapped the circle and escorted the Bride and her children within the chain stole. He read to them from *The Book* and led them in the singing of several ancient hymns and chants. They offered their thanks and praise to the Bridegroom. The children who were ready received the Bridegroom when the sacred meal of bread and wine was distributed. Bestman Clemence led the Bride in a rehearsal for the Great Dance. His proclamation to them concerned the need for them to be able to voice their belief.

"... and as a result, we'll remain here and prepare for another six days. What is ahead for the entire assembly or for any one of us is known only by the Bridegroom. We know his promise and the blessed end for those children who remain faithful to him. As we travel through the city, there will likely be many attacks against the Bride, as well as against you individually. We have the special privilege to use these assaults to bear witness to the Bridegroom. Nothing is known of the Liege in this city, or of the man, Opacus, if indeed Opacus is a man. As children of the Bride, we may render allegiance to the authorities of cities, but only as long as such pledges don't conflict with or deny the Bridegroom or the life he has called us to lead."

Throughout the week, the children and Bestman Clemence worked with the Bride to draft a declaration of belief. Included

193

were sections on the Father, the Bridegroom and Ruach. On the evening of the seventh day, during the time of the gapped circle, the Bride and her children first used the declaration of belief. Known simply as *The Declaration* and derived only from *The Book*, it stated what the Bride and her children believed and taught. *The Declaration* provided a way for the children to stand together and bear witness to the world and to each other.

The next day, Bestman Clemence led the Bride and her children into the city. Marketplace loiterers inventoried the children's persons and possessions. Petty officials and randomly positioned militia made note of the caravan. Unseen by the Bride, one of the officials left the scene to report to his superiors. Artisans and shopkeepers ceased their labors, noticing the company processing into the city. If the children had been more stately in apparel or commanding in posture and gait, the Bride in the white cloak from the snow leopard might have been received by these citizens as an aged and distinguished queen.

Travel within the city was slow. The children of the Bride were fascinated by the hand-crafted articles fashioned by the minds and hands of others. Alluring enchanters, moaning unknown phrases and uttering strange sayings, enticed the children. Too often sons and daughters fell to the temptations, leaving the company of the Bride and never returning.

In the years that followed, many children were summoned to appear before the Liege and profess allegiance. Opacus stirred the heart of the Liege and puffed him up with the desire to be worshipped. When the Liege discovered the children professed a loyalty limited to the Bridegroom, a reign of terror began.

Children of the Bride were scattered throughout the city. Those identified as sons and daughters of the Bride were seized and brought before the Liege. Each was given the opportunity to respond to one question, "Do you claim the protection of the Liege, or do you claim the protection of the Bridegroom?"

If the answer was given, "I claim the protection of the Liege," then the authority and protection of the Liege extended to the individual and he or she was freed with commendation and praise. If the Liege heard the words, "I claim the protection of the Bridegroom," then the protection of the Liege could not cover the individual. The Liege announced, "Then the Bridegroom must deliver you from the consequences of your claim. None of those who have preceded you in their trust of the false deity known as the Bridegroom have ever been rescued. He has left them and they have all died. I say this not by way of inviting you to change your claim, for you may not do so. I am announcing this for the sake of those who are witnesses here this day. Do not claim the Bridegroom."

The servant of Opacus selected a repercussion from the box of punishments. More often than not, the sentences involved combat with the city lions. However, slow death by impalement, entrapment, frying, burning or flaying was not uncommon. Thanatos and Pale Rider reaped a grim, abundant harvest in The City of The Lions.

In the early days and years, many of the Bride's children, having lived under the relative ease of being a follower of the Bridegroom, fell away from him when threatened with death. Bestman Clemence was martyred in a calculated, agonizing death over the course of four days. His successor claimed the Liege. The failure of a bestman to claim the Bridegroom had a sobering, puzzling effect on the Bride and her children. Many children, having seen the failure of the bestman to remain faithful, fell away themselves.

After a decade of such testing and refining, the children who remained with the Bride were devout and resolute in their faith. While they did not seek martyrdom, they did not shrink from it when called to appear before the Liege. These children victoriously and valiantly claimed the Bridegroom, not only when asked the question, but also during their executions. The bestmen became younger as each, in turn, wore the wool robe from the black sheep and donned the chain stole. Daughters and sons of the Bride stepped forward to stand in the place and service of the many whose lives were taken by the wave of terror inspired by Opacus.

Amazingly, the Bride begat many daughters and sons during the following decades. Residents of The City of The Lions, appalled at the cruelty of the Liege and captivated by the determined witness of those dying such horrible deaths, believed in the Bridegroom. One of the greatest blows to the Liege occurred when the oldest living son of the Bride was brought before the court on a pallet. The old man, the last of those who had actually seen the Bridegroom, was no longer able to walk. Before being asked, the aged man, with both failing eyesight and resolute voice, made his claim.

"With these eyes, I have seen the Bridegroom. I saw him die for me. I saw him after he emerged from the net. O Liege, he endured the trap for you and all these people."

The Liege, furious and enraged at these words, grabbed a shield from one of the guards and slammed it across the old man's face. He never saw the shield coming and took it at full force. He struggled to a semi-standing position where his one hand still touched the floor and the other clasped his torn lip. He coughed blood and stabilized himself in the presence of many witnesses. He spoke once again.

"O Liege, how can I hold this transgression against you, when the Bridegroom has already taken it upon himself? I claim the Bridegroom and pray that you do as well."

The livid Liege, in a fit of wrath, ordered a sentence of death by slow, public flaying. The skin was to be peeled back in thin strips and left attached to him. The grotesque sight and the putrid smell of the rotting flesh strips turned the stomachs of all, even the executioners. The old man, staked out in public, was forced to drink water so he would not die by dehydration. In the midst of the intense pain and suffering, he spoke to passersby of the wrath and the love of the Bridegroom. He told them that the present sufferings, no matter how severe or painful or horrid, were mere, temporary discomforts. They were nothing compared to the glory of paradise for those who love the Bridegroom, or the agony of the never-ending second death for those who reject him. Through parched lips, the old man invited them to seek the Bride before the day of the Bridegroom's grace was gone.

For a week and more, the old man sounded forth. Day and night, whenever he was conscious, he recited long sections from *The Book* which he had heard and memorized. After receiving water he would thank the Liege's executioners for giving him water to remain alive and enabling him to sing. Then he would sing the ancient hymns, one after another, each bearing witness to the Bridegroom. Seven times a day, he recited *The Declaration* and prayed. Soon the executioners and others at the place could recite *The Declaration*. They heard the account of the promises given and fulfilled by the Bridegroom.

The old man's body was netted but his witness continued to strengthen the Bride and her children. The story of the old man became known, both by the children of the world and those of the Bride, as *The Old Man's Song at Lions.*

This martyrdom marked the turning point for the gradual downfall of the Liege. The people, whether for or against the Bridegroom, were shocked at the depth of cruelty exacted by the Liege and his unwillingness to end the old man's suffering by either granting life or death. The executions continued, but the populace lost its appetite for the Liege's power craving. Reports of public sightings of the Bride's children ceased.

Years later, Bestman Nigel, the Bride and her children approached the northern edge of The City of Lions and prepared to leave. The Liege's death accompanied the decay and destruction of the city. The Bride, weary with the struggle and stronger from the trials, begat many more sons and daughters than were lost throughout the years in the city.

As the Bride crossed the city limits, she gasped with a sudden fear that unnerved her, causing her to gather her children together. On the plains below the city, their eyes beheld the end.

CHAPTER 26

THE CITY OF THE CAVES

The horizon to the east now mirrored the west as the long, black net trailing behind Thanatos encircled the earth for the second time. A quick glance to the rear and the city behind revealed the waiting rider in pale apparel. To the north, the two coils converged at some distant point. Now restrained on two sides and unable to go back, the Bride and her children were being funneled to the north and to a time when the two meshed coils of death met. Thanatos was hemming them in, drawing them ever closer, firmly coiling, ever constricting and slowly cinching the Gordian knot that bound the earth and all who dwelt upon it.

"We must proceed," stated Bestman Nigel, noting the Bride's hesitation.

"Yes," replied the Bride, her attention obviously elsewhere. She remained mesmerized by the unfolding, yet ever converging landscape before her.

Noticing her stare and focus, Bestman Nigel gently gripped her elbow, to direct her.

Brought back to the present by the gentle touch, the Bride stated, "Yes ... uhh, dear children, let us follow the wise counsel of Bestman Nigel."

For more than seven decades, they journeyed slowly to the north. The children grew strong in the trek as they were fed and led by bestmen who cared deeply for the Bride and her daughters and sons. These faithful men gapped the circle, marked the foreheads of the newly begotten with the water from the cruse and led the Bride and her children in the Great Dance.

In the seventy-third year after leaving the previous city, they approached another. The sign posted near the southern entrance brought back pensive reflections.

Welcome to ...

The City of the Caves

(no worship of the Bridegroom is permitted)

A great discussion followed at the base of the sign. The first question focused on the need for them to pass through the city. This was quickly resolved since any travel to the east or west was blocked by the black tubes of death. Since time did not permit them to return whence they came, and because remaining in place was not the will of the Bridegroom, they resolved to enter the city.

The second question involved extended deliberation among the children. The issue concerned gapping the circle, not if they would do so, but how and when the divine service of the Bridegroom would take place. After extended discussion, a son of the Bride stood and asked a question.

"Before us is a sign at the city limits. We all agree that we will not stop gapping the circle or being led in the Great Dance. We will not stop believing in and trusting the Bridegroom. But right now, if we were to have the service, would it take place right here on this side of the sign, or over there on the other side?"

The answer to the question had a great impact on the Bride's journey through this city. After extended discussions, the bestman gapped the circle outside the city limits. Leading the Bride in the Great Dance was intended to give the children of the

199

Bride an opportunity to be fed and to hear the Bridegroom's word, not to be an open flaunting of the children's freedom or an occasion where they might be subject to arrest and danger.

The City of the Caves appeared inviting, and was, ... if approached without the Bridegroom. Many deities were accepted and openly worshipped by the people. Reports had come to this city about the doctrines of the Bridegroom. The laws prohibiting worship of the Bridegroom had been enacted because of the exclusive claims made by his followers. The Sovereign of the city encouraged the people to have many deities but not to have just the one named the Bridegroom.

The Bride and her children sought to gather for the Bridegroom's services quietly and away from public attention, often at odd times. Both the times and the places changed to prevent detection by the authorities of the Sovereign. Word spread from house to house concerning the location and time of the next gapping of the circle. The children arrived quietly, entered the circle through the gap and were led by Bestman Zeke in the service of the Bridegroom. Less than two hours later, no sign remained that a gathering had ever occurred at that place.

Rumors and reports of these events reached the Sovereign. His officials and soldiers responded quickly to reported sightings, but did not arrive while the children were still in the gapped circle. The frustrated Sovereign offered a reward to anyone whose efforts led to the Bride and her children being caught in the act of worshipping the Bridegroom.

This invitation to betrayal eventually proved fruitful when one of the Bride's sons fell to the temptation of easy money, reporting where and when the next service would be conducted. Though given only an hour's notice, the time was sufficient for the officials to set the trap. The soldiers waited until the circle was gapped and the children had entered with the Bride. When Bestman Zeke began by invoking the name of the Bridegroom, the Sovereign's men descended upon the place. Though many children fled in chaos, forty-two were caught and arrested. They were brought before the Sovereign. Those denying the Bridegroom would be released. Thirteen of the children, overcome by fear, denied the Bridegroom. Those refusing to deny him were executed. The first to be martyred, a nineteen year-old daughter of the Bride, stood calmly before the feared Sovereign and her executioners. As death came to her, she encouraged her brothers and sisters to remain faithful.

Her quiet witness and fearless approach to her own death unnerved several of the executioners. While they carried out their duties, two of them no longer slept peacefully. Months later, as a result of a conscience that gave him no rest, one of the executioners visited Bestman Zeke at night. The man confessed what he had done and how "it ate at his insides." Bestman Zeke told him what the Bridegroom had done for the executioner and for all people. That night the man became one of the Bride's children. That same night the other executioner took his own life.

Throughout the city, caves led below the surface to a tunnel system harboring "criminals, critters and creed confessors." When gapping the circle was to take place, the report spread quickly and the children filtered their way to the site. The location changed from time to time, usually occurring in a cavern with multiple tunnels providing several escape routes from the large room.

Bestman Zeke quickly placed the chain stole in the circular shape and invited all to enter through the gap. He removed *The Book*, the loaf of bread and the flask of wine from the substantial wooden box with the hinged door and began the service at once. The bass voice of Bestman Zeke resonated in the large rooms while the *a cappella* chanting carried throughout the tunnels. Citizens of the city above ground and near the cave openings heard the liturgical singing of the hymns, particularly the mighty hymn of invocation, *The Great Three in the One I AM.*

On cool, still nights in the city, the voice of the children wafted through the streets and into the homes. Many people became familiar with both tune and text of the hymnody and liturgy of the Bride. At times of persecution and whenever one or more of the children was martyred, the congregation sang the triumphant hymn, *The Old Man's Song at Lions*. The most moving was the chanting of *The Eulogy of the Bridegroom* by a single alto voice. The sound seemed to pass through the rock walls of the cavern and arise at the surface from everywhere and from nowhere. Those who believed the message of the children's singing were begotten by the Bride. At the next gapping of the circle, they were marked on the forehead with the water from the cruse and covered by the white cloak from the snow leopard.

Others, however, were not pleased with those who hid below the surface and broke the law of The City of the Caves. They complained to the Sovereign. He, in turn, grumbled and swore revenge.

The repentant executioner remained in the service of the Sovereign, but at a new position which did not require him to carry out the sentences. He listened carefully, and if he overheard any plans against the Bride and her children, he relayed the information to one of the children. He organized a number of tunnel watchers who warned the main group if one of the Bride's enemies was drawing near. This gave time for the children to escape through the other tunnels.

One cold winter, just after the *Celebration of the First Entrance*, a spy from the Sovereign infiltrated the children of the Bride. The spy learned the location of the next gathering and where the tunnel watchers would be posted. Near the end of the service, the Sovereign's soldiers captured three tunnel watchers and twenty-eight children. They were martyred immediately in the tunnels. The pale beast pulled the black tubing to the bodies and Thanatos netted them. Like a deadly snake, the black net wound its way through tunnels, up to a cave opening, across part of the city, down another cave opening and into a cavern. From a hill far away, the light brown city appeared as a great, rough piece of fabric stitched with a giant strand of black yarn.

The tunnel watchers were brought before the Sovereign. It was there that Opacus inspired the Sovereign to order an especially repugnant death for the tunnel watchers. The three naked men were impaled on poles in such a way as to produce as slow a death as possible. Placed in the arena, they were left in the bitter cold to die. Days later, hungry beasts were released in the arena to devour them.

The spy incident led to the necessary practice of advocating. In order to be permitted to know where and when a service was to be held, and before anyone could enter the circle through the gap, there had to be two advocates for each person. In addition, other safeguards were initiated. Not only were the tunnel watchers increased in number, but door keepers were assigned near the cave openings. Disguised or hidden from view, the door keepers provided an early first warning.

Nearly a century to the day, the Bride and her children left The City of the Caves. While she suffered much, she begat many children who were strong in the faith. During that time she was escorted by eight successive bestmen, each one doing, in turn, what the Bridegroom desired for his Bride.

CHAPTER 27

THE CITY OF THE SWAN

From the moment the Bride and her children crossed into the wilderness, the black walls to the east and the west threatened. The death snake had coiled the earth twice and pushed the faithful congregation ahead and forced the assembly to the end. Staring straight north into the worldly hallway, the two walls converged. The corridor formed by the tubing of bodies narrowed gradually. The canyon walls steadily closed, confining the troop as it moved northward. Some years the corridor decreased only by inches, other years by as much as forty feet.

The consequences of enmity, endemism and entropy over a thousand years is stunning and frightening. The trenching, snorting red horse and Polemos decimated entire families and cities and cultures and regions of the earth. Limos and Loimos changed the face of the land with the two plagues they sowed. Thanatos and its pale horse never stopped moving for decades at a time. Some battle grounds and plagued cities had bodies on the fields and in the streets for months before they were scooped into the net and the black tube became their abode. Since none of the children lived more than 120 years, no child ever noticed the gradual narrowing of the land between the two dark walls. The black tubing was simply there, for as long as any of the children had life on earth, from beginning to end.

The Bride, however, was painfully aware that every step she took to the north brought the death tubes closer together. It also brought her closer to the Great Wedding. Now an old woman, the Bride's appearance revealed the strain of a life with no death to die and the loneliness of continually outliving her children. The Bride appeared older than she was. Her weather-beaten, tanned face had crow's feet on both eyes that willowed around her cheekbones and to her jaw. The deep furrows in the tough hide of her face carried many tears. Seams of salt formed in the deep crevasses as tears dried without being wiped. With the bitter weeping, she also shed tears of joy and gladness. They came whenever a child was begotten by her. If the child was an infant son or daughter, her gnarly, knuckled hands held the child. At such times, her broad smile revealed a heart filled with joy and a set of teeth now neither white nor straight nor complete.

Since leaving The City of the Caves, the Bride had been escorted and served by fifty-eight bestmen. Each man, in turn wore the black robe and the chain stole with the trap and the large wooden crate with the hinged door. The bestman was called to serve, served and died. The body of each was snatched and tossed into the net of Thanatos and pulled along by the pale horse.

There were changes in the bestmen over the one thousand years and the changes came as a result of the Assassins aiming their potent arrows from a great distance. At first, the bestmen fiercely guarded and protected the Bride and her children. They faithfully fed, led and read to them. The children who strayed from the will of the Bridegroom were confronted and brought back to the circle, if possible. Those who needed a comforting word to calm the soul were served as the Bridegroom desired. These bestmen joined in the hymning of the ancient chants, psalms and songs. They proclaimed the Bridegroom entrapped to death, bursting from the net and on the other side of the Portal making all the preparations for the Great Wedding.

On a spring day, one of the Assassins fired an arrow from its bow. The invisible arrow hit the right arm of the bestman and began to fester. As a result, a small shift in emphasis took place during the new few centuries. The sideways movement was made with a subtle shift from a resolute commitment and calling regarding the welfare of the Bride, to a determined profession and pledge to protect the black robe and the stole. After six hundred years, the men who occupied the ministerial office of bestman were serving themselves while neglecting the Bride and her children.

One hundred years later, only the bestman drank the wine from the flask. The children were coerced out of their livelihood and forced to pay large sums of money to the bestman and do whatever he desired and ordered. Outright lies were told as the bestmen began selling invitations and passes into the Great Wedding. They sold to the Bride's children as well as to those outside the circle. The children suffered at the hands of these bestmen and the Bride was frustrated at not being able to use the white cloak from the snow leopard more often.

As the Bride and her children were forced over a hill one morning, they came upon a small city in the woods. Descending to it, they discovered its sign engraved on a rock.

THE CITY OF THE SWAN

The residents of the city, though aloof and wary of the bestman, received the Bride with cordial respect. In order to provide the basics of life, the people of the city worked hard, many in the woods, mines and tanneries; others in service or the trades.

As the years passed, many of these hard-working citizens and their families were begotten of the Bride. Instead of the bestman caring for and feeding them, he used both the opportunity and his position to fill his coffers with their money. He portrayed the Bridegroom as an angry landlord who was willing to let the people remain on his land, but for a price. If the children wanted to be seated at the Great Wedding, they would have to earn the right. If they weren't good enough, they could bypass the process by paying the bestman a large sum of money. "Nobody," the bestman said, "was good enough."

Whenever the circle was gapped, the bestman used the opportunity to speak about everything other than the loving, gracious Bridegroom. The Bride, in addition to her aged appearance, looked gaunt from lack of nourishment. Suffering from hunger, her daughters and sons were skinny and the outline of their ribs could be seen. However, unbeknownst to the bestman, the Bride and her children were being fed and kept alive by the marking with the water and the ancient rituals. The rituals always followed the same order and included readings from *The Book*, the confessing of *The Declaration*, the announcing of the white cloak from the snow leopard, the prayers, the partaking of the Bridegroom's bread and the singing of the hymns, odes and psalms.

It came to pass that one day, at the beginning of the winter season, the Bride begat an infant son when he received the marking with the water. His name was Hanson and as he grew, he desired to please the Bridegroom. Being a bright boy, he listened carefully to Bestman Romulus and discovered that pleasing the Bridegroom would not be an easy thing to do. The Bridegroom demanded perfection and Hanson knew he wasn't perfect. But the young man would attempt to please the Bridegroom by being the very best he could be.

As he approached adulthood, Hanson grew in wisdom and stature. He received the favor of the bestman and the Bride. While this would be a great accomplishment for most people, it was not for Hanson. He had earned the favor of everyone except the one he desired it from the most, the Bridegroom.

"The favor of the Bridegroom," Hanson said, "how can I achieve it?"

He watched and listened. Those who had money were told they could buy the favor of the Bridegroom. He watched many such transactions taking place. He saw the deals struck, but observed no change in the lives of those who bought the favor.

Could the Bridegroom be pleased simply by money and not a change of life? he pondered in his mind. *If so, do I want anything to do with the Bridegroom?*

Oh yes, he answered silently and with a rush of dread. *I will do what I must do to earn the favor of the Bridegroom.*

But Hanson did not have enough money. Indeed, he thought that the entire world did not have enough money to buy the favor of the Bridegroom. He was right.

Hanson watched and listened again. Bestman Romulus often made reference to his being closer to the Bridegroom than anyone else. The bestman said that by being the bestman, he gained the favor of the Bridegroom. Hanson heard the same claim over and over from the mouth of Bestman Romulus. He thought, *If he said it, it must be true.* Then and there, Hanson resolved to become the bestman and earn the favor of the Bridegroom. Then his mind would be at rest and his soul would be comforted. Entry into the good land on the other side of the Portal would be guaranteed and his place at the Great Wedding reserved and confirmed.

Hanson made a point of helping Bestman Romulus and letting it be known that he was interested in the worship services and the duties of the bestman. This curiosity did not go unnoticed by the bestman.

"Boy, come here," he ordered.

"Yes sir," Hanson answered, coming to a rigid stance of attention.

"What's your name?"

"Hanson, sir."

"Well young man, why the great interest in me and what I do?"

Usually not at a loss for speaking bluntly, Hanson followed form, answering him, "I want to become the bestman some day."

208

Bestman Romulus snickered and said, "That's a noble pursuit, but there are a number of prerequisites before that will happen. Tell me, boy, why do you want to be the bestman?"

Hanson hesitated as he thought. Bestman Romulus noticed and pushed him, "Come on! You know what the reason is. Are you man enough to speak it."

The young man spoke, "Because I want to gain the favor of the Bridegroom. I can't achieve it by payment because I will never get enough money in my life. Therefore I want to do it by being the bestman."

Bestman Romulus turned a bit red, "And so you think, -- what's your name?"

"Hanson, sir."

"So you think, Hanson, that by being the bestman you will acquire enough money to buy the favor of the Bridegroom."

"Oh, no, sir," Hanson replied quickly, "I didn't mean it like that. What I meant was that simply by being the bestman, I would earn the favor of the Bridegroom. That is correct, isn't it? I mean, that's what you have been saying, isn't it?"

Bestman Romulus became bored with the conversation and wanted to end it. "Hanson, if you only knew your letters I would let you look at *The Book*."

"I do know them, sir, and I would be most pleased to read *The Book*."

"Yes, I'm sure you would, Hanson, but you need to be able to know more than just the letters of The City of the Caves. *The Book* is written in the two ancient languages."

"Yes, Bestman Romulus, I know both the language of *The Book of Ancient Promises Given* and the letters of *The Book of Ancient Promises Fulfilled*."

With skepticism, Bestman Romulus asked, "So, Hanson, you know the letters of four languages. Is that right, Hanson?"

"Yes sir, and their numbers, too."

With the intent of exposing the pompous young man, Bestman Romulus opened the hinged door on the large, wooden box and took out *The Book*. He turned to a page in the front portion and said, "Here, Hanson, read this to me, in the original letters and then translate it to the letters of this city."

Hanson took *The Book* into his trembling hands and could not speak. He looked at the binding, the pages and the letters and seemed spellbound.

"As I thought," said the bestman in a voice of condemnation. "You are not able to read a single--"

"Wait, sir. Please excuse me. I am overcome by the fact that I have, in my very hands, *The Book*. I am able to read this and translate it as well."

Hanson slowly read *The Psalm of the Headbanger's Advent* in the ancient language and then gave a clumsy, but acceptable, translation of it into the letters of The City of the Swan. Bestman Romulus, impressed by the young man's ability, interrupted the translation and turned to Bestman Juan's *Thistle Epistle*. Hanson's reading and translating were even more impressive. The bestman did not hear the latter part of the translation as his mind was occupied with a possibility.

"Hanson, you may be of great help to me. Would you be willing to work in *The Book* and prepare a detailed analysis of a topic?"

"Oh, yes! Thank you, Bestman Romulus! What is the topic, sir?"

"The favor of the Bridegroom," he answered.

"When do I begin?"

"Tomorrow morning. You will report to me to receive *The Book* for the day's study. Before the evening meal you will return *The Book* to me."

"How long do I have to complete the work?"

The bestman laughed and replied, "However long it takes."

Bestman Romulus made Hanson pledge unconditional faithfulness and allegiance to *The Book*. This Hanson did and for three months, he studied *The Book* and made notes. He received permission to make a copy of it and to make a translation copy in the letters of the people of The City of the Swan. The study and writing passed the five year mark and during this time, Hanson and Bestman Romulus became great companions; the younger soaking up the words in *The Book* and being able to recite long portions in the letters of the languages; the elder wondering if Hanson might not be a good replacement for himself.

The work itself, however, was disturbing for Hanson. While he was immersed in *The Book*, the topic troubled him. Everywhere he read, the favor of the Bridegroom was the compelling factor for entrance into the Great Wedding and life on the other side of the Portal. He began to hate the Bridegroom's favor because there was no room for any relief. The favor must be complete and must be perfect. Without complete perfection and perfect completion, all was lost and entry through the Portal was absolutely denied.

Then a strange wind blew through The City of the Swan and gave a perspective to Hanson he had never seen before. While out in the woods, it occurred to him, as he was reading the copy of *The Book*, that the favor the Bridegroom required was the favor the Bridegroom gave. It was the Bridegroom who earned the favor and it was the Bridegroom who gave it as a gift. Late into the night, Hanson raced through his copy of *The Book*, looking at places where the favor of the Bridegroom was mentioned. Each time, it was revealed to him that the favor was a gift and any attempt to earn or buy the favor of the Bridegroom was a denial of the Bridegroom and his gracious love. Near dawn, the truth suddenly confronted him.

He shouted to himself, "The Portal is open wide!"

After a few minutes, he stopped and considered an undeniable truth. His heart pounded when he realized that either Bestman Romulus was wrong or *The Book* was wrong.

"Bestman Romulus, in my study of *The Book*, I find that the favor of the Bridegroom is a gift, given by the Bridegroom and announced by the bestman to the Bride and her children."

"I see," he said. "I don't want you working on the topic any more. Your training seems to be complete in this area. Now I want you to concentrate on music and the intoning of the various hymns."

"No, sir. You required of me my unconditional faithfulness and allegiance to *The Book*. I have found great comfort in the reading and studying of it. I am not willing to depart from it. In good conscience, I must stand on what I am convinced is the truth."

Furious, Bestman Romulus fumed, "Your faithfulness and allegiance is to me."

"No, sir. It is to the Bridegroom and *The Book*. You may err, but the Bridegroom and *The Book* do not err. Show me in *The Book* where I am wrong."

"I declare to you that you are wrong. That's all you need to know and hear."

"No, sir," Hanson declared defiantly.

Bestman Romulus roared in anger, "Then you must leave and I must announce that you are no longer one of the children of the Bride."

Hanson retorted in rigid determination, "I will tell her myself."

This the young man did. The Bride listened with close attention for several hours as Hanson related his personal findings and where they were found in *The Book*.

Finally the Bride asked, "Hanson, what do you believe about the edicts that recent bestmen have made and practiced concerning the earning of the favor of the Bridegroom?"

He replied immediately, "Dear Mother, they are attempts by the forces of Footstomper to turn your children away from worshipping the gracious, merciful and loving Bridegroom who willingly died for all. Instead, these forces of Ophis portray the Bridegroom as a blood-thirsty, vengeful and wrathful beast who is looking for a reason to send your children to the second death. These Assassins' agents, disguised in bestman's clothing, have pierced the souls of many of your children and are now lining their purses with the treasures of this world."

"You seem rather sure and opinionated, Hanson."

"Dear Mother, think back to the other side of the Portal. What was it that you did that made him forgive you? Did you earn the favor of the Bridegroom, or did he announce your forgiveness by giving you the white cloak of the snow leopard that you wear to this day? What did you deserve from him, and what did you receive from him?"

The old woman thought carefully and invited, "Go on, Hanson. I am listening."

"Dear Mother, does the Bridegroom's entrance at the Small House of Bread, his sin-atoning death by entrapment or his triumphant departure from the meshed net indicate that he is your loving Bridegroom or an angry, irrational brute? Has he given you any reason why you should think of him as a vindictive judge seeking any excuse to condemn your children to the second death? Isn't he our redeemer who wants you and everyone to be with him at the Great Wedding?"

The Bride inhaled deeply and held her breath for several moments. She scanned her sons and daughters as they gathered about her, their ears hearing these words concerning the Bridegroom for the first time in their lives. Her facial expression did not change. She cast a resolute stare at Hanson and put her fist up to his nose. It trembled before his eyes. She opened her hand and placed it on top of his head. As she exhaled, the Bride smiled and spoke two words.

"Bestman Hanson."

CHAPTER 28

THE CITY OF THE DOUBTERS

While Hanson stood stunned and in disbelief of his hearing, the wool robe from the black sheep instantly replaced his other clothing. The chain stole appeared and hung over his shoulders and breast. The iron trap hung on the one end and offset the jumbo, weathered, wooden box with the hinged door fastened to the other. Bestman Hanson opened the rough-grained door and inspected the cruse of water, the flask of wine and the loaf of bread. This led him to discover that *The Book* was missing.

"*The Book*-- It's gone! It's no longer here."

The Bride thought a moment and said, "Do not let this trouble you, Bestman Hanson. Do you not think that if it were the will of the Bridegroom, that it would be here along with the robe and the chain stole?"

"Yes, but the Bride and her children need to hear from *The Book*."

"Did you make a copy of it?"

"Yes, and a translation."

"Try putting your copy inside the box, along with the flask, loaf and cruse."

Bestman Hanson opened the hinged door on the jumbo, wooden box, placed the copy of *The Book* inside and closed the faded door.

The Bride continued, "Now Bestman Hanson, put the translation inside."

He tried to open the hinged, wooden door, but it would not budge.

"Bestman, read to me from the copy of *The Book*."

The weathered door opened easily at his hand and he removed the copy and read to her. After reading, he replaced the copy of *The Book* and shut the old door. She then asked him to put the translation inside the jumbo box with the hinged door. The wooden door would not open. The puzzled young man thought for a moment and then understood what to do.

"Bride, there is a man in the city who has one of the new presses for making many copies of a book. With your permission, I will take this translation to him and ask him to produce many copies of it. Then, any one of your children who wants *The Book* in the letters of this city may have one."

The Bride agreed with great delight, "Then each one of my sons and daughters will be able to read about the promises of the Bridegroom at any time."

"Yes, and," replied Bestman Hanson, "will be able to compare what the Bridegroom says in *The Book* with what is being heard from the bestman. That will be a great blessing to everyone, the bestman included."

"Yes, and from now on during the gathering of the circle, read from the translation. I want all my sons and daughters to hear the word of the Bridegroom in their own language."

Several decades later, Bestman Hanson, the Bride and her children left The City of the Swan. The dark walls from the coils of the death net blocked all travel except to the northwest. From the edge of the city, they could see the next city. They arrived at the entrance to the next city in only two years. On the left side of the city gate was a plaque.

The City of the Doubters
finitum non est capax infiniti

From the first step inside the city gate, the Assassins launched invisible arrows from their long bows. Since they did not cause immediate death, these arrows were particularly sinister. The individual struck by the arrow was neither aware of being attacked, nor being hit, nor that the poison was festering an infectious wound. Many children of the Bride were afflicted and their stories were pathetically sad.

In the front of his closed shop, a watchmaker has been examined by a local doctor. Rudy is an older man, though certainly not old. He is a man who never married and has made his living with clocks and watches. Rudy the Watchmaker has just learned from the doctor that nothing will stop the disease from consuming him. The doctor, unable to say anything more, becomes silent and returns a few medical items to his worn, brown bag. He leaves. Rudy the Watchmaker leans on the counter staring through its surface. After the sounds of the doctor leaving the shop and shutting the door subside, Rudy the Watchmaker is immersed in a world of thought. The only sound he hears is the passage of time as the timepieces throughout his shop mark the chunks of his remaining existence. He hears the clocks tick off the seconds in his life. The shining pendulum on the grandfather clock swings in tempo and Rudy sees it in his mind. A huge scythe, sweeping in an unstoppable cadence, cuts people down with each swing. The unemotional, relentless, sterile, sweeping scythe will soon be swinging in his path and taking him.

A peasant girl, hired to clean the bachelor's shop and living quarters, has entered from the back and has heard everything the doctor said. She makes no noise, but continues to listen from the back room of the dying man's shop. The peasant girl regrets the eavesdropping and thinks of a way to leave by the back. She wonders about the floor boards creaking if she attempts to retrace

216

her steps. She does not want him to know she heard the deadly prognosis. As the peasant girl considers leaving quietly, Rudy the Watchmaker begins to sob and speak to himself.

"Dying. ... Not me; oh, please, not me! ... I don't want to die. No, no ... no, not me."

Through his tear-filled eyes, he catches a glimpse of someone outside the front door of his shop. He wipes his nose with a rag and calls, "Who is there?"

There is no answer as the clocks continue to tick.

The dying man stares at the front door and commands in anger and fear, "Who is there, I said? Answer me!"

"'Tis me, sir. 'Tis Whispe'en, sir."

Rudy jerks his head around and faces the back of his shop. He blurts out, "Is my shop surrounded?"

"'Tis not surrounded by me, sir."

In confusion, he speaks, half asking and half declaring, "Whispe'en?"

"'Tis me, sir, yes."

Rudy moves to the front of his shop and looks out the window. He sniffs and mutters to himself, "Must have been my imagination. It's the shock. My mind is playing tricks on me." He continues to peer through the front, wooden shutter as he speaks to the peasant girl, "Come here, Whispe'en."

"Sir?"

"How long have you been here?"

"Sir, I began coming here with my aunt when I was three. But by myself, I've been cleaning for you five years."

Rudy spoke sourly, "No, you foolish girl. How long have you been here today?"

She answered, "'Twas not long, sir."

Exasperated, he asked, "Whispe'en, were you here when the doctor was here?"

"Was the doctor here, sir?"

"Stop avoiding a direct answer, girl. You have always been an honest cleaning girl. Nothing has ever been missing after you leave. I trust you and I am asking you a simple question. No harm will come to you for your honest answer."

"Sir, I'm sorry. I didn't mean to listen in and hear everything. I just came in the back door as I usually do and I just heard what 'twas that the doctor said. I'm sorry. Please forgive me, sir."

Rudy the Watchmaker rubbed his eyes and ran his hands through his thinning silver hair. He sighed and continued speaking, though more to himself, "Well, it doesn't matter much anyway. When a man is facing his own death, nothing really matters any longer."

"Sir, isn't now when the matters are the most?"

He breathed heavily and said in resignation, "You speak of the life-after?"

Whispe'en affirmed his question with a nod, adding, "I see you every time the gathering takes place in the gapped circle."

"What? You do? Are you there?"

"Yes indeed, sir. But I'm nobody of any special worth, just a daughter of the Bride."

Rudy laughed a snort and said, "I suppose this is the time to make confession and get things set right. Whispe'en, I don't ever recall seeing you there. Oh, the irony and the appropriateness! How would that read on my epitaph? *Rudy the Watchmaker: No Time For Others.*"

The peasant girl frowned, "But sir, you do believe in the Bridegroom and trust in him, don't you?"

"What does that mean, girl?"

"You belong to the Bridegroom. His promises are yours, sir. If I might be so bold to say it, whether you live or die, you belong to him."

"How am I his? Why are his promises mine?"

Startled by his questions, the peasant girl asked one of her own, "You have received the marking of the water, haven't you sir?"

Rudy the Watchmaker erupted with a mocking guffaw.

"Little girl, you are so young. There is nothing to a little ceremony when the bestman pours water from the cruse over his filthy fingers and marks a baby while speaking some words. It is strictly a symbolic action, conveying nothing but the Bride's rite handed down from some dark time."

"Sir, at your marking, the words spoken by the bestman were not his own. The words are the promise of the Bridegroom. They contain his power. He marked you and you belong to him."

"He was not at my marking."

"Why, yes, the Bridegroom was at your marking."

"Whispe'en, you need to pay closer attention to the reading of *The Book*. The Bridegroom is in the good land on the other side of the Portal. He can not be there and here at the same time. He is there and there is where he stays."

"Sir, the Bridegroom's everywhere."

"Yes, of course. Spiritually, he is everywhere."

"Sir, it's more than that. He's really present everywhere."

"I doubt the Bridegroom even knows where I am right now."

"Sir, 'tis wrong to say such a thing."

Rudy the Watchmaker waved the peasant girl aside and turned his back to her. While doing so, he caught another glimpse of someone outside the front door. He screamed in fright.

"Whispe'en! Hide me. Help me get away."

Turning his back to the door and leaning on it, he slumped to the floor. Rudy was terrorized and beads of sweat formed on his brow and cascaded down his face.

"Sir, what--"

"Outside! Look outside. Are they still there? Look! Oh my dear Bridegroom, I am afraid. Help me!"

The peasant girl stared through the window and saw no one.

"Sir, I see no one. 'Tis nothing there."

The trembling man answered in a subdued tone, speaking more to himself than to Whispe'en, "They are out there. Just because you can't see them doesn't mean they're not out there."

"True," the peasant girl replied slowly. "Sir, who is out there?"

Rudy the Watchmaker shivered as he answered in a forced whisper, "Death. Death is outside my door."

She continued, "In a spiritual sense, you mean. Death isn't really outside your door, right? I mean, since I can't see Death outside the door, then it's all kinda make-believe."

He replied in anger, "You mock me, peasant girl. Thanatos and the pale horse are out there, on my doorstep, really and not figuratively. The net being pulled and readied for my body is not symbolic."

"Forgive me, sir," she said, "but who is inside your door?"

"What? Stop being silly!"

"Please, 'tis not a foolish question and I'm not being silly, sir. I plead with you to answer. Death is outside your door. Who is inside?"

"You and I are inside!"

"The Bridegroom is also here, sir. He is really here, on the inside of the door. He stands with us."

"How can he be here? He's in the good land on the other side of the Portal. It's not possible."

"He's here because he's the Bridegroom. He's here because he's promised to be here. He's given his word. He's here because he marked you. Besides, just because you can't see him doesn't mean he isn't here, right?"

"Would you have me think like a child, Whispe'en?"

"'Tis the only way to think."

"Am I to think that the Bridegroom I can't see on my side of the door is going to protect me against the death I can see on the other side of the door?"

"Yes, for 'tis true, sir."

"Will the Bridegroom defeat death for me?"

"He already has."

"But he was not fully the Bridegroom when he was entrapped to death."

"Really? *The Book* declares he was, and that he still is."

"But he couldn't really die if he were true deity in all the fullness of the deity."

She urged Rudy to continue, "What happened at the Small House of Bread?"

Rudy the Watchmaker pondered her question and said, "He came to be like us ... in order to die for us. He couldn't die for us unless he was one of us. ... But I doubt that the fullness of the--"

A knock sounded at the wooden door. All present thoughts were removed from the consciousness of Rudy the Watchmaker. He trembled with fear.

"Whispe'en, don't leave me. I am dying and I am terrified!"

"Sir, I'll stay."

"Whispe'en, did you hear the knock at the door?"

"Yes."

"Death is knocking for me on the outside of the door. Death wants me and I am afraid."

"Sir, how do you know that the knock came from the outside?"

CHAPTER 29

THE CITY OF THE REASONERS

A dark gray haze hung over the distant city, foretelling its destruction and providing ample warning to those who sought to enter its gate. The only way to the future on the other side of the clouded city was through its streets. The eastern and western walls of death continued their slow convergence. These barricades funneled this world's people to the last day when the walls finally would touch and the sojourning on the land would cease.

Bestman Andreas rested on the rise of the hill that provided the prophetic view. The Bride glanced at him as she passed him and continued walking, hip-carrying one daughter. Her bowed, aged legs strained to keep up with the little ones who scurried about her. These little children laughed and played into the future. Bestman Andreas smiled at these little ones who were passing him. He breathed heavily from the steady climb to the rise of the hill and took a few moments to recover and rest. The huge wooden box with the old hinged door strained his arms and winded him in the ascent.

His vantage point not only gave him a view of the city ahead, but an opportunity to watch the Bride and her children as they began the gradual descent. The strong sons of the Bride led the company while striding and talking into the great adventure. They were unaware of the in-coming arrows of the Assassins, as these archers stood on the walls of the city ahead and began finding the range for their invisible projectiles. The Bride and her strong daughters accompanied the younger ones. Older children followed in small groups, some discussing and debating the topic for the day, others singing songs and making melody in their hearts. The oldest sons and daughters came last and were the quietest, many immersed in personal thoughts and prayers.

One of the oldest sons stumbled and fell forward onto his frail knees. He caught himself with one hand on the ground and clutched his chest with the other. Bestman Andreas hurried to the old man and bent down to help him. A moment later, he opened the hinged door on the huge wooden box, removed what was needed and served the dying man. Several minutes later the old man died as Bestman Andreas read to him from *The Book*. Both men now had their eyes closed, one in death, the other in thought. The latter opened them at the snorting sound of the pale horse. He didn't look back. Rather, he put the holy things away, picked up the huge, weathered wooden box with the ancient hinged door and began the descent to the city.

A fortnight later, after crossing marsh, moor and bog, the Bride and her children approached the lush, broad-leaf vine that covered the old gate of the sooty city. A swampy slough, five feet across, separated the troop from the rustic gate. The city was immersed in a dense fog. The few days of sunlight and the abundant dampness aided the growth of a type of moss more black than green. No city sign was visible. No gate handle could be located. Only a small plaque near the far, top left corner of the gate could be seen. Standing in the still water, one of the sons was lifted to read the words on the plaque. In a loud, clear voice, he read the words to those below.

```
        Instructions for
     opening the gate of
        this great city:
               you
         must locate the
       button in the very
      center and push it
```

223

The troop inspected the center of the gate thoroughly, time and again, but was unable to locate any button. They climbed to the top and read the plaque. They scrambled down and searched the center of the gate for the button. They removed all moss and vines from the surface of the gate and examined it for any blemish or spot which might be the mysterious button. The mystery remained. During the gathering in the gapped circle that evening, Bestman Andreas petitioned the Bridegroom for wisdom in locating the button and opening the gate.

The next morning additional attempts were made to solve the puzzle of the gate, all without success. The children of the Bride sat to discuss the matter. The younger children played near the gate, pretending to be able to solve the mystery. A small, three year-old girl asked one of the others to lift her to the instruction plaque so she could, as she said, "read it." The others laughed at her and one of the taller men decided to play along. As he hoisted her, she became aware of how high she was and leaned against the gate.

From the ground below, one of the older children laughed and said, "Go ahead. Now that you're up there, start reading."

The little girl said, "'Kay." She pretended to be reading, following the words with her fingers as she had seen the others do. "One, two, phree, pive, sic."

The children below chuckled. The man supporting the little girl on his shoulders laughed, causing him to stagger. As he regained his balance, the girl hugged the gate, grabbing onto the edges of the plaque and pressing her face against it.

"Are you just about done reading?"

"Uh-huh," she replied, continuing to read as before, "jus' 'bout done, 'kay?"

"Hurry."

"'Kay," she said and began reading the letters quicker and with both her mouth and finger.

Without warning, a cracking sound emanated from the gate and it began to open from the top. The small girl screamed as she fell into the arms of the man. He carried her out of the water as the gate, hinged from the bottom, was lowered by supporting chains on both sides. The gate served as a small bridge across the moat, permitting entrance into the city.

"She opened the gate," someone shouted.

Another asked, "How did she do it?"

Still another added, "Where was the button?"

Other than saying, "I open it," the smiling girl was unable to tell them what she did to make the gate open or where the button was she had pushed.

Someone suggested that the man supporting the girl hit the button with his elbow as he was regaining his balance. Another thought that it was a delayed opening from some action done the day before. There were many suggestions made, not one of them the correct one.

"Let her try to read this," an older son of the Bride said.

The children focused their attention on the older son. He kneeled on the deck of the small bridge and pointed to a polished bronze sign fastened to the deck of the small bridge.

```
LHEKE,2 LHE KEV2OWI LHIWK VBONL LLi
NKSB CVKEPNCi WIWD YONKSELPi
KNOKSB HEKEi
YKN HEKEi
ONK HEKEi

LHE CLLY OE LHE KEV2OWEKS

MELCOWE LO
```

The children of the Bride marveled at the number of factories in The City of Reasoners. The industrial district gave way to the lower class neighborhoods with street sewers, the business district with the guilds and the middle class section where residents dreamed of life on the terraces. Broadleaf trees and bristly hedges concealed and sheltered the estates and mansions purchased by the families with old money. Ivy-covered university buildings housed the academics. These intellectuals elevated the human mind one degree at a time and expounded the exaltation of the human spirit to the highest level. The benchmark for everything good and right was human reason. The high water mark was viewed in the eye of the dreamer.

Sirens from these luxurious havens attracted the inquisitive children in general and unsettled bestmen in particular. From the open windows of the lecture halls and the conventicles, the arrows of the Assassins rained upon the children of the Bride.

Arthur and Charles sat with their backs leaning against the ivy-covered brick wall of a university classroom. Both young men had been studying to be the bestman one day and enjoyed adding to their studies by listening to the enlightened. The professor, obviously intelligent and articulate, delivered his lecture with such conviction and force that Arthur and Charles were fascinated with its implications and mesmerized with the consequent possibilities. When the lecture ended, the two remained deep in thought.

"I didn't think these things were even possible to think," began a stunned Arthur.

"Your statement proves the whole point of his lecture."

"How so?"

Charles answered, "The creative mind of man is the highest good, capable of thinking beyond what was once thought to be impossible."

"Then the creative mind, along with the awareness of our being, is what separates us from the animals. Mankind has only taken an additional step or two."

"Yes, and, as you and I have heard today, the step or two we have taken in the past, what we call history, should move us to take a step or two in the future."

"A knowledge that we have and are able to take such a step is, in itself, a step."

"Very true, an affirmation itself of the evolving mind."

Arthur thought and spoke, "What could be done as we walk about on this land creating?"

"The wrong perspective, Arthur, what could not be done?"

"Sure," he answered excitedly. "For example, someone could create a story in which two men are sitting on the grounds outside a university classroom. These two did not have any being until they were created by the story teller. They could talk about whatever the story teller wanted; the newest type of cobblestone, the value of the insane, or snow."

Charles frowned, "I think, dear friend, you miss the point? Your examples tell, once again, of what could be done. All your illustrations already exist. In order to take the next step, we must answer the question, 'What could not be done?' How do you answer the question?"

"Nothing," Arthur blurted out in newly found joy, "Nothing could not be done!"

"Exactly. Now turn around and look back. You and I have just taken one more progressive step in the consciousness of the creative mind."

"Charles," his friend said, "how do we create something which does not already exist, if not in reality, at least which does not exist as an idea in our minds? How do we create out of nothing? I mean, to use the story teller theme, there already are two men sitting outside a classroom talking. And even if a story teller invented a race of creatures with three arms and two heads, arms and heads already exist."

His friend, earnestly desiring to defend his position, suggested, "Does deity exist?"

"Certainly."

"How do you know?"

227

"He is sensed by our consciousness. He exists because we are aware of a higher being. Deity has created us. Besides, he has told us about himself in *The Book*."

"I believe that you have the whole matter backwards. Though not really, 'you' in particular, but 'we' in general. It suddenly occurred to me that we, humanity since the beginning, have gotten it backwards. In reality, we have created deity, doing so out of nothing but our desire and need to exercise our creative, collective mind."

"Charles! You better be careful, here."

"Arthur, you sound like a man who has just watched another man take a step forward and, not willing to step with him, can only stand frozen in fear and begin criticizing."

Arthur, not wanting to be left behind and not knowing whether to take the step, asked, "Charles, are we serious here, or, are we only exercising our minds with a little frivolity?"

Charles guffawed and responded, "Hey, we're just playing a little, harmless game. Come on, please walk with me a little while more. Okay?"

"Alright," Arthur conceded. "So, what are the implications of your proposal that mankind has created deity?"

"Well, first of all, we have each become deity."

"Wait," demanded Arthur, "that means we have to become what we have created. It's not possi--"

"Stop, with all of your limitations! Step up and stay with me. We have each become deity by creating deity, Arthur. In the collective, creative mind of humanity, deity now exists. We have created the standard for what we strive to become. Our task is to achieve it, and today, you and I have taken a large step. So, dear friend, it is your turn. Here's your examination for the day. Since you are the creator of the deity, what is *The Book* ?"

He closed his eyes and thought. Arthur didn't like doing this, but convincing himself it was still a game, he responded, "As we took the one critical step of being aware of our need to exercise our creative mind, we created deity -- totally unknown and completely unknowable. In doing so, we now desire to become deity and to live up to the standard of deity whom we have created. *The Book* is the historical record of our ancient longings and creative accomplishments. Instead of being *The Book* of the Bridegroom, proclaiming the account of our salvation earned for us by the Bridegroom, it is *The Rulebook*, telling us how to think, what to do and how to be in order that we might, individually, become deity."

"Outstanding! You're really getting into this. Consider this. *The Book* is also an honest record of the past failings of mankind in becoming deity. You and I, today, are called to build on the errors of the past and go beyond them in becoming deity."

"Called by whom?"

"Called by the deep, hungry, inner yearning; called by the same desire that created deity out of nothing."

"I don't like it at all, Charles. I'm not comfortable with this, even though we have termed it an academic exercise."

Charles ignored him and continued, "Think about this implication. The Bridegroom is the creative incarnation and manifestation of our minds in order to have the standard a little closer. He was created by us to be the intermediary step. We recognized that we could not make the one giant step forward so we created deity in our image and after our likeness."

Mockingly, Arthur asked, "And the suffering entrapment and death of the Bridegroom? Have we not changed it from his sacrifice for our sins? Isn't it now but a model, a way that he has shown us what we must do to become like him?"

"Yes, that is the new, enlightened meaning, my friend."

Soberly, Arthur continued, "Then we have not only become creators. We have just learned to uncreate."

"Uncreate!" exclaimed Charles. "I say, you are forcing me to take another step. What an expansion of the mind! Uncreate. Let's hear more of this."

Sometime during the conversation an invisible arrow from the Assassins pierced one of the two young men directly in the heart, pinning him to the ivy wall of the university building. He never left the university, one day becoming a famous professor and, for many, a sought-out mentor. The other young man was hit with an arrow as well, though not directly in the heart. The poison-tipped, invisible arrow festered for years, causing him great doubt and sorrow, especially after he became the bestman.

CHAPTER 30

THE CITY OF THE BATTLE GROUND

"What are they doing, Mother?"

The old Bride felt a shiver pass down her back as she raised her slightly dimming eyes to the landscape ahead. Limos and Loimos plodded along at a walking pace, scattering the seed of pestilence and blight in the world ahead. Wherever the seed was sown, nothing grew. If the place was already green, it turned a dead brown.

"Not again," she muttered to herself, ignoring her son who asked the question. "Oh, please, my Beloved, do not permit this to happen again," she petitioned, watching the land being choked of life.

The bestman asked her, "Who are they?"

She answered him, "They are a prelude, first to plague and then to war. The plague will rise forth from the land as the fog forms during the night. I fear many will die."

"And of war?"

"Polemos will come," she announced as the thundering sound of hoofs beating the ground caused the Bride and her children to turn as they looked back. They narrowly missed being trampled as the fierce, red stallion, at a full, galloping charge, parted the children. Swirls of dust billowed as horse and rider passed, carrying not only dirt into the lungs of the Bride's daughters and sons, but also the tiniest seeds of pestilence.

Two hundred yards from the Bride, the red beast reared. When all four hoofs were on the earth, Polemos slammed a stake into the ground. At the top of the stake was a sign. The red rider dropped the giant hoe and released the bloody beast. The animal bolted to the west at full speed, pulling the metal scalpel across the face of the land. In a few seconds it was at the western wall of the death net. The beast charged into the net and rebounded, travelling at full speed to the east. The same happened at the eastern wall of the death net as Polemos zigzagged across the surface of the land until they disappeared from sight. Horizontal lines were now stacked upon one another to the ends of the earth.

"Not again," spoke the Bride with tears welling to the brim of her eyes. "Oh dearly beloved Bridegroom, please come and deliver us before we have to enter the land ahead. Is it time? Oh please, let it be time for the Great Wedding."

While the dust settled and, as the scarred land turned brown, the Bride realized it was not time. The Bride asked the children to follow her through the land of enmity and thorn, rather than leading as had been the custom of some.

Beholding her downcast appearance, they agreed without asking for or being given further explanation. The Bride called the bestman to hold her elbow and guide her as she walked. He did so, after having several men lift the immense ironwood box with the hinged door onto his back for easier traveling. Everyone remained quiet, keeping their eyes on the old, frail woman they called Mother. In front of them was a deserted, exposed land. She walked slowly, leading them to the first trench and the posted sign.

The City of the Battle Ground

You are NOWHERE.

You win some. You lose some.

"Mother," said a daughter softly, "tell us what the sign means?"

"There is much war and strife ahead in the City of the Battle Ground. Thanatos will be reaping a large harvest in the years ahead."

"But the land is empty," noted the daughter.

"From the trenches, my daughter, nation will rise up against nation, and people will die. From the trenches, a people will rise up against a people, and children will die. From the trenches, children will rise up against children, and they will kill each other."

"Please, tell me which people and children will die, Mother?"

She answered, "All nations will suffer; many people will die; too many children will be among them."

"Whose children?"

"Some of my children will war against each other and will kill one another."

"Mother, what is this place? The city sign says that we are n-o-w-h-e-r-e. Are we *no where* or are we *now here*?"

The Bride replied, "Yes."

The daughter could only wonder at her reply and consider what it meant. One of her sons asked, "The sign says, 'You win some. You lose some.' Does that refer to the wars of the nations and the battles of the armed forces?"

"No," she said with a degree of somberness that no one recalled hearing before. She sighed and said, "No, I believe it refers to the children of the world and to my children. As I travel across this land, I will beget many new children. But, many will leave me too."

A long silence, when no one spoke because the Bride was in reflective thought, prevailed. She said with a spirit of joyful determination, "Bestman, please gather my children about me and feed us."

233

The bestman gapped the circle, inviting the Bride and her children to worship the Bridegroom and to feast on him. This they did as *The Book* was read and the bread and wine were distributed. Many of the ancient hymns were sung and several psalms were chanted, including *The Psalm of Battle Done* and *The Old Man's Song at Lions*.

Nearly a century of war took place in the trenches upon the earth. The people on the earth killed one another with cannon balls, mustard gas, machine guns and tanks. Some trenches filled with water and the people of the earth killed one another with depth charges, deck guns and torpedoes as submarines and battleships ruled the waters in the trenches. From the skies, the people of the earth rained down attacks and killed one another with flak, cluster bombs, mines, missiles and the Bomb. Wars were fought in the steaming jungles and the bitter cold. More children of the land died from disease, starvation and freezing temperatures than died in the many wars. Battles were fought and answers were sought. The battles always came; the answers never did.

Despite national borders and cultural differences, the Bride begat many children from the land as she won some. She begat them during battles, at night, when ships were sinking and in foxholes when soldiers were dying. Often there was no time for the bestman to mark them with water and the word. The circle was gapped in haste and, many times, only three were near enough to gather in brief worship: the Bride, the bestman and the newly begotten.

Of particular sadness for the Bride were those all too frequent occasions when one of her daughters or sons left her. Wars and battles, pain and suffering provoked many of them to leave. One day, during the divine service, a son of the Bride stood while listening to the responsive reading of *The Psalm of the Good Shepherd*. After looking at the children seated with him and responding during the half verses with them, he stared at nothing and began speaking in a quiet, firm voice.

"If good, then not powerful. If powerful, then not good. Either way, not mine."

The congregation and the bestman became silent as he repeated the words three times. The man gazed at the Bride, said good-bye and left the circle. At an unusually slow pace, he walked across the entrenched land, looking neither to his right nor to his left. He never stopped as he continued his journey. He disappeared from the sight of the Bride.

On another occasion, a daughter came to speak to the bestman after she learned of the death of a loved one in a bombing run. She said, "If this is the kind of deity you worship, then I want no part of him, the Bride or you." Having said that, she denied the Bridegroom and departed from her mother.

Another daughter, in the presence of the Bride, confronted the bestman with a vehement assertion, "There is no deity. The Bridegroom is a fraud. You, Bestman Whatever-Your-Name-Is are the most worthless person on the face of this earth."

The Bride listened attentively and thought sadly, "While I win some, I also lose some."

CHAPTER 31

THE CITY OF THE MESSENGERS

Several decades slowly became a century as the era of Opacus-driven power subsided momentarily. In the wake of Opacus, that heinous offspring of Footstomper, the meshed, black net of Thanatos swallowed millions of slaughtered men, women and children. Now the deep trenches changed to shallow ditches and, more often as the Bride continued her journey, rolling mounds on the face of the land.

Though the outlook seemed free of the brutal beast, Opacus, the dangers increased as the Assassins launched the invisible, soul arrows from the shadows. The dark walls of the death net, now a mere quarter mile apart, blocked out the remote mountain ranges on the eastern and western horizons.

Bestman Manoah surveyed the countryside ahead with the eyes of concern. He spent the first sixty years of his life in the trenches, the last thirty-seven as the Bridegroom's bestman. He gave sincere thanks to the Bridegroom for deliverance from the trenches. He also feared for the future and eagerly anticipated the same. His heart often beat faster when he meditated on the promises declared by the Bridegroom.

While life had been difficult in many ways for him as bestman during the Battle Ground travels, he knew what to expect each step of the journey. He was raised in the trenches and was fully aware of the dangers. Individual links of the chain stole dug deeply into his aging shoulders as he slung the enormous wooden box with the hinged door onto his back. The old, ironwood box, once highly polished, was more of a heightened crate, now weathered and sun-faded. The gray, cracked door creaked on its ancient hinges.

Faithful bestmen gladly bore the load and opened the box and shared its contents. They comforted the dying and grieving They gapped the chain stole and proclaimed the promises of the Bridegroom among the children. These bestmen confessed and taught The Declaration. They led the others in the singing of the ancient liturgies, feeding the life-giving food to their sisters and brothers and spoke of hope in a land that offered none. They led the Bride in the Great Dance.

Now the contours of the ground ahead signaled a new land, with differing problems, challenges and opportunities for the older man. Many questions surfaced as Bestman Manoah ushered the Bride to the next city. He would be the bestman of transition with one foot in the trenches and the other in the unknown city ahead. The city sign, flashing brightly with a rainbow of electric lights and beaming broadly with an orchestration intended to dazzle and entice, prophesied of the difficulties awaiting the Bride, her children and the bestman.

Welcome to all persons who enter

The City of the Messengers

Where objective truth varies according to personal opinion.
Where corporate reality is defined according to individual concept.
This is the land of the tolerant and the home of the permissive.
Intolerance is not tolerated.
There are absolutely no absolutes.
Please, dear person, enter and indulge yourself.*

The Bride asked Bestman Manoah to gap the circle every morning and evening for six days. He agreed and they invested nearly a week listening to the words of the Bridegroom given to them in *The Book* and partaking of the blessings he had bestowed on his Bride to sustain her and her children. In his teaching and proclaiming, Bestman Manoah emphasized the necessity of remaining steadfast in the word and the work of the Bridegroom. The children were admonished not to allow a single teaching to be taken from them. He told them, "When any teaching from *The Book* is compromised, children get hurt."

The sons and daughters soberly listened to their leader, wondering what evil awaited them in The City of the Messengers and swallowing hard in proper fear. The circle was gapped within sight of the radiant sign and Bestman Manoah often referred to it during the proclamation. One of his great warnings during those six days was, "Beware of Footstomper." He appears as the "Effulgent Messenger of Luz." He told them what those words meant and where in *The Book* the warning was given.

At the same time, he reminded them of the need for all the people of The City of the Messengers to hear the bitter word and the sweet word of the Bridegroom. As begotten sons and daughters of the Bride, they were to be messengers to those they found along the way. Many people would be found who were abused, abandoned and hurt by the philosophy, machinery and subtlety within The City of the Messengers. The begotten of the Bride were charged with bringing the truth to those dying from the arrows of the Assassins.

The children were taught the differences between freedom and license, laws of creation and laws of opinion, proven fact and posited fabrication, and propagation and propaganda. He explained to them that, as both almighty Creator and the great Communicator, the Bridegroom is the source of truth. Thus the source of truth was not the prevailing popular opinion of an individual's desire, a people's fad, a group's agenda or a society's trend.

A time comes, however, when the theory, learning and recitation must be put into practice in the city and outside the circle. Thus, on the morning of the seventh day, after the gapping of the circle and the feeding on the Bridegroom, Bestman Manoah escorted the Bride through the gate of the city.

Silently the children eyed the schools and shops, wondering what evil watched them and what horrid people stalked them from the shadows of these buildings. A young son of the Bride suddenly ran into one of the stores. A great gasp was heard from the other children and cries of anguish came from those closest to the unfortunate boy. A moment later a woman came out of the hardware store holding the boy's hand and returning him to his family. The woman smiled at the newcomers and waved to them. Many of the Bride's children were confused at the evil woman's good deed.

Just before noon, they passed through *Feminist Memorial Park*. A group of young people were playing a game of baseball and one of the batters hit the ball over the short fence and into the midst of the Bride's children. A girl retrieved the ball and tossed it over the fence to the outfielder. The outfielder responded with a word of thanks. Several children looked at Bestman Manoah and wondered.

Two days later an elderly son of the Bride tripped at the curb of a sidewalk and hit his head on the concrete. A man rushed out of his home and treated the injured man with ice, a bandage, a comforting hand and an understanding word. He advised the man to see a local physician whom he knew who would suture the wound. He gave him his card and told him to show it to the doctor. He informed the old man that if anything else was needed, he would be cared for.

GRANT R. MANSON, PH.D.
6 PERSONA DRIVE
THE CITY OF THE MESSENGERS

ATHEIST   PHILANTHROPIST   HUMANITARIAN

The old man received excellent treatment from the physician. Many of the children began to feel that the bestman's criticisms of the city and warnings of the philosophies were excessive, if not totally unfounded. Weak or naive children felt betrayed and claimed brainwashing as they recalled past and present warnings by the old man of the trenches. Several newly begotten children felt Bestman Manoah was a man living in the past and that it was time for a new bestman, one with a perspective consistent with the present, to lead them.

Soon the children isolated the truth of the bestman's words to those times when the circle was gapped. As he had no authority in the culture and society of the city, so his words carried no weight outside the chained circle. The children listened to the bestman, but always put his words in the context of prevailing societal trends and personal opinion. Many daughters and sons of the Bride developed two allegiances and maintained dual lives, thereby attempting to serve two masters.

As Bestman Manoah and the Bride continued to walk through the city, many children left. Fascinated by the stock market and enticed by the possibility of being a corporate executive in a fast-growing company, sons and daughters abandoned the Bride. When the Assassins started firing their arrows with modems, satellites, computers, television and micro-waves, thousands of the Bride's children were slowly poisoned.

Four years later, Bestman Manoah became gravely ill and was put in a private room at one of the city's major hospitals. As he waited, Bestman Manoah was depressed, no longer able to carry the immense wooden, box-like structure with the hinged door and no longer capable of even gapping the circle. His condition worsened. With a respirator keeping him alive, he was now incapable of reading to the Bride from *The Book*. The doctor told him he had cancer and would soon die. Bestman Manoah imagined his death would be much different, perhaps martyred by an agent of Opacus or being hit during a firefight in one of the trenches as he was attempting to serve one of the Bride's children.

The Bride visited him in his sterile room setting. The IV pump stood as a sentinel over him. Bestman Manoah's eyes were mournful and distant as the Bride spoke with him and read to him. The doctor entered and told the Bride that the man would be taken off the respirator and IV pump that night. If he was not dead by morning, he would be given an injection. The Bride objected sternly but was forced to leave the hospital. So the Bride's son who was named Manoah, a faithful bestman for many years, died. The black net wound up the stairway of the hospital to the room where Manoah's body was and Thanatos scooped it into the great net. The Bride wept. Some of the children in the circle wept great tears of sorrow because of Bestman Manoah's death. Many children did not shed tears of grief.

A great struggle took place as the Bride began to prepare for calling a new bestman. In the evening, two daughters came to the Bride and spoke with her.

"Dear Mother," one said, "my sister and I have been talking about the possibility of a woman being the bestman."

"Right," chimed in the other, "and while we don't think it is necessarily the right time for a woman to be the bestman, we want to know from you if the possibility exists."

The first daughter continued, "Please, Mother, tell us that, one day, a woman will be the bestman."

The Bride did not speak for a moment as she studied her two daughters. With a silent prayer for wisdom, she began.

"In terms of intelligence, physical strength, education, mental toughness, emotional stability, wisdom or courage, there is no reason why a woman could not be the bestman. Still, I must tell you that a woman may not be the bestman."

The first daughter exploded in anger, "And why not?"

"There are three reasons. First, it goes against the nature of the wedding party. A woman can no more be the bestman than a woman can be the Bridegroom. Second, it goes against the nature of creation. A woman can no more be the bestman than a man can be the Bride. Third, *The Book* does not permit it, speaking against it in diverse places and not supporting it anywhere."

The first daughter argued in return, "Listen, the popular opinion of these times supports a woman being the bestman; or maybe we should say *bestperson.* As far as *The Book* is concerned, we can get around that by saying it is a culturally conditioned book and it only bound the people during the time and society in which it was written."

"Please, dear daughters," the Bride said calmly, "I do not want to get around it. Your wanting it does not mean the Bridegroom permits it. An entire city might decide in favor of a woman being the bestman. This is all a momentary fad and will soon pass. Even if the present trends favor a woman as the bestman, that does not change the objective truth of the Bridegroom's will. From the other side of the Portal to the Day of the Great Dance, I will continue, to the best of my ability and strength, to do what is pleasing to the Bridegroom. Please, let us be of like mind in this matter and continue to the day of the Great Wedding."

The first daughter shot back, "Then, old lady, you will continue without us. Let's go sister."

Shocked and embarrassed, the second daughter replied, "I don't think I want to leave our mother."

"She's not our mother. She's yours. I'm leaving."

The word of the incident reached the ears of the other children. More than half of the other daughters and sons left the Bride because of her decision. Shortly after, the Bride called a young man to be the bestman of the Bridegroom. On the afternoon when his call was confirmed by the children in the gapped circle, Bestman Victor led the Bride in the Great Dance.

Bestman Victor was a loving man who served the Bridegroom well for nearly eleven years. It was during his service that the Bride faced a most difficult time.

One morning, a proclamation sounded forth from the city and it shook the entire land. Contrary to the law of creation, the popular opinion of the city prevailed. The decision of whether or not an underage child would be permitted to continue living became the judgment of another. As the announcement was made, the Bride collapsed to her arthritic knees, raked her swollen hands through her gray hair and wailed in anguish to the women of the city.

"Please, I want them. Please, oh please, let me beget them. I beg you, let them live and come to me and live again. Do not, I plead with you, do not destroy your little underage boys and girls."

Hardly anyone listened to her and thousands and millions of underage children died each year. A great depression fell upon the Bride during these years. She was quieter and often subdued for months at a time as the dark net, pulled by the pale horse and loaded by Thanatos, bulged with the multitude of tiny corpses.

Bestman Victor spent many nights reading to the Bride and singing with her. She was comforted by him, but changed little in her words and actions. She walked slower, taking but a few steps each day. Bestman Victor encouraged her to pick up the pace. His words seemed ineffective. Then he died. After the days of mourning had passed, the Bride called Bestman Regal.

Bestman Regal was a gifted man and one genuinely concerned about the Bride. Her quiet moods troubled him as both the number of children begotten by her decreased significantly and the losses of sons and daughters within the gapped circle increased dramatically. The entire scene reflected badly on him personally and he questioned his own effectiveness as the bestman. He did not have any desire to be blamed for the losses within the circle or the lack of children begotten by the Bride.

Hoping he might be able to reverse both of these trends, as well as present a positive public image to the other children and feel good about himself, Bestman Regal hired a psychologist, a sociological consulting agent, an executive, an accountant and a statistician. Their initial recommendations led him to retain the services of a financial planner, a fund raiser, an entertainer, a builder of self-images, a pop musician and three motivational speakers.

With the team in place, it actively began changing the character and nature of the gapped circle. At first, the changes were small and seemingly insignificant. Background music came from a new age and not from the ancient hymnbook. One of the readings from *The Book* was dropped in favor of a testimonial, while the proclamation decreased to half time.

Once the children of the Bride became used to change itself, the changes increased. The marking of the water upon the foreheads took place at a time other than when the circle was gapped. The harsh words of the Bridegroom were omitted. Instead of being fed with the ancient promises, the children were given a steady diet of popular thought. Songs, which contained no reference to the Bridegroom or his work or word, were to be introduced to the children. Entertainment replaced worship. The number of children entering the gapped circle increased dramatically. Offerings overflowed and the Bride soon found herself the owner of several businesses.

Tensions heightened among the sons and daughters. Grumbling increased. An impending confrontation among the children needed only a spark to ignite it. The catalyst came when Bestman Regale permitted Eddy the Entertainer to lead the Bride in the Great Dance. Eddy the Entertainer guided her outside the gapped circle and continued to dance with her in the streets of the city. The Bride jerked away from him as the children streamed through the gap.

With an indignant demeanor never before shown, the Bride fumed, "Stop it! What in the world do you think you are doing?"

Startled by the Bride's stern words, Eddy the Entertainer replied, "Don't get so uptight!"

The Bride's voice shrilled and quaked in anger and fear, directing her accusations against both the entertainer and the bestman, "You have greatly offended me! You have accosted me and attempted to violate me!"

"What?" asked Eddy the Entertainer.

"Who?" interjected Bestman Regale.

"You tried to lead me in the Great Dance apart from and outside of the gapped circle. Scandalous!" She looked at her children and continued, "What must these few children of mine think?" She glared at Bestman Regale, "And you, the one given the authority and charged with the responsibility. You let it happen!"

"What are you talking about? You have never had so many children."

She replied, fuming at Bestman Regale, "Less than half of the children who claim me as their mother have been begotten by me."

Bestman Regale defended himself and interceded on behalf of Eddy the Entertainer, countering, "Change is the name of the game and we have kept you from dying alone."

The Bride took a deep breath and continued slowly, "When did my journey begin with Bestman Dusty?"

"According to the tradition, it started at the Portal?"

"Tradition? What is this tradition business? It began there in fact. How long ago was it?"

"Thousands of years, I suppose."

The Bride pressed him, "You suppose? Tell these people, then, how long and how far have I traveled."

He sighed and said, "Thousands of miles and thousands of years."

"Yes," the Bride continued, "as many miles as years. Now, Bestman Regale, tell us, where are we standing? What is the name of this street?"

"Hayes," he answered.

"Where did you become bestman?"

"I became bestman at the intersection of Third and Hayes."

She continued her questioning, "What is the name of the next intersection?"

"It's Fourth and Hayes," he replied.

"Now, tell these people assembled on this street, how long and how far have you have escorted me."

"Eleven years and half a block."

"Eleven years and half a block? Why you?"

Bestman Regale was puzzled. "What do you mean?"

"Why you?"

"Why me, what?"

"What has given you the right to refrain from singing the old hymns and chanting the ancient psalms? Who gave you the authority to cease confessing The Declaration and proclaiming the person and work of the Bridegroom? Are you able to produce any document that has empowered you to withhold the cruse of water from the head of my children?"

Bestman Regale remained silent.

The Bride demanded again, "Why you?"

"What do you want--"

"One bestman with only eleven years. Out of hundreds of other bestmen from the beginning until now, it is you. One bestman escorting me half a block! Thousands of miles and as many years. Eleven years and half a block. Why you?"

In front of the entire assembly, Bestman Regale repented of his sin, confessed it and asked for the Bride and her children to forgive him for the sake of the Bridegroom. Forgiveness was announced to him. On that day, Bestman Regal began being the bestman once again.

CHAPTER 32

THE CITY OF THE CLOWNS

The old man chuckled as he summoned his final breaths, "I prayed ... to see ... the land ... beyond ... this city."

The Bride held him closely and thought about him. The old man was the last of her children who had been in the trenches. He was a boy of six when the last trench was crossed. It was all a great adventure for him. Amazingly, he had fond memories of those battles and wars, and often, as he grew weary of The City of the Messengers, he stated his preference for those days of his youth.

With his passing, the children of the Bride reduced in number to twenty-seven. The years in the city and the fever poison from the Assassins' soul-arrows decimated the ranks. The Bride's begetting of children rarely occurred, the last being about a year earlier.

Corrupt bestmen had abused the Bride for nearly twenty years, especially when Bestman Pawky and Bestman Err were in power. Recently she had been particularly blessed to have a faithful and loving man serve her and her children, Bestman Mimbocha. His kind heart and firm dedication to the Bridegroom, *The Book* and the Bride kept several of the children from leaving the Bride. His deep voice, when hymning *The Psalm of Eventide* soothed and comforted his troubled brothers and sisters during the evening devotions. One of the great blows to the Bride and her children occurred the morning they arose to find Bestman Mimbocha murdered. He had been strangled with the chain stole.

Seven days later, the Bride called a strong, young man from her children to be the Bridegroom's bestman. While her choices were limited, she did have a man who studied under the recently martyred Mimbocha. In a solemn ceremony one evening, she placed the chain stole on his shoulders. He received it and asked everyone to sing *The Psalm of Eventide* as it had been sung to them on so many nights by Bestman Mimbocha.

Now, with the Bride and her children beyond the boundary of The City of the Messengers, a limited landscape awaited them. The eastern and western walls of the black net of death were but a hundred feet apart. The height of the walls exceeded fifty feet, blocking out direct sunlight for most of the daylight hours. With every step taken into the future, the walls closed on the travelers and heightened to eliminate the sun. Ahead in the lifeless wasteland of rock and sand, the dark walls converged.

Bestman Harold stood in front of the tall, massive wooden structure with the hinged door and read from *The Book*. After a young woman died in the arms of the Bride, a fallen son of the Bride ran into the desolate land ahead. As Thanatos netted the young woman's body, the fallen son of the Bride piled rocks against a wooden post to which he had attached a sign.

---

behold the land ahead of you, you are now entering

The City of the Clowns

only children of the bride may enter
(have a nice day!)

When the man braced the sign sufficiently and signaled his triumph in accomplishing this difficult task, the crowd of heckling taunters applauded and whistled. Bestman Harold tilted the tall, massive box with the hinged door onto his back and began lugging it out of the city and into the rock desert. While the crowd shouted obscenities, the Bride and her children followed Bestman Harold.

The Bride, now with a dowager's hump, embraced an infant daughter in one arm and guided the shoulder of a young son with the opposite hand. With each step forward, her toes extended beyond the yellowing cloak from the snow leopard. Her gnarly feet had thick calluses that were cracked to the quick and oozed some sort of thick fluid. Her toenails, some split to the root, matched the brown rock in the wilderness. The Bride's weather-beaten and sun-baked face bore wrinkle upon wrinkle.

Bestman Harold, though a young man, struggled with the tall wooden structure, often only able to carry it for fifty feet before resting. A quarter mile became a day's journey.

The forces of Footstomper waged a fierce attack. Limos and Loimos appeared in front of the troop and began sowing extra seed upon the dry desert floor. Immediately cocklebur and puncture weed sprouted in the crevasses and fissures. The noxious plants matured and awaited the travelers. Cocklebur clung to the wool robe from the black sheep and began to weigh the bestman down. The spikes of the goatheads penetrated the thin shoes on the children and found the quick in their feet.

While the troop crossed a valley, Opacus blocked out the sun and sent a torrent of rain clouds. The rains fell as never before and a flash flood raced through the dry stream bed. The roar of the flood preceded the wall of water by mere seconds. The juggernaut struck, splitting the small caravan, leaving several on each bank. Only Bestman Harold in the lead, the Bride at the back of the troop and five others with them had not been swept away.

From the heights of the walls, now only fifty feet apart, the Assassins launched a silent volley of darts using blowguns. As the deadly projectiles approached the seven, the dark darts suddenly became ravens. The birds began an attack on the Bride, pecking at her head and attempting to rip swatches of her scalp. Several times the ravens were successful, flying away with gray strands of her hair still attached to flesh. The barrage lasted only minutes, ample time to send blood streaming down her face and neck in several places. The others rallied around their mother and drove off the birds.

Each morning and every evening Bestman Harold gapped the circle and invited the Bride and the others into the presence of the Bridegroom. The service began quietly and softly as the small group reflected on their situation by singing a penitential hymn. The readings were read confidently, loudly and triumphantly. The announcement of the white cloak was greeted with a sigh of thanksgiving, and The Declaration was confessed with boldness and determination. The morning service ended with the small congregation confidently singing an ancient hymn. The evening service ended in a quiet spirit with prayers for the night and the recitation by all of *The Psalm of the Shadowed Valley of Death.*

After the evening service on the day when the walls of net were forty-three feet apart, the Bride and Bestman Harold sat. The others were asleep as the two spoke.

"The darkness stays so long now. The walls of the black net tower above us. We have direct sunlight only a couple hours and indirect light for a few more."

"I don't know how much longer I'm able to continue."

"The others are weary as well."

"Our water supply is low; maybe enough for one day."

"You know what we will have to do?"

"Yes, and we'll do it."

Bestman Harold woke everyone up two hours earlier than usual. After the morning devotions, they started before they could really see. With the heavy load on Bestman Harold's back, their pace was slow enough to prevent any injuries from unseen rocks.

At daylight Footstomper's beasts began another assault. The black pair cast a pestilence that removed all water on the land ahead. After moving several hundred feet, the year old baby needed water. Bestman Harold opened the hinged door and took the cruse of water and, beginning with the baby, gave each a single swallow. He replaced the cruse in the tall, wooden structure.

Just as the sun was rising over the eastern wall, now only twenty-eight feet from its western counterpart, Opacus conjured a rain cloud ahead of the caravan. The dark cloud covered the sun and threatened to rain. The older daughter and sons, anticipating the cloud burst and seeking to satisfy their thirst, bolted to the land ahead. Arriving in time to collect the downpour, they received instead the dry lightning bolts that killed them instantly.

The Bride wept dry tears and mournfully cast her eyes upon the little one in her arm and the child at her side. She was not comforted when told the others hadn't felt a thing and never knew what happened. She said she knew and still felt their loss. Bestman Harold understood and agreed.

At noon, the quartet ate some of the bread. The children appeared in good physical condition, but needed water. The bestman poured water into their mouths from the cruse.

The Assassins aimed crossbows at the four and fired heavy bolts. As the missiles neared the Bride and her children, the bolts changed into a flock of buzzards and vultures. The large birds circled and, when given the opportunity, silently perched on the massive wooden box. There they stayed as Bestman Harold continued to haul the structure on his back. He supposed the added weight was due to his decreasing physical condition. When the Bride turned to see if the bestman was still walking, she noticed the handful of birds riding on the tall, wooden box. The couple spent themselves trying to keep the large birds off the roof of the tall box. Exhausted, they stopped for the day.

"We traveled 250 feet today."

"I can't straighten my back anymore."

"I know."

"The walls are only twenty-two feet apart now."

"Please get more water for the little ones."

A moment later he replied, "What? I'm sorry, you said something. I can't keep my thoughts straight anymore."

"Water for the children."

"Yes, water for the little ones," Bestman Harold said in order to concentrate on what he was doing. He removed the cruse of water and gave each a swallow, though they wanted more. He took the half-loaf of bread from the tall wooden structure and, having given thanks to the Bridegroom, tore pieces off for everyone. He handed the flask of wine to the Bride and she drank from it, as he did after her. The two children received a couple more swallows of water before everyone fell asleep for the night.

The buzzards and vultures remained on the roof of the massive wooden box until morning. When Bestman Harold opened the hinged door and grabbed the cruse of water, he discovered it was empty. After loosely gapping the circle, he and the Bride crawled into the center. With parched lips and a tongue that stuck in place due to a lack of moisture, he muttered and clucked the words to a psalm. The infant and the child continued to sleep.

"Bride?"

"What?"

"The cruse of water is empty."

"It has always had water in it, even from the time at the Portal. It is empty? Are you sure?"

"Yes, not even a single drop of water."

"Do you know what that means?"

"Yes," he said in a state of stupor, "the little ones will be given bits of wine-soaked bread."

"True, but it means something else, something so very important."

"What's that?"

"I have begotten my last child. The water of marking is needed no more. I will beget no more children."

"Uh-huh. The end must be near."

"I pray so."

"Pray," Bestman Harold said and repeated softly, almost to himself, "pray that he will come and end this."

Everyone slept in the circle until the sun had passed behind the western wall. The bestman opened his eyes without moving his body. The black walls towered over him. Thanatos and the pale beast stood at the ready. The tall wooden box, now soiled with fecal material from the birds, stood on the ground before him. He struggled to his feet and opened the hinged door, taking out the flask of wine and the crust of bread. All ate from the supernatural bread and all drank from the set aside wine.

Before attempting to travel, the Bride removed a puncture weed from her face and checked the condition of her children. Bestman Harold cut off a five foot section of the cocklebur train that accumulated on the back of the black robe. He attempted to hoist the tall wooden structure onto his back and could not manage it. Determined to continue, he tilted it onto his shoulders, reached above his head for the chain and pulled the box across the ground. After an hour, the skid marks from the small building testified that he had moved it only thirty-five feet.

The Assassins placed razor stars in the slings and flung them at high speed in the direction of the four. Only one razor star found its target. The large tendon on Bestman Harold's left foot was severed above the heel by the slicing projectile. He cried out in pain and fell to the ground, the massive wooden box falling on him and further injuring him.

The Bride put the infant on the ground and moved quickly to lift the tall wooden structure off Bestman Harold. The young son helped as he could. The bestman hobbled to his feet. The Bride turned in time to see an enormous owl making an attack run on the infant. She shielded the baby at the last instant, thus thwarting the latest assault by Opacus.

Bestman Harold became dizzy with shock, his injury and dehydration. He leaned his back against the wooden closet and slid to the rocky ground. He muttered, "Bride, please, ... I need to rest ... just for a few minutes."

"Rest," she said, putting the young son next to him. The infant girl was cradled in the arms of the Bride.

Bestman Harold gazed at those under his care and begged the Bridegroom, "Please, no more."

The next day the four gained some strength from the few morsels of bread and the last sips of wine. Bestman Harold slipped the chain over the heads of the others, encircling them rather than having them move into the gapped circle. After a hymn, a psalm and several prayers they stood to continue walking. The severed tendon caused sharp pains to shoot up the bestman's leg. The foot would not bend but his leg did support weight. With the tall wooden structure tilted onto his back, Bestman Harold slid forward on his healthy foot and leg. He then pulled the old, disjointed ironwood box and his trailing foot forward for a short step.

The Assassins fired smoke canisters and Opacus summoned a dense cloud to form and descend on the Bride and her children. The thick fog in the dark valley prevented them from seeing each other and the ground. The Bride stumbled and let loose of the boy's hand to stop her fall and protect the infant girl. The boy was pulled forward as she released his hand and he disappeared into the fog. She cried out for him but he did not answer. Bestman Harold tilted the tall wooden structure back to a self-standing position and clipped the trap onto his black robe. He hobbled to the point where the chain stopped him and found the Bride. She was crying for the boy and both realized her crying was in vain.

They followed the chain back to the tall, wooden box and huddled in silence, hoping to hear the boy cry out and let them know where he was. No sound was heard.

Bestman Harold asked, "How's the baby girl?"

Clutching the blanket-covered baby in her arms tightly, the Bride answered, "I am afraid to look and see. She has not whimpered or cried in a long time."

The pale horse stepped forward and nudged the Bride. A hissing language emerged from the unseen Thanatos in the fog above, "Mine. It is mine. Put it down. It goes in my net."

"Never," said the Bride.

The pale rider took the baby's body from the Bride and hissed, "The right is mine."

"Stop," Bridegroom Harold shouted in vain.

The pale horse nudged the back of Bestman Harold and Thanatos hissed, "You are next."

The bestman snapped back, "Maybe, but I know something you know as well. I may be the next; but if so, I am most certainly the last."

Thanatos hissed once more.

On the eighth day, a wind arose from the north and began blowing in the faces of Bestman Harold and the Bride. They shielded themselves as it removed the fog from the valley. The sun was nearly at its pinnacle. The walls of death were now ten feet apart. Thanatos and the pale horse stood at their backs. Above them, six vultures and buzzards sat upon the tall wooden structure with the old, creaky, hinged door; their defecation sliding down the outside.

The Assassins stood on the top of both walls and hurled large boomerangs in the direction of the sun. When the boomerangs converged at the farthest point, they joined together and became a fierce, flying dragon bearing down upon the Bride and Bestman Harold. The beast breathed fire and extended its claws in attack. It blocked out the sun as it approached at a frightening rate of speed.

Bestman Harold moved the Bride to huddle in front of the box as he put the chain stole around both of them. He slid down the face of the weathered door on the tall wooden structure and joined her on the ground. The ancient dragon lusted after them and increased its attack velocity. The Bride and Bestman Harold watched the dragon's descent.

The Bride cried out, "Please!"

Bestman Harold whispered to her and himself, "I don't think the Bridegroom is going to make it in time."

An instant later the Voice was heard.

CHAPTER 33

THE OPENING OF THE PORTAL

When the initial vibrations of the Voice began, the earth strained from its foundational roots and groaned to the heights of its lofty mountain pinnacles. The word spoken originated from the point of intersection ahead, where the dark walls of the death tubing finally touched. Out of the depths of that darkness stood Logos. The word that fulfilled the ages and brought history to its conclusion was uttered a second time, "*Tetelestai!*"

A bolt of lightning flashed from the sword of Logos to the peak of the tall wooden structure with the ancient hinged door. The splash of lightning disintegrated both buzzards and vultures. As the concluding vibrations of that word dampened into the forever, the whole creation remained fixed.

Nothing moved in eternity, whether in the heavens above or on the earth or under the earth or in the seas. The Assassins became as dark statues on a distant ridge. Thanatos and the pale horse resembled a spalling, sallow rock sculpture. The great dragon, in mid-air with talons exposed to the quick, remained motionless. Its jaundiced eyes, with a fixed gawk of seething hatred and evil, stared at its intended victims. Nothing moved after the end of time and before eternity, except what was permitted to live and move and have its being.

Bestman Harold slid his shoulders under the chain and jumped to his feet, doing both with unexpected ease. He reached down to assist the Bride who was already arising.

She said, "I saw Logos."

The bestman replied, "I saw a great white charger with trappings of pure light and a magnificent rider in dazzling white apparel. But they are no longer here. Both disappeared when the lightning bolt struck."

The Bride agreed, "You are right, Bestman Harold, they are no longer here. No indeed, he is closer than here."

"I don't underst--"

Bestman Harold's reply of confusion was interrupted when there came a rapping sound behind them. Both turned and neither saw anyone. The rap sounded again.

"It's coming from inside," replied the Bride, referring to the tall wooden box with the hinged door. She inhaled deeply and said, "Behold, someone is standing at the door and knocking. Bestman Harold, would you please open the door for me?"

"Yes," he said slowly as he extended his hand.

The knob turned easily and the door swung open on its ancient hinges. There standing before them in the doorway was the Bridegroom. His omniscient eyes never moved from the Bride as he stepped over the threshold. He extended his right hand and touched the chain stole. He fingered it to the end where the iron trap was attached, all the while keeping his eyes on the Bride. His hand followed the chain, link by link, over Bestman Harold's shoulder, around his neck and to the top of the tall wooden structure with the ancient door. He lowered his hand to the shoulder of the man standing next to him, squeezing it firmly but gently.

"Well done, my bestman. You brought my Bride to me. Well done, good and faithful servant."

"But sir," he responded, "I traveled neither a long time nor a great distance with her. There were others who--"

"I know, but you brought her as far as you were called to bring her. Others brought her as far as they were called."

The Bridegroom drew near the Bride.

She spoke to him, "Sir--"

259

"Sir?" He asked. "Do you call me, sir? I am your Bridegroom."

She continued without addressing him by any title, "So much time has passed and I am quite old. Just look at me."

The Bridegroom spoke, "I am looking at you, my beloved Bride. You are younger and more beautiful than you have ever been. What do you call me now?"

Indeed, the Bride's appearance had changed in the twinkling of his eye. The calluses and wrinkles and pock marks and scars disappeared. Her skin became a creamy color of perfection. Her balding, scraggly, snarled, gray hair was replaced with a shining, radiant head of hair. The Bride, with the eyes of her youth, noticed the difference, but did not smile.

Once again, without addressing him, she spoke, "Though I have had many such fine men as Bestman Harold escorting me to this place of when and to the fulfillment of time, there have been others who have used me ... I mean, I am not pure, I am not clean, and ..."

"You are what I have declared you to be. I have declared you clean, and you are clean. You must not call unclean what I have declared clean. I have declared you pure, and you are pure. You must not call impure what I have declared pure. Now understand this, there is no difference between my declaration and what you are."

She spoke again, "Look at my cloak. It is old and worn and soiled and tattered."

The Bridegroom spoke, "Look at the white cloak from the snow leopard I placed upon you. It is your wedding dress."

The Bride gazed upon the cloak and saw that it was perfectly pure and clean and white and brilliant and without any spot or blemish.

He continued, "You have something to say to me."
"Yes."
"Say it, for you need to hear yourself say it to me."

260

The Bride extended her left hand and placed it into his right hand as she said, "My beloved."

"Indeed," the Bridegroom responded. "Please, dear Bride, step through the Portal and await me. I have a few matters to attend to before the Great Wedding commences and the Divine Dance begins."

The Bride followed his lead and was escorted across the threshold of the ancient wooden box and into the Great Wedding Hall. Once his Bride was inside, the Bridegroom closed the door and remained outside with Bestman Harold.

"Are you afraid, my bestman? You need to hear yourself answer my question."

"I'm not afraid, sir. I am uncertain."

"Of what are you uncertain, bestman?"

"I don't know."

"You do know, bestman. Answer."

"I don't know about them," he replied, pointing to the dragon, Thanatos and the pale horse.

"What do you not know?"

Confidently, he said, "I know they aren't able to hurt me. But, sir, are they alive?"

"They are not alive. Although they are dead, they are conscious. While they hear us and are aware of us, they are not able to respond or move. They are dead and dying. It is part of the eternal sentence of their unending destruction."

"Where will they go?"

"The place called *Second Death* has been prepared for them and they will be sent there. They will stay there forever."

"Who are they?"

The Bridegroom answered, "Footstomper and the Two Conjurings, Opacus and the Nameless One of the Assassins. Thanatos and the pale beast will be cast in that place as well."

"Will there be others?"

"Yes."

"Will you send them there?"

261

"Yes, I will send them, but also permit them."

"Sir, you make it sound as if that's where they want to go."

"It is not so much that they want to go to the place called Second Death, as it is that they want to get as far away from me as possible. The only place far away from me is the place called Second Death."

"I don't understand."

"True. However, you will understand shortly, and yet, you will not remember later."

"Sir?"

"I speak of the Judgment. You have another question that you need to hear yourself ask."

"Yes, sir. You're going to take care of the death tube aren't you?"

"Yes."

"How will it be done?"

"I will speak the word and the thread will be pulled."

"The thread, sir. What thread?"

"The red thread."

CHAPTER 34

PULLING OF THE RED THREAD

The Bridegroom spoke, "You have another question that you need to hear yourself ask, bestman."

"Yes. Have you created the place called Second Death?"

"Again, that place is not so much created as prepared, bestman. For it exists because I, who am everywhere, am not there."

"Is the place prepared?"

"It is. I am not there," replied the Bridegroom.

Motioning to Thanatos, the dragon and the pale horse, Bestman Harold asked again, "Are you going to send them there now?"

"One more deed must be fulfilled before they are imprisoned," stated the Bridegroom. "I will speak the word and pull the red thread."

Bestman Harold continued, "I understand part of what you say, Bridegroom. These forces of darkness hear what we speak and know what will happen. Your fulfilling of the deed in their presence is part of their punishment."

The Bridegroom affirmed the truth, "Yes, as is your knowing and declaring these matters within their hearing."

"I understand, sir."

"Yes, you understand that now. Later you will not remember it."

"I won't remember any of this?"

"You will remember only the good that is good for you to remember. However, the pain and death and hurting and grieving and suffering and sorrow and a host of other realities experienced and known in this fallen land will not be remembered by you. It will be as in the morning when you have an awareness or vague recollection of a dream, but are not able to recall it."

Bestman Harold asked, "Is that one of the blessings of life on the other side of the Portal?"

"Yes, but there are many more. Some, because you are still on this side of the Portal, you are not able to understand or know. However, you are perplexed about something else."

"I am, sir. I wonder about the red thread."

"I will explain by showing. Before I do, the chain stole needs to be lifted from your shoulders. When my Bride's hand was given to me, your work as my bestman was fulfilled."

The Bridegroom removed the chain yoked to Bestman Harold. The one end remained attached to the top of the tall wooden box with the hinged Portal. The Bridegroom lifted the other end with the trap and examined it for a moment, obviously immersed in divine thought. He placed the chain and trap on the ground in front of the Portal.

Harold's burden had been removed from him and a weight much greater than the chain stole and its two attachments ascended from him. He inhaled at the relief and held his breath for an instant.

Exhaling slowly, he asked, "Sir, do you want me to remove the wool robe of the black sheep?"

"No. You will wear it longer. Walk with me."

Harold followed the Bridegroom's command and walked beside him. The Bridegroom moved between the tall wooden structure and the rigid, and now plainly visible, Thanatos and pale horse. Approaching the open end of the dark, meshed net immediately behind the pale pair, the Bridegroom directed Harold's attention to a single, thin, red thread.

"Sir, I can barely see it."

"The red thread runs from here to the other end of the death net. You never looked closely at this meshed net, did you?"

"No, sir, I confess I did not."

"I am not being critical of you, Harold. The inspection of and the meditation on the long net of bodies are not enjoyable activities. Thinking about having one's body dumped into this net does not produce pleasant thoughts. Anticipating one's death is an unnatural, wretched, humiliating, horrid business. I know."

"We tended not to think about Thanatos and the pale horse, at least not in our daily lives. But they were always there, in the back of one's mind on restless nights and in the forefront of one's life on days when death snatched a loved one away."

The Bridegroom did not continue the discussion. Rather, he reached out with the forefinger and thumb of his right hand and pinched the end of the red thread, holding it tightly.

"This is to be done," He announced. He pulled the red thread and uttered the Word, "*Ephphatha!*"

The red thread instantly unraveled the black net from beginning to end. As the bodies spilled forth from the ruptured receptacle of the dead, Ruach hovered above and along the entire length of the net, restoring the breath of life to all humanity. Every infant, child, youth, woman and man who ever died was returned to life. At once, the people of the earth were drawn to the place where the Bridegroom stood. They waited silently in front of him. As for the net, from one end to the other, it closed and assumed the shape of a hollow tube.

The earth heaved and mounded forty feet in the vicinity of the Bridegroom. Below him the ground sloped gently to the plain. All humanity looked to the hill and beheld the Bridegroom.

He raised his voice in declaration, "The judgment has begun!"

"Footstomper, slither forth and behold."

The limbless Footstomper squirmed forward, still bound and only able to slaver from either side of its mouth.

The Bridegroom thundered, "I summon the two conjurings of Footstomper!"

Opacus and the Nameless One of the Assassins immediately and involuntarily presented themselves before the Judge.

"Opacus and Assassins, go to the place of the Second Death," the Bridegroom ordered. They were lifted off the earth and violently cast onto a spot of desolate dirt in the distant plain. The ground swallowed them and belched forth sulfur.

The Judge grabbed the pale pair, each one by the throat with one in each hand. He roared, "Thanatos and pale horse, where is your victory? Your work has come undone and your net emptied. Thanatos and pale horse, where is your sting? Be ye swallowed up!"

After the Bridegroom spoke these words. He arose and hurled the horse and rider into the place of the Second Death.

"I summon Limos and Loimos. Present yourselves."

Even before the Judge finished speaking, Limos and Loimos appeared. Their throats clutched by the omnipotent hands of the Champion, the black pair could only listen to him say, "There is no more pestilence, famine or plague permitted here or anywhere else that I am. You may do your work only where I am not."

The Bridegroom cast them into the same abode of eternal dying. Immediately, the whole earth, except for the spot of desolate dirt, turned a lush green.

The red horse and rider were summoned and presented themselves before the Judge who grabbed the war hoe and broke it in half. "Wherever I am, there will be neither war nor rumors of war nor fighting nor strife nor enmity. These things are no more where I am and may only be done where I am not." Having declared this, the Bridegroom flung the polemical pair and the two halves of the war hoe into the place where he was not.

In like fashion, the Judge summoned Ophis, M'Lordonsi and the other conjurings of men, along with the demons,

266

phantoms, witches, fallen messengers and abysmal minions. They, too, were cast into the eternal abode.

"Footstomper! There are none left here whom you may claim. All your forces are where I am not. At my word, you will join them. Footstomper, I am Headbanger! I suffered, was entrapped and netted, but I have conquered death and emerged from the net. I am alive and I reign again. Footstomper, be gone!"

Throat-throttled by a clenched fist, Footstomper was lifted from the earth and launched in a high arch. Still accelerated by the invisible word, Footstomper was propelled headlong into the place of the Second Death. The ground heaved, shook and imploded. An instant later, the sink-hole erupted with a mournful, wailing belch of venom, ash, carcinogen, vomit, anthrax, grit, excrement, blackdamp, enmity, dust and friction. The Bridegroom forbade anything from the spot of desolate dirt to escape the place and the foul cloud settled back into the spot and became its eternal atmosphere.

When the earth stopped shaking and the vile haze disappeared into the sink-hole, the Bridegroom spoke to the people, "All bestmen will assemble and wait behind me while I judge the rest of the people."

Many men in black robes stepped forth from the great mass of humanity. Every man whose neck had been yoked with the chain stole walked behind the Bridegroom and silently assembled beyond the tall wooden box.

He turned and said to Harold, "Go and wait with the other bestmen. I will return to judge all of you."

Harold walked the twenty feet to join the other bestmen. When he arrived at the spot where they gathered, he turned to watch the events. He was startled because the Bridegroom stood there, no more than three feet in front of him.

"Sir, is there something more you want me to do? Have I disobeyed you in some way?"

"No, judgment is now to be announced to the bestmen."

"But sir, I thought you were going to announce the judgment to each of the billions of others first."

"I just did. Judgment has been rendered on all people, except for the bestmen, Harold. Each person's case was handled justly, individually, personally and thoroughly."

Harold replied, "But how could that be? You just spoke to me and ..."

With a short laugh, the Bridegroom interrupted him and said, "Do you forget who I am, Harold? No need to answer. Now the announcement of judgment for bestmen will take place."

CHAPTER 35

ACCOUNTING OF THE CHILDREN

The Bridegroom explained, "The announcement of judgment has taken place with everyone except you men who have held the office of bestman. Those who are perfect in my eyes have been given entrance to the Wedding Hall through the Portal. They are now awaiting those of you who will be joining them. Those who are not perfect in my eyes have scattered and are presently heading for destruction. You may look in the direction of the place of the Second Death and see them approach the only spot in all creation where I am not."

The assembly of bestmen gazed across the land. The people heading for destruction were only the size of small dots on the light green plain. No two dots were near each other as they traveled to the same place.

"Many of you have questions," the Bridegroom noted. "You may ask them."

One of the bestmen called out, "Sir, they appear to be in a great hurry. My first question is, 'are they running?' And second, 'if they are running, why are they running to the place of the Second Death?'"

"Yes," he responded, "they are hurrying as fast as they are able. However, they are not running to get to the place of the Second Death as much as they are rushing to get away from me."

The questioner added, "I don't understand."

"Some of you will understand, but later will not remember," the Bridegroom noted. "Others of you will always remember, but never understand."

Another questioner spoke, "Sir, the way you speak, it sounds like some of us will be joining those in the Wedding Hall, and others will be running away from you. Is this true?"

"Yes," came the answer from the Judge.

Another asked, "What is the basis for our judgment? How will we be judged?"

The Bridegroom answered, "You will be judged on the same basis as everyone else. Those of you who are perfect in my eyes will step through the Portal and be given entrance to the Wedding Hall to partake in the Wedding Celebration and the Great Dance. Those of you who are not perfect in my eyes will not be able to stay with me, but will go to the place where I am not."

Someone else spoke, "That, as you have said, sir, is the same as everyone else. But isn't there something else that figures into the eternal outcome of the individuals in this gathering? I speak of the accounting. Sir, what of the accounting of the children's souls?"

Headbanger's response surprised the bestmen, "Truly, truly, I say to you, the accounting of the Bride's children has already taken place."

The questioner continued, "Sir, I don't understand. In *The Book* it is written that we will have to give an account of those under our care as bestmen. I don't believe I have given you my accounting of the Bride's children under my care when I was your bestman, have I?"

"Yes, for I received your accounting from each soul of the Bride's children under your care."

"Sir, how can this be? Don't we have to give the account? I don't think I want my eternal reward based upon the testimony of someone else. Don't I have the right to hear and argue my own case?"

270

"No," the Bridegroom responded. "I represent you. At the accounting, each of the children could do nothing other than tell the truth."

The man objected, "But everything they say comes from their perspectives. Though they may be declaring the truth, it is from their points of view; perspectives, I might add, which are not always reliable."

"There is only one truth."

"But didn't we have the right to-"

"No," He replied interrupting the man, "no indeed, you have no right. You do not know the entire story of the life of each of the Bride's children under your care. Your memory is limited and your knowledge of their hearing of my word is incomplete."

"Sir, I don't understand. Please explain what you mean by giving us some examples."

"Certainly," the Bridegroom responded to the man. "Consider one example about you in particular. I asked one daughter of the Bride if you had proclaimed my word to her. She said no. I asked her why and she had to admit that she never attended the services of the gapped circle while you were the bestman. Now you proclaimed the word but she would not come and listen. Her blood is on her own head and not on yours. Her accounting of your work with my word is complete and I say to you, 'Well done, good and faithful servant.'"

"Is that all that was required, sir?"

Headbanger responded, "It is required for a bestman to be faithful; nothing more and nothing less. Several times you invited her to come into the gapped circle and to partake of the Bride's white cloak from the snow leopard, but she was not willing. You encouraged her and admonished her. The responsibility was hers."

Another among the gathering of bestmen requested, "Sir, tell us an example of my accounting of the word."

"Indeed," the Bridegroom responded, "oh yes, indeed. There was a specific and troubling number of the Bride's children who, under oath and the compulsion of truth, told me that you,

271

while wearing the wool robe from the black sheep, sowed the seeds of doubt when you proclaimed and taught. The proclamations were not based upon *The Book* and you chose to speak on secular topics of sociology, psychology and, on one occasion, unknowingly promoted the worship of Mother Earth and human nature."

With regret and remorse, the man remarked, "The accounting report they gave condemns me."

"No, not quite," the Judge noted. "They also told me that you repented and there were times in every gapping of the circle when they heard about me, my love for the Bride and the salvation I wrought for all people. For all your faults, and they are many, you stayed with the ancient orders of worship. Since these orders included the readings from *The Book*, the singing of the psalms and a confession of *The Declaration*, the word they needed was given to them in spite of your atrocious and unacceptable negligence. The children of the Bride were fed in this way, despite your personal departure from the proper proclamation."

"Then I have a favorable accounting from the children of the Bride and am perfect in your eyes?"

"Yes, but not in the way you think. For, in many ways your thinking is quite wrong," continued the Judge. "Your being my bestman is not the basis for perfection or lack of it. Even if the accounting I received from the children of the Bride were perfect, and surely, there is not one which is perfect, that would not be the basis for either your perfection or your imperfection in my eyes. Truly, truly I say to you, there are some standing here whose accounting is nearly flawless, but who will not be judged perfect in my eyes. They will be forced to the place of the Second Death. A place at and in the Great Wedding is not yours by virtue of being a bestman, or by the fine and nearly flawless work you may have done."

The Bridegroom directed himself to the most recent questioner, "In your case, though you have been quite negligent in many ways, the accounting of your ministration of my word is favorable because it was still proclaimed in a few ways. My demand was for you to proclaim it always in all ways. My expectations were for you to do the maximum, not simply get by on the minimum. However, the power of my word is to be credited for its working in these matters and not the fact that you did either a few things or many things properly."

Another man stepped forward and asked, "Sir, you have declared that the basis for our judgment will be the same as the others, namely, whether or not we are perfect in your eyes. I beg you, tell us what is done with our transgressions as we occupied ourselves with the work of being bestman?"

Several in the gathering began talking to one another. They were silenced when the Bridegroom raised his hand. When he knew he had their attention, the Judge responded.

"Whether intentional or accidental, whether ones of omission or commission, whether done in word or deed, whether ones done in fleshly desire or mournful regret, whether known or unknown, whether committed with or without choice, all your sins in the office of bestman have been taken care of in the same way as the others. All of you, listen to me. All your transgressions, and there are many, were also placed on my foot. I bore them and suffered on account of them and died because of them."

Another man asked, "Then what, good sir, is the advantage of being a bestman?"

"Much in every way," the Bridegroom answered. "First, you have been entrusted with the care and protection of my Bride. Such a responsibility is an office of serving and is a great honor. You have also been entrusted with the care of my Bride's children. That obligation carries with it both privilege of duty and burden of serving. In addition, you have been given two more treasures, *The Book* and the time to study it."

Another man quietly approached the Bridegroom and petitioned him, "Logos?"

"Yes."

The man did not immediately continue. His hesitation to speak, combined with a desire to choose his words carefully, resulted in a halting awkwardness. "I must ... well, tell you something. ... No, it's more of a confession. ... But, is the time for confession ... Lord, you know, don't you?"

"Yes, I do. However, you need to hear yourself speak of these matters."

Calmed by the invitation, he spoke slowly and without breaks in his speech, "Right. Well, as you know, I was your bestman for awhile, although that title before my name describes more of your desire than either me or what I did. Although, having said that, I know it's not right."

The man hesitated, waiting for a response. Receiving only silence from the Bridegroom, he admitted, "I fear."

"I know. Speak of it."

"Am I to be denied entry into the Portal?"

"Speak of it."

"I wanted to tell the Bride and her children about you and about the deep, wonderful, sacrificial love you had ... you have for them ... for us. But, as you know, my intentions were not always so noble. Pride was involved too; as was a lack of faith. However, I believe, or at least, I want to think my primary intention was to tell as many people as I could the account of your love for all people, as well as encouraging the bestmen to care for your Bride as you would have them, or us, do."

"Do you expect to cross the Portal's threshold because of your good intentions"

"No, absolutely not."

"Do you deny my atonement for your impure intentions?"

"Oh no."

"Continue, for you need to hear yourself."

"As you know, I wrote a story, hoping many people would read it and begin, or continue, trusting you. The work was a story - a confessional chronicle, a narrative of time from within time, a parable of history from the start at one end to the beginning at the

274

other end. It was a story following alongside and touching the story. I intended it as another way to tell the truth of your word to people; the same truth but using a story to do it. I questioned whether or not I should do it. I was uncertain, but in the end, I had it published and encouraged people to read it. In doing this, am I guilty of adding to or taking from *The Book*?"

Logos answered with questions, "Did you read *The Book* to my Bride and to the children?"

"Yes."

"Did you read it perfectly?"

Frightened, not only at the question but at his answer, he replied, "No, I did not read *The Book* perfectly."

"Did you gap the circle perfectly? Did you lead my Bride and the children in the Great Dance without error? Did you teach without mistake? Did you sing with perfect pitch? Did you utter my odes as I would have them spoken? Did you give perfect counsel to my Bride and to the children?"

"No. Perhaps, I never did anything perfectly, never spoke a perfect word or never thought a perfect thought. Perhaps. What a foolish use of the word, *perhaps* !"

"In order to pass through the Portal, you must be perfect."

"I know."

"Do you desire to step across the threshold of the Portal based upon your personal perfection, bestman?"

"Sir, I have none. If I am permitted to enter, it will be because of your perfection, not mine; your works, not mine; your love, not mine."

"True. Continue."

"It is by your entrapment, suffering, atoning death and victorious exit from the death tube that I have the right to hear your word of permission to go through the door of the Portal."

"This is most certainly true, bestman. What, then, might prevent you from having a place at the Great Wedding Feast?"

"Doubt."

The Voice deepened, "Doubt? Is there doubt about who I am or what I have done? What is the source of your doubt, bestman?"

The bestman answered quickly, "Oh, no sir! The doubt is with me, not with you. It's me. I don't doubt you, your work or your word; I doubt me, my work and my word. I doubt the story I wrote."

"If you look to yourself, you will have doubt. If you look to me in repentant faith, you will have assurance."

"I understand, sir, and have confidence about you. But I still question the story I wrote for the children."

"Did you add sections to *The Book* or delete any portions from it."

"No."

"Did you write a perfect book in your story for the children?"

"No, sir."

"Well then, consider what you have just heard, from my mouth and from yours. Think on these things."

The Bridegroom finished speaking and waited a moment before turning to address all the bestmen congregated before him.

"The questions remaining in your minds deal with the judgment. Each question is best answered, not by my words, but by the act itself. The Bride and her true children await us inside."

Having said this, a deep silence fell upon the black-robed men. All eyes stared in his direction. The Bridegroom stretched forth his arms and placed the palms of his hands over the assembly of bestmen and opened his mouth. The ancient Voice proclaimed the word.

"Let the judgment of the bestmen begin!"

CHAPTER 36

JUDGING OF THE BESTMEN

The Bridegroom sat upon a bench and presided over the judgment scene. His holy face reflected the majestic royalty of his being and the objective impartiality of the impeccable adjudicator. He announced to the bestmen assembled before him, "Judgment is simple and quick. Each one of you will be summoned. You will step forward and look into my eyes. If you are perfect in my eyes, you will be invited to pass through the Portal and enter the Wedding Hall. If you are not perfect in my eyes, then you will leave where I am and go to the where I am not."

The Judge called for the first bestman to step forward for the judgment. An elderly, gray-haired man presented himself before the Bridegroom.

"Approach me and peer into my eyes."

The gray-haired man leaned forward and gazed into the eyes of the Bridegroom. The man asked, "Sir, what do your eyes behold?"

"Closer. Let your nose touch the tip of my nose and look into my eyes. Are you able to see?"

"Me, sir, am I supposed to be the one seeing?"

"My eyes are wide open for you. Peer inside them and you will see yourself in the reflection of my eyes. Focus your eyes to behold your reflection."

The elderly, gray-haired man had some difficulty making his eyes do as directed.

"Wait," he said in excitement. "I ... I am able to see my reflection in the pools of your eyes, sir."

The Bridegroom directed him, "Announce to me what your eyes behold. How do you look? How do I see you?"

"I am mesmerized by what I see. Can this be?"

The Judge answered him, "Not only can it be; it is and ever shall be."

The gray-haired man could not move from his stance. His nose continued to touch the Judge's nose. His eyes continued to stare into the Bridegroom's eyes, beholding his reflection.

"Your Honor, what I see is ... is, I mean, all I see is perfection."

The Judge agreed, "That is all I see as well."

The man half-heartedly objected, "But sir, I know myself. I know that many of my thoughts were absolutely filthy. I am aware of my words which were often biting and vengeful. Many of my deeds and actions were cruel and done with vindictiveness. I know ..."

The Judge interrupted, "I see none of these things of which you speak. My eyes behold nothing except perfection in thought, word, deed, motive and desire."

"But I know I am not perfect."

The Judge raised his voice slightly, "What my eyes behold as perfect and what my mouth declares as clean, you will not call imperfect or unclean. Do you not remember or recall the central message of *The Book* and the Bridegroom's salvation; the message you repeatedly proclaimed to the Bride's children?"

"Yes, I do, sir," the elderly, gray-haired man conceded, "but it is better than what I ever thought or believed. The message of salvation is far more beautiful than I have ever imagined or proclaimed. In my proclaiming and teaching, I under-stated the good news to the Bride's children. Your love and pity and mercy and grace and care and benevolence and kindness and goodness far exceed anything I ever told the children. How inadequate I was. How-"

The Bridegroom interrupted him once more, "Enough. Look again and tell yourself once more, how do you see yourself in my eyes?"

The man marveled as he admitted, "I am perfect; absolutely and totally and completely perfect. It is amazing."

The Judge declared, "That is the way I see you. You may stand by the Portal and wait for the others to be judged."

"Must I stop looking at myself?" the man asked.

"Yes," he was told. "For there are many others awaiting judgment and there are manifold blessings awaiting you on the other side of the Portal."

"As you say, sir."

The elderly, gray-haired man backed himself a few steps from the Judge. Willingly, he bowed the knee and confessed with his tongue, "The Bridegroom is Lord; my Lord." The man, deep in thought and smiling as a result, walked to the Portal.

After two similar declarations, a thin, balding man moved near the Bridegroom. While the others exhibited fear, this man was more nervous and jittery.

"Approach me and peer into my eyes," the Judge ordered.

The thin man hesitated and shook noticeably as he leaned forward to gaze into the Bridegroom's eyes. He stayed close a moment and jerked away.

"I see nothing."

"You have not looked closely and you have not seen yourself. Step forward again and peer deeply into my eyes."

Unable to do otherwise, the thin man approached the Judge and after a moment, saw himself in the reflection of the pooled eyes of the Bridegroom. The thin man leaped back and screamed in horror.

"No! Acghh! Horrid! You have tricked me. What an awful thing to do to anyone."

"I have not deceived you," declared the Bridegroom. "You have only seen yourself as I see you and as you truly are."

"No! That was not me I saw in your eyes. What I saw was loathsome and putrid, vile and repugnant. I am not that way and I know myself better than you do."

"For the first time, you have seen yourself as you are. With me, there are no masks or screenings, no deceptions or makeup. With me, you see yourself as you are in reality. Step forward and look again."

"No," the thin man replied as he was forced to draw near and peer into the eyes of the Bridegroom again. The man wriggled and squirmed as he saw himself in truth.

"No more," he screamed. "Let me go. I don't want to look into your eyes any longer. I don't want to be in your presence a single second more. Even being near you makes my skin crawl and my tongue cleave to the roof of my mouth. I am dying in your presence. I don't want to be near you. I beg you; let me go."

"Where will you go?" asked the Judge.

"I will go where you are not. It is better than being anywhere you are. I crave release from you. I loathe the way I feel in your presence. I hate myself when I am near you. Let me go. Will you have pity on me and free me from you? I beg you."

The Bridegroom responded, "One deed must be done and you may depart from me."

"Whatever," the thin man blurted out, "I will do anything if it means getting away from you."

The thin man knew what must be done. He bent the knee and confessed, "The Bridegroom is Lord. Permit me to leave now. I feel cursed in your presence."

The Judge answered him, "Depart from me, you accursed, into the place of the Second Death which was prepared for Footstomper and the others."

"At last! I go, at last," the thin man cried. Immediately he ran down the grassy mound and headed in the direction of the desolate spot.

After the Judge watched for a moment, he ordered, "The next bestman, approach me and peer into my eyes."

A quiet, dark man somberly presented himself without speaking. He closed his eyes for a minute and pinched his upper lip between his teeth. Knowing that the dark man was immersed in serious thought, the Judge waited. Finally the dark man inhaled deeply, held the breath at its apex and slowly exhaled. He opened his eyes and leaned forward to gaze into the Judge's eyes.

"Ohhh, ... I don't ... How can this be?" he asked as he leaned back. "Sir, I am perfect in your eyes."

"Yes, you are perfect."

"Sir, don't you know what I did to your Bride and to many of her children?"

"At one time, yes, I did know. But I do not know about these things of which you now speak. I have forgotten them."

"Forgotten them? How can this be? You can't forget, can you?"

"It must be this way. I can not deny myself. I have forgotten."

"I don't deserve this."

"Yes, you do," the Judge quickly replied, "you are perfect in my eyes and you are perfect throughout. This is exactly what you deserve. What you will receive and enjoy for an eternity is also precisely what you deserve. Please, stand by the Portal and wait for me to finish here."

With a smile of admiration and astonishment, the dark man bent his knee and confessed, "The Bridegroom is Lord; my Lord!"

After the dark man joined the others by the Portal, a light-haired man heard the Bridegroom call for the next bestman to approach and be judged. The light-haired man strolled to the Judge and confidently leaned over to view himself in the eyes of the Bridegroom.

"What? Ughh! How awful and ugly you make me appear."

The Judge replied, "You only appear as you are in my eyes. I know everything and you are imperfect."

"Well, if you know everything, you know just how much good I did as a man and, particularly, as the bestman. I increased the number of children in the circle and organized a program for providing many people with shelter. In addition, I single-handedly gave up the right to-"

"Imperfectly done," noted the Judge with an interruption. "Everything you listed is nothing more than filth in my eyes."

"What about all I did as one of your bestmen?"

"Filth," the Judge declared.

"What about-"

"Filth."

"Not fair! You didn't even let me finish what I was going to say."

"Not fair?" repeated the Judge. "I am completely fair, impartial and just. Look into my eyes and tell me if you see anything perfect."

The light-haired man was incapable of resisting. He peered into the Bridegroom's eyes and recoiled in disgust. "I am horrid in your eyes. But the problem is you, not me. I will not be a part of this any longer. I want to be where you are not. May I leave and get as far away from you as possible?"

"You are permitted."

The light-haired man moved to leave immediately. He stopped suddenly. Then he kneeled and confessed, "The Bridegroom is Lord."

The light-haired man arose and left. As he was leaving he suddenly turned and shouted, "Didn't I do all these things in your name? No matter, don't answer. I know what you would say."

CHAPTER 37

LEADING OF THE BLIND

Two blind men were some of the last bestmen to be judged and, upon being summoned, they approached using their walking sticks as guides. One stopped to wait while the other approached the Judge.

"Sir, where are you?"

"I am here, draw near," replied the Judge.

"Sir, I, along with my friend here with me, will not be able to peer into your eyes, for we are blind, having lost the sight of our eyes in the service of the Bridegroom. What would you have me do?"

"You may look into my eyes."

"Sir, I can not see and will not be able to be judged like the others. Do you want me to stand by the Portal?"

"No," answered the Judge, "you are to be judged as the others."

"But sir, I have told you that I can not see. It is impossible for me to peer into your eyes as the others."

The Judge declared, "There is a great difference between can not and will not."

"Sir?"

"You will not be judged by sight since you have announced your inability to see. Are your other senses heightened?"

"Oh yes, for I have relied on them as one normally would and much more so, sir, to compensate for the tragic loss of my sight while in your service."

"Draw near and touch me," the Bridegroom commanded. "You will feel yourself as I feel you. You will discover how you really are."

The blind man probed around with his walking stick and found the feet of the Judge. After saying he was sorry and receiving no reply from the Bridegroom, the blind man reached with his free hand and lightly touched the face in front of him. The blind man recoiled in horror.

"Achhh! Clammy and crawling. My skin spalls with the maggot fodder that cleaves to my bones. Do not bid me touch you again, sir. I desire to back away from you. Nothing good dwells within me when I touch you."

"Remain," the Judge ordered, "draw near and smell me. You will smell yourself as I smell you and as you are."

The defendant slowly leaned forward, stopping at intervals to sniff with a shallow breath.

"Inhale deeply," came the order.

The blind man did so and began coughing violently and choking as he fell back holding his nose with both hands. His walking stick landed near him on the ground.

"Pfew! Ughhh! The stench," he said, continuing to back away from the Judge. "The vile and putrid smell of my own body is even tasted in my mouth. The vomit and the bile drawn up through my gullet is better tasting than my own tongue. I will leave your presence now."

"No, you will remain," stated the Judge.

"Let me go!"

His request was denied and the Judge continued, "Speak to me and hear yourself as I hear you and as you are."

"I don't want to do such--," the blind man started to say. His words, however, echoed off the Bridegroom. "Aghh! My ears! Cacophony," the man whispered, "Let me go. I beg you.

I bend the knee. Let me go. The Bridegroom is Lord. Away, I say, away! Let me get my walking stick and leave your presence."

"The walking stick is on the ground in front of you. But remember, the walking stick is part of my creation. You may not want it back again."

"I'll be the judge of that," the blind man said, groping on the ground. He found it, picked it up and dropped it immediately. "You contaminated it," he yelled and then began whispering again, "You have turned my walking stick against me. I don't need it. I will find the place where you are not. I will wait for my friend to be judged by you and together, without walking sticks or anything else from you and your precious creation, my friend and I will leave."

"Enough!"

The blind man stepped back and waited and stepped back farther and waited and inched farther away.

The Judge ordered the next defendant to be brought forth and presented. The second blind man, aided by his walking stick, moved forward.

"You may look into my eyes," the Judge informed the second blind man.

"At your invitation, I will draw near. Please, sir, lead me to you and when I am close, take my face into your hands and guide me into your eyes," the second blind man requested.

"I will," replied the Judge.

The walking stick located the feet of the Judge and the second blind man slowed his approach. He leaned forward and awaited the hands of the Bridegroom. His face was cradled in the cupped hands of the Judge and the second blind man was drawn near so their noses touched. The huge hands were lowered and the invitation repeated.

"Open your eyes and look into mine."

The man opened his eyes and commenced blinking and focusing. A moment later the man uttered a joyful moan.

"Are you able to see?"

285

"Yes," the man replied, "not since the hot poker blinded me in the arena have I seen. The last image imprinted on my mind was the beast tearing apart my wife and son. Oh, how good it is to erase that image with what I see now."

"On the other side of the Portal, these same eyes of yours will soon see the woman and the boy again. What do you see?"

"Sir, in your eyes I see a perfect man. Is it true that I see myself?"

"What you see is what I see. What I see is what you are. My eyes behold a perfect man and that is what you are."

The man bent the knee and confessed, "The Bridegroom is my Lord."

When he arose from his subjection, he spoke softly to the Bridegroom, "Sir, my friend is still blind and I would like to assist him. We have come a long way together and he is my friend and he needs my help. Do I have your permission to do so?"

The Judge answered, "He will not let you help him. The two of you are different now. That difference will keep you from coming together and will drive you apart forever."

"May I hand my walking stick to him? I have no need of it anymore."

"You may try," invited the Judge.

The man approached the blind man, intending to assist his old friend. The blind man sensed someone coming and began to back away from him. He waved his arms about and turned his head aside.

"Stay away from me, Judge. I don't want you to torment me."

"It's not the Judge. It's me, your old friend. I want to help you. Please take--"

"Deceiver! You are playing a cruel trick on me. Stay away and leave me alone, deceiver and sadist! If you were my friend, you would not be the way you are. But I doubt you are my old friend. I sense that you are no different than that awful Judge.

286

Get away from me!" The blind man stumbled away and fell in doing so.

The man tried to help him to his feet.

"Leave me alone and get away from me. I know who you are. You are the Judge. Oh, Bridegroom, you are a tortuous deceiver, taking pleasure in taunting me like this with your perfection."

"But I am not the Judge. I am not the Bridegroom. I am your old friend."

"Liar!"

The blind man jerked his arm away and started running down the grassy slope. He could not keep his balance and fell to the ground. He assumed a sitting position and wiped the grass from his face and hair, all the while saying things like, "Stinking grass! It has the scent of the Bridegroom permeating it. Isn't there a place where he isn't?"

His nose lifted slightly, as a faint scent of the desolate spot came into his nostrils. The blind man, attempting to determine a bearing for the place where the Bridegroom was not, turned his head and sniffed the air again. He rose to his hands and knees, now proceeding in the general direction of the desolate spot. He alternated arms, waving in front of his path to prevent running into any obstacles, particularly the Bridegroom.

CHAPTER 38

SPEAKING OF THE CHASM

When the judging of the bestmen was completed, the royal Bridegroom walked to the edge of the high, grassy mound. He said nothing as his eyes scanned the scene before him. Scattered on the plain below, the imperfect undertook the pilgrimage to where the Bridegroom was not. Each traveled in isolation, keeping as far away from everyone else as possible. The desired separation became increasingly difficult as they approached the desolate place. The craving to be away from the Bridegroom was stronger than the yearning to be separate from one another.

The green landscape became littered with clothes from those running to the desolate place. Clothing was part of the Bridegroom's creation and they had his creative hand's smell about them. Any hint of his goodness caused the skin of the imperfect ones to crawl and their internal organs to burn with a consuming tingle that never consumed. The aching to be rid of such clothing was stronger than the desire of covering their nakedness.

Thus, they loathed one another and the anguish increased as they approached the desolate place. Usually, an individual hesitated at the entrance, looked to the Bridegroom standing on the hill far away, turned his back on the Bridegroom in one last act of desperate defiance and quickly entered the barren abyss.

The Bridegroom turned to the bestmen and said, "Soon."

One of them responded, "Sir, what do you mean."

"Several of you are wondering when we will go through the Portal and join the others for the Great Wedding. Soon."

The same bestman spoke, "Sir, was I wrong in thinking you a question? Or were we wrong in wondering in our minds when we would enter the Portal? Have we sinned?"

"No," the Bridegroom answered, "you have not sinned, neither are you capable of transgressing my will any longer. You may think, speak and act freely."

"Sir," one replied, "we do not enter the Portal yet. Is it because of something that must take place on the other side or here?"

"There are a few remaining acts to be accomplished here. However, they can not be accomplished until the departing ones have all arrived at the desolate place."

"Sir," another said, "tell us why we are standing here with you and are not walking on that plain and heading to the barren abyss."

"I chose you to be mine in time and forever in eternity."

Pointing to those below, the bestman continued, "Did you choose them to go to the desolate place?"

"No. It is their choosing to go there."

"Sir, did you create that place for them?"

"No. The place of the Second Death came into being for Footstomper. Properly speaking, it is not a creation of mine. I prepared it by not being there. It was not ever my intention that people would go there."

"But sir," another man asked, "please tell me to be silent if I overstep the line, but they are going there."

"Yes," the Bridegroom responded, "but I would have all to spend eternity with me on the other side of the Portal."

"That does not seem to make sense."

"It does make perfect sense if you were able to understand my thoughts and ways."

The man asked, "You bore their transgressions on your foot, died for them and became alive again for them, right?"

"Yes, that is correct, for I cannot deny myself."

"Sir," the man continued, "how does that make you feel as you watch them head for the place of the Second Death?"

"Feel?"

No one answered his question.

"A time, long ago, I stood on a rise like this, looking down upon many people. They were heading for the desolate place even then. I wept for them there. Many other times my tears were shed for those who opposed my good, gracious, merciful, kind, benevolent intentions for them. But they resisted me. Here and now, there are no tears, no sorrow, no pain, no suffering, no sin. This is the only way it is and always will be for us. The opposite is the only way it is and always will be for them."

The bestman who had been blind said, "My old friend waves his arms and staggers about in pursuit of the desolate spot. He is the only one left who has not made it to that place. In a few moments, he will find the barren abyss and will be gone. It is a most pitiful sight, sir. I could wish to do something for him."

The Bridegroom spoke, "He would not accept it, either now or an eternity from now. You have seen how he loathes being in your presence. He seeks only to be away from me. Now he wants no part of you either. He wanted no part of me in time when he enjoyed a part of my goodness. In the barren abyss, where neither I nor any of my goodness abides, he will not suddenly desire me."

The man said, "I begin to understand, but it is only a beginning."

"A beginning is all you ever will have," the Bridegroom responded, "and even that will be taken away from you when you go through the Portal."

"A part of your goodness, sir, that we will not remember this scene before us?"

"You do begin to understand," the Bridegroom said smiling. A moment later, his face became formal again. "The last man has entered the place of the Second Death."

The good man started to speak, hesitated and then said to the Bridegroom, "Neither door nor lock nor seal nor rock is needed at the entrance of the place of the Second Death. There is a great chasm between us and it will never be crossed by anyone, either from there to here or from here to there."

"True," came the majestic reply.

CHAPTER 39

WHITENING OF THE ROBES

The meshed, black net of death shivered as the Bridegroom grasped its open end. The coils that encircled the earth vibrated upon the green grass. After inhaling deeply, the Bridegroom blew a mighty breathe into the death tubing, declaring as he exhaled, "I am Headbanger!" The Voice carried down the dark corridor of the tubing, echoing and causing the coils to unbind the earth. The closed end extended into the heavens and the net bulged to the point of bursting at the spirit-filled words of the Bridegroom. The black conduit, now straight as a piece of rigid pipe, remained fixed in the atmosphere.

"Dance and enter!" boomed the voice of the Bridegroom as his eyes scanned the grassy plains below. At his command the clothes littering the ground from horizon to horizon began to twitch and tingle, vibrating on the surface of the land. Appearing as enchanted characters from a fantasy cartoon, the clothing moved across the grassy fields and ascended the mound where the bestmen stood. When within twenty feet of the open end of the black piping, the clothing accelerated into the meshed net as if drawn by a monstrous vacuum cleaner.

When the last piece of clothing was inhaled by the dark pipe, the muscular arms of the Bridegroom began reeling in the net. As it was pulled in, the Headbanger's large hands compressed the netting and the clothing. Hundreds and thousands of miles of the black tube were worked into a small ball in the palm of his hand. After the last inch of netting was drawn into the strong hands of the Bridegroom, he worked and compressed the little black ball until it became smaller than the tiniest speck of black pepper.

"Be gone!," whispered the Bridegroom and the minuscule dot of darkness left his hand and went in the direction of the desolate place.

He walked to the edge of the grassy mound and scanned the whole earth. Except for the desolate spot of land with the brown earth surrounding its open entrance, everything was green. An emerald carpet covered hill and valley, mountain and desert. The sparkling waters of ocean and sea reflected the clear blue sky.

The Bridegroom turned and approached the mass of bestmen. He studied each one and smiled as he did. "No longer do I call you servants. You have been faithful in leading my Bride and I am eternally thankful to you for what you have done."

"Ah, yes, very good and quite typical of you men. True, you consider yourselves unworthy servants, only doing that which was your duty. But you are no longer servants for I have declared you my brothers. You are no longer unworthy, for I have declared you worthy."

He continued, "My beloved brethren, all things are now ready. When you step through the Portal, your wool robes from the black sheep will become a dazzling white. A pristine vestment of blazing righteousness is the only proper attire for the wedding ceremony and the occasion of the Great Dance which commences shortly."

Once again, the Bridegroom addressed his own, "My dear brethren, you led my Bride over the centuries from the distant Portal to this one. After crossing the threshold of this Portal and having the proper attire, I ask you to escort my Bride one last time. Upon crossing the Portal and stepping outside, you will go to the room where my Bride is waiting. You will remain there until the music stops and all eternity is quiet. When the music begins again, all of you will escort my Bride to the altar during the wedding processional."

The bestmen smiled with thankfulness and laughed with joy. They would be privileged to escort the Bride to the throne where the Bridegroom would be waiting for her. Now, collectively and for one final time, they would escort her down the aisle of the Wedding Hall and present her to the Bridegroom.

One of the bestmen inquired, "Dear Brother?"

"Yes."

"Did I understand you correctly when you said that as we crossed the Portal we would be stepping *outside* ?"

"Yes."

Gesturing in the direction of the tall wooden structure with the ancient Portal, another asked, "But we will be going *inside*, won't we?"

"No," the smiling Bridegroom answered, "you will be leaving this little closet of a place and going outside. You need to orient yourself to the fact that this universe is but a dot of space and time; nothing but a single, momentary thought of mine. This is the inside; through that Portal is the great outside. To understand the reality of this petite place you will need to experience the eternity on the other side of the Portal."

"Dear brother, this is small?"

"Very small. Tiny. A jot."

"But the dimensions of this earth are amazing. We have sent a space craft to the farthest parts of this solar system. A telescope has enabled us to view galaxies light years away. The distances of our galaxy are astounding. The staggering expanse of the universe is overwhelming. And yet, dear brother, this is small?"

"Yes, a tittle."

"Will I understand once on the other side ... uh, once I cross the Portal and am outside?"

"No," the Bridegroom responded, "not anymore than you remember today one particular step you took in this small universe in the second year of your life."

The bestman continued, "Even though I do not remember any step I took in the second year of my life, I do understand that I did take many of them. Let me think about this. ... Uhh. Okay. So, I will not understand in this small world, but once outside, where I might be able to understand, I will not remember. Is that the way it is?"

The Bridegroom laughed, "Yes, you express the truth well. However, I will grant you a special gift. My beloved brother, you be the last one to pass through the Portal and I will permit you, for a moment, to remember and to understand at the same time. Please remain standing here beside me."

The Bridegroom swung his hand to the Portal and lifted his voice to the mass, "My dear brethren, please enter the joy of your brother."

He opened the hinged door and held it for his bestmen. Each bestman, one by one, crossed the Portal and went outside. The Bridegroom smiled the smile of genuine delight as the bestmen stepped forth from this closeted space known as the earth and into the outside. As each man crossed the threshold, his black robe changed into a brilliant white robe.

When all the others went outside and donned the dazzling vestments, the Bridegroom turned to the last bestman. He directed him, "Here is how you will understand and remember. As you cross the threshold of the Portal, stop with one foot here on the inside and one foot on the outside. Take a long look outside and then peer back into this closet."

The bestman nodded his head and stepped halfway outside. The inside half of his robe remained black while the rest of it turned a sparkling white. He beheld the majesty, grandeur, glory and holiness of the outside and was mesmerized by its magnificence, beauty and splendor.

The Bridegroom spoke to him, "Beloved brother." The bestman did not respond. The Bridegroom touched him and said, "Beloved brother, turn around and look back here."

"Huh? Oh, yes."

The bestman forced his head to turn. His face wrinkled and furrows formed in his forehead.

"Oh, I remember. Now I understand. A tiny, dark niche in the wall. Sir, I am filled with anxiety. May I please go outside? I have no desire to be inside that place any longer. It makes me itch. Please, may I go outside?"

"Certainly," said the Bridegroom.

The bestman leaped outside, his robe turning completely white as he exited.

CHAPTER 40

SMILING OF THE BRIDE

The bestmen were immersed in the preludes as they entered the spacious anteroom. Music permeated their revitalized bodies harmonizing with both the instruments in the symphony and the heartbeats of the men as they all blended to create a woven fabric of euphony. Beat after beat the hearts of those waiting arose in joyful expectation. Note upon note, the flow of the music soared in anticipation of the Great Wedding. Breathing lungs harmonized with heartbeat and instrumental note. Measure built upon measure and line upon line as one instrument surged forward while others receded slightly. A harp danced up the higher steps, hesitated and was beckoned to wait by other strings. A flute and a horn, urged upward by the organ of Paradise, approached a peak and an oboe ebbed a wave of awe.

Stunned by the thrilling sounds and by their own bodies participating in the prelude, the bestmen were incapable of either movement or speaking for several minutes. The rich air of the good place filled their lungs rendering the bestmen somewhat light-headed. The sights about them, even within the small fifty acre anteroom, were greater than their eyes could receive and their minds process.

While the bestmen recovered from the effects of their new world, the Bride entered the anteroom through a forty foot high set of double doors trimmed in pure gold. Every bestman turned to face the Bride. Never had anyone, not even the first bestman, seen the Bride more beautiful. Her vibrant, youthful body, restored beyond what she had ever been, was beyond description.

Her bouquet consisted of a single, perfect, trumpeting Easter Lily surrounded by pure Baby's Breath. A fine, white-laced veil was held in place by a thin, golden diadem. The white cloak from the snow leopard was restored to impeccable condition.

The music continued to soar ever higher as ten and twelve instruments joined in an ascension to the pinnacle. Now only a few others, a clarinet and a trombone, hesitated on the slopes of the climb.

The Bride slowly walked through the midst of the bestmen, moving forward to the larger double doors at the far end of the anteroom. The bestmen parted for her and formed a line on each side. She looked into the eyes of each man and communicated a look of love, respect and thankfulness.

She smiled at each one, each bestman returning her smile in like fashion. Her eyes met those of the bestman who served her for twenty-six years and another who had the privilege of leading her for eight years. She smiled with pure joy at the young man who was bestman for only three years before he was martyred. Standing beside him was a man who served her a thousand years later, during the horrid times of tolerance. The Bride grinned widely when she noticed the bestman who had been blind now watching her and smiling at what his eyes beheld. Hundreds upon hundreds of bestmen looked upon her whom they served, each in his own day and for as many miles as the Bridegroom allotted.

All instruments combined, soaring to the highest peak. Every heartbeat and each breathing sound of every person in all of Paradise synthesized and surged upward. The music rose to a heightened pinnacle, a point where it certainly could go no higher. When it reached that ultimate peak, where no greater elevation could be attained, the sounds soared farther.

The Bride reached the large double doors, the ones of pure gold. When she arrived and stood still, there was total silence in Paradise. Though hearts still beat, they made no sounds. Though everyone continued breathing, nothing was heard.

Silence reigned in Paradise.

After the silence passed, the gold, double doors swung silently and slowly outward, revealing the grandeur of the Wedding Hall. At the far end of the hall, standing on the green jasper dais, the Bridegroom gazed upon the congregation and awaited his Bride. He wore a robe of pristine light and a brilliant crown of pure gold with twenty-four diamonds evenly spaced on its circumference. Behind the Bridegroom stood the rose-crystal altar and beyond it, seven marble steps higher, the Bridegroom's Father sat enthroned in splendor and majesty. Ruach hovered as a thick, transparent, glistening incense over the entire assembly.

When the double doors were fully open, the sounds of the processional commenced. The music of the processional was more magnificent than before and the people perceived what they heard before was but the prelude. The height, width and depth of the music increased geometrically as the strains invaded every pore and caused every hair to tingle. Any mouth that dropped open in awe began sounding forth with the music of the processional.

The Bride stood in the doorway and her children rose to face her in the forty square mile Wedding Hall. The sides of the floor sloped and provided an opportunity for each of her children to see her. The Bride would have the occasion to behold each of her children, as she was escorted by the bestmen to the Bridegroom. Her children; women, babies, men, little ones and youth from every nation and tribe and people and culture and race and tongue; were assembled in the Great Wedding Hall.

With neither cue nor direction, two files of bestmen preceded the Bride down the polished silver carpet covering the aisle. Those preceding the Bride were the men who served her prior to the Bridegroom's entrance at the Small House of Bread. After these bestmen entered the Great Wedding Hall, the Bride began her processional. Following her were two files of the bestmen who served the Bride after the Bridegroom's entrance at the Small House of Bread.

By design the bestmen and the Bride walked slowly down the ten mile aisle. From side to side the Bride looked into the faces of her children, seeing everyone of them and remembering each one. On the aisle was the old man who never missed an opportunity to enter the gapped circle and be blessed by the Bridegroom. A bit farther away was one of the many sons who returned to the Bride later in life. High on the right side stood the woman who bore witness to the truth and paid for it with her life. Beside the woman was a boy, marked with the water of life and who died in the projects as the result of a drive-by shooting. She smiled at him, as the Bride had done with all the others. The peasant woman was there, the one who taught the old hymns to young boys and girls by singing with them. Near her were many of those men and women who had learned the truth by her hymnody. The red-haired boy with blue bib overalls gave a little wave to his mother as she walked by. She smiled in return, as she did to the little boy who had disappeared into the fog, the old fisherman, the hillbilly, the university professor, the former witch doctor, the flautist, the stuntman, the rice planter, the switchboard operator, the riveter, the six-fingered baker, the blacksmith who memorized hymns, the prison guard, the orthodontist, the miner who laughed, the ballad singer, the twin girls who had been kidnapped, the defensive line coach, the grave digger, the former atheist, the charwoman, the stock market broker, the brother and sister who foraged through garbage dumps, the sentinel, the alchemist, the runner, the rich woman, the whaler, the distiller, the boy from the well shaft, the orphan, the creation scientist, the migrant farm worker, the man who never married, the princess, the teenager who lived in her parent's prairie schooner, the woman who worked in a slaughterhouse, the funeral director, the slum dweller, the cobbler who played the harpsichord, the hospice volunteer, the miller who tasted wines, the man who made canoes, the woman who had owned six head of cattle, the janitor, the man who once stuttered, the ice hockey referee, the man who had been staked out in the desert, the acolyte, the girl who played instruments by ear, the woman who had been killed by a drunk driver, the jeweler, the former prostitute who wrote poetry, the submarine commander, the farmer, the woman who once had a pig valve surgically placed in her heart, the miner once trapped in a cave in, the pharmacist, the cosmonaut, the western scout, the beautician, the boy whose legs had been painful, the steeplejack, the man who made tongue-and-groove paneling out of curly maple, the grip, the girl who gathered seeds, the slave, the poor man from the inner city, the young woman who had been scarred from burns, the inscriber, the tanner, the housewife, the man who restored old pickup trucks, the cave dweller, the wine-maker, the lackey of the count, the theatre usher, the astronomer, the slave and the master who cared for one another, the elephant attendant, the author, the abused teenager, one of the entrappers, the standup comic, the baby boy abandoned in a dumpster along with the young girl who found him, the harbor master, the man who grew tulips, the playwright, the mule skinner, the resident orthopedic surgeon who thought about many things, the scavenger, the woman who never left her house because of fear, the under rower, the slender man who hunted mastodon, the mill worker, the solicitor general, the paramedic who collected stamps, the physiognomist who played dominoes, the glazer, the girl who made truffles, the camera operator, the cartographer, the hod carrier, the embalmer, the mercenary, the president, the ostler who wrote short stories, the medic, the gleaner, the cave-dweller, the bosun's mate, the marathon runner, the underground railroad assistant, the notary public, the man who had hidden in a hay crib during the war, the glass blower, the mute den-dweller who aged cheese, the gravedigger, the man who raced minnows, the financial consultant, the girl who never spoke a word, the congregational chronicler, the lawyer, the watch maker, the man who operated a linotype, the bootmaker who thought about philosophy, the slave driver, the proofreader, the draper, the spelunker, the fat man who had been missing an ear, the cobbler, the gandy dancer, the soldier, the cabinetmaker, the exchange clerk, the forger, the boy who hiked the mountain passes, the truck driver who had lost the tips of two fingers in an accident, the bounty hunter, the earthworm farmer, the falconer, the housewife who brought her husband to the Bridegroom, the biologist, the woman who was wife of a bestman, the doughboy, the woman who had pet squirrels, the keeper of the bridge gate, the woman who had been a leper, the well woman, the man who operated a swing-saw, the carpet cleaner, the feudal landowner, the organist, the woman whose eye had been injured when she was born, the turnkey, the chimney sweep who read poetry, the woman who fished in the fjord, the nuclear physicist, the woman who helped with her children's and grandchildren's education, the grenadier, the man who made flint tools, the waiter, the explorer, the young woman who worked in decontamination, the waif, the electrician, the refugee, the scullion, the soldier abandoned on an island during a war, the woman who loved her husband, the elementary education teacher, the storyteller, the trawlerman, the legal secretary, the sawyer who operated a headrig, the pony express rider, the gymnast, the woman who collected baseball cards, the miller who played the lute, the fireman who canned asparagus, the boy who had a lisp, the young woman who had gall stones, the fireman who had been poisoned with mercury fillings, the environmental engineer, the woman whose son disappeared, the general practitioner, the recluse, the writer of limericks, the woman who wove baskets from river reeds, the speech pathologist, the organ donor, the stage coach driver, the prisoner, the woman who was brought to the Bridegroom by her husband, the child who climbed trees, the frogman, the hermit, the basket bearer, the delivery truck driver, the huntress, the woman who twirled locks of her hair, the man who was executed for being a serial killer, the groomsman, the prospector who talked to himself, the zoologist, the market researcher who studied linguistics, the barrel maker, the man who picked raspberries, the gang member, the blacksmith who painted, the journalist, the emperor's sister, the whittler, the used-car salesman, the mason, the spy, the marine biologist, the fuller, the comedian, the cheese maker who lived in an attic, the baby girl who was the last one marked with the water, the thief who died by crucifixion and millions of others begotten by the Bride.

The preceding files approached the Bridegroom. He looked upon them with reverent approval. One file continued to the side at his left and the other to his right. They turned to face the Bride and rejoiced to see this day. The Bride stopped at the bottom of the steps and waited. She lifted her eyes to the Bridegroom and smiled with sheer joy in his presence. The two following files of bestmen processed to their respective places at the Bridegroom's left and right.

The entire assembly faced the Bridegroom and the Bride at front of the Wedding Hall. When the bestmen were in place, the processional music stopped.

Silence heightened the anticipation. The Bridegroom descended the steps to his beautiful Bride. He extended His hands to receive her, saying, "My beloved."

The Bride gave her hands into his and answered, "Behold, here am I, and the children whom thou hast given to me."

Thus, the Great Dance commenced with the wedding of the Bridegroom and his Bride. The marriage feast continued forever as the children laughed and ate savory foods at the Father's banqueting table with each meal more delicious than the previous. The Bridegroom escorted the Bride and her children to different places with each land more spectacular than the last. The Spirited celebration continued as the children played in the eternally dawning day with each moment more wonderful.

The Beginning